THE BLACK MADONNA
OF DERBY

THE BLACK MADONNA
OF DERBY

Joanna Czechowska

SILKMILL PRESS

The Black Madonna of Derby

The Polish edition, Goodbye Polsko, was published in 2006 by Foran Media

Published by Silkmill Press
Copyright © Joanna Czechowska, 2008

This book is set in 11/12pt Palatino

Cover design and author photo: Isobel Cianchi

ISBN 978-0-9558840-0-9

Printed and bound in Great Britain by
CPI Antony Rowe, Chippenham, Wiltshire

Acknowledgments

Many thanks and love to my cousin Anna Kanthak who translated the Polish edition. Also thanks to Hazel Pedley for her advice and comments, and to Debi Alper and the members of the East Dulwich Writers' Group.

This book is dedicated to
Tim, Joseph and Isobel
and also to my father and mother.

Chapter 1

Derby, East Midlands, 1964

Babcia folded her mottled, 69-year-old hands in her lap, looked up at the brooding icon of the Black Madonna hanging on the wall above the fireplace and then lowered her gaze to the sepia photograph of her husband on the mantelpiece. She noticed with annoyance that someone had stuck a curling black and white print of her three grandchildren into the edge of its gilt frame. Her husband's elegant pose (seated sideways on a straightback chair, legs crossed, pretending to read a book) was thus half concealed by a cheap Kodak image of Wanda (scowling), Zosia (smiling) and Janek (poking out his tongue to the camera). Babcia tutted and looked round the sitting room to see what else could inspire her displeasure.

Television – one thing Babcia hated was television. The little black and white box was blaring out some nonsense about tin monsters. Six-year-old Janek was throwing himself around on the sofa with excitement. This aggravated Babcia, partly because she didn't think children should behave in this fashion in the sitting room (and another thing Babcia hated was badly behaved children) and partly because she didn't understand a word being said on the television and the child did. Not that Babcia lacked talent for languages – she spoke fluent Polish, Russian, French and some German. Yet her seven-year sojourn in England had so far only seen her learn the words 'hello', 'goodbye' and 'parsnip.' Wanda had taught her these words and informed her grandmother that parsnip was a formal English greeting only to be used in polite society.

These three words had seen her through well enough as she could buy food in the little Polish shop in Irongate where the staff spoke her language. If she went elsewhere she took a grandchild with her to translate. But recently things had changed, there had been a subtle shift of power, a slight change in the undercurrent and this was the underlying cause for Babcia's bad humour.

Janek had mastered English.

When he'd stayed at home with her, Polish had been his one and only language but now he'd started school, Babcia found she was the only one in the family who couldn't speak the language of the host nation. She felt annoyed and frustrated by this fact but she wasn't going to do anything about it.

She turned her attention from Janek to her daughter Helena who was thumbing through *The Derby Evening Telegraph*. Why did Helena allow her children to have the television on all the time, stifling conversation? Even her favourite grandchild, 10-year-old Zosia, was transfixed by the hideous flickering box. It was true that Wanda, the fat cheeks of her ample bottom splayed across a dining chair, was not watching it but was engrossed in painting her nails at the table. Nor, judging by the slurping sound coming from the little table in the corner, was her son-in-law Tadek interested in the programme, preferring to drink tea from his saucer like a peasant and meddle with his silly hobby of taking watches and little clocks apart then putting them back together again.

Babcia sighed in an exaggerated fashion. The whole family was consumed by some kind of pointless activity, letting life tick along, marking the minutes until the next meal. It was time for a change of pace, it was time for an explosion and Babcia was going to detonate one.

She rapped her daughter's newspaper with the end of her walking stick and said, 'How much would it cost to have a body flown to Poland?'

Helena looked up and stared at her mother.

'What kind of body, Babcia?' asked Zosia.

'A human body, of course.'

'Whose?' said Helena.

Babcia raised her eyes to heaven. 'Mine, obviously. I want to be buried in the land of my fathers next to my beloved husband. But if it is too expensive to move the whole body, you could cut out my heart and just take that to bury in Warsaw. If it was good enough for Chopin...'

'Yummy – is it liver for dinner tonight, Mum?' said Wanda nonchalantly without looking up. She began applying another coat of pearl pink varnish to her ragged, bitten nails.

'Mama, I have no idea how much it would cost. Maybe Tadek could ring the airline people and find out,' said Helena.

Tadek looked up from his tea. "What?"

'Could you please ring, Tadek? It's important.' Babcia's voice was shrill.

'But which department would I ask for?' Tadek pleaded.

'Maybe baggage handling,' suggested Wanda holding her hand up to the light.

'Baggage?' asked Tadek.

Wanda shrugged. 'All right then, maybe cargo, freight, catering – I don't know.'

'Just ring BEA at East Midlands airport and see what they say.' Helena looked pleadingly at her husband.

'Now? Do I have to do it now ...'

Tadek sighed and dragged his attention away from the half-hunter pocket watch he'd been dismantling. Telephoning some stranger in an unknown department of a large organisation was the last thing he wanted to do, but crossing his wife, and more importantly his mother-in-law was unthinkable. Tadek found the number in the telephone book and called. It was a Saturday afternoon and he was sent from department to department trying to find someone on duty. He had no idea which area of the airport he was finally connected with. A gruff voice with a strong Derby accent answered the phone.

'Good afternoon, Sir. My name is Tadeusz Baran.' Tadek tried hard to speak his best English. 'I want to know, please, how much would it cost to take a body to Poland?'

'A body?' said the man on the other end. 'You mean a corpse? It'll cost you. We can't just prop a stiff up on a seat you know. It will cost a fair bit with refrigeration, handling etc.'

'Yes, I know, but have you a rough idea of the cost?'

'Well, how long has the body been dead?'

'Oh, she's not dead.'

(Pause)

'I see. So you're planning to knock off this woman and hide her body by transporting it to Poland. I'd have thought it would be much easier to chuck her in the garden and throw a bit of earth over her.'

'No, you don't understand – she's my mother-in-law.'

'Oh, well I do understand, then.'

Tadek could hear the man's colleagues laughing in the background.

'She is 69 years old,' Tadek spoke patiently. 'She thinks she will die fairly soon and she wants to be buried in Poland where she was born.'

'I see. In that case it would be much easier and simpler if she went back to Poland now while she's still alive and we could sit her in a seat. It's easier than sending a dead body back – refrigeration, handling, that's where all the cost would be.'

'I think you're probably right,' agreed Tadek and put down the phone. He looked at his wife's questioning eyes, his mother-in-law's threatening scowl.

'He says you should go back now while they can still put you in a seat.' He looked at Babcia who gripped her walking stick and stared straight ahead. He was just the messenger, he reasoned, he couldn't be held responsible for what the man had said. His duty done, Tadek went back to his watches.

'But you could live another 10 years, or even 20.' Helena gently took her mother's hand.

'Three score years and 10. I'll die next year so I must go back home now.'

'But, mother, we need you here.'

'I'm not needed anymore.' Babcia felt her voice burst out in an uncontrolled torrent. 'Since he started school, Janek replies in English when I speak to him in Polish, Wanda is only interested in her hair and nails, you and your husband work all the time, the people at the Polish Club are all peasants. I have no one to talk to, I don't understand what you all laugh at on the television – I just want to go home.'

'Learn to speak English, then,' muttered Wanda.

'Oh, mama, you're just feeling a little depressed. Your home is here now.' Helena stroked her mother's hand.

'My home will never be here. My home is and remains the land of my ancestors.'

'Please don't go, Babcia, I want to you stay.' Zosia came over to sit by her. 'Who will look after me if you go?'

'*Kochana*, I know you want me.'

Babcia looked round the room expectantly, but there was silence. Helena was reading the newspaper again, Tadek was staring at a tiny little screw in his half hunter, Wanda seemed to be removing the pearl pink nail varnish and opening another bottle and Janek was rolling on the floor as a tin rocket exploded on the TV and in his imagination.

Chapter 2

'I can't believe that's really you, Babcia,' said Zosia staring at the sepia image of a little girl wearing tiny lace-up boots, a stiff dress and an enormous bow in her blonde hair. The picture showed three-year-old Babcia sitting on a little chair, her feet sticking out in front of her while her four-year-old brother stood rigidly by her side. In white ink on the thick black paper of the elegant, leather-bound photo album was written, *'Witold and Barbara, Warsaw 1898.'*

'I remember exactly when that picture was taken,' said Babcia tapping her finger on the image. 'I have an excellent memory – that has always been my curse. Witold was cross because he wanted to sit on that little chair but father let me. I can still remember the photographer's studio. He had a duck puppet to keep us amused and large painted backdrops made to look like a scene in a house, or park.'

Zosia stared at the picture. 'What happened to uncle Witold?' she asked.

'He was killed fighting the Germans in the Second World War and my husband, The Prince, was wounded fighting the Russians during the 1920s and died a while later. That's the way it is with us Poles – it's always either the Germans or the Russians, the Russians or the Germans.'

Babcia sighed exaggeratedly, but in reality she loved these Saturday evenings. This one had taken on its usual formula. Helena and Tadek had gone off to a dance at the Polish Club *Dom Polski* where the usual entertainment would be provided by the usual band, Tempo Trio, the gins would be sweet with Britvic orange juice and the fug of cigarette smoke would hang in the air like gauze. The restaurant upstairs would serve its usual selection of barszcz and bigos and as usual someone would get too drunk, complain loudly about British duplicity during the war in abandoning Poland to Stalin's tender mercies, rip the Union flag that hung above the Polish eagle in the reception and be thrown out on the street.

Babcia always stayed at home to babysit. She hated the idea of sitting in the smoke-filled rooms of the Polish club, talking to a group of uneducated peasants while loud modern music blared out. She preferred to stay at home with the television off and Zosia for company, Janek safely tucked up in bed. Babcia and Zosia would usually start the evening sitting in the small and cluttered front room, doing their needlework. This was an activity Wanda had long ago given up and these days she preferred to spend her time up in her bedroom listening to pop singles on her little record player.

'The back of the embroidery should look just like the front,' was Babcia's mantra. This was certainly the case whenever Wanda had attempted needlework; there were just as many knots, missed stitches and pulled threads in the front as the back. Wanda's resulting handiwork was always torn, puckered and yellowed with sweat. Zosia, on the other hand, managed to produce the most delicate blue and yellow flowers stitched perfectly onto small white mats. Her efforts were then used to decorate the shelves or serve as a centrepiece for a tiny ceramic pot, sea-shell bird or small wooden figure.

By eight o'clock on that particular evening sewing proved too difficult in the dimming light. Babcia suggested they look at photographs instead. She took the precious album down from the shelf and she held the book on her lap while Zosia leant against her arm. The clock ticked, the coal fire spat and hissed in the pink-tiled grate, bathing Babcia's white, bun-bound hair in a warm glow.

She gently moved the crackling tissue paper covering each page. 'This is our estate in Southern Poland, not far from Tarnow. We had a 10-bedroom house with elegantly laid-out lawns and a team of servants and gardeners.' She pointed to a large white, balconied house with a few servants standing in the grounds outside, hoes and pitchforks at the ready. 'Father kept two carriages and six horses. I can remember the barefoot peasants bowing their heads to us as we swept past in our carriage on the way to church. We had our own pew there, high up so we were raised above the common people.' Babcia turned the page. 'Ah, this is a picture of me when I was 16 playing tennis on our private courts.'

'How could you wear so many clothes to play tennis, Babcia? Weren't you too hot?'

'Too hot, too restricted, too uncomfortable but that was the way for girls then and we had to put up with it. Witold and I had a nursemaid called Katerina and later a French governess, Mme Bertrand. Katerina made supper for us and brought it to the nursery and she kept our clothes tidy. She read me folk tales and plaited and brushed my hair. Witold had a train set and I had a beautiful rocking horse with a red saddle and a mane and tail made from real horsehair. My mother would kiss us goodnight in the evening. She sat me on her knee and called me her pearl, her darling, her sweet princess. We were so happy – such an idyllic family.'

Babcia turned the page, her eyes shining.

'And this is me aged 17 at my first ball in Moscow. I was a student at the Smolny Institute for Gentleborn Ladies at that time. The girl next to me is my dear Russian friend, Tatiana. She was from an aristocratic family, name of Bessov, and they took me to the dance. I met the brother of the Tsar there.'

Babcia stared at the 50-year-old image and sound waves transmitted through time and space brought back the words of the long-dead Tatiana as if she were standing in Porton Crescent's tiny sitting room – 'This is my friend,

Barbara Ostrowska, she's a Pole but she can't help it – don't worry, we won't need to count the silver...' Her shrieking, mocking laughter lived on in Babcia's ears. She paused in a daze until Zosia's words cut through.

'Just think, Babcia, what if you'd married him, the Tsar's brother I mean. You'd be, I don't know...'

'Dead, certainly. Now this picture is later – during the war between Poland and the Bolsheviks. It was taken in the military hospital where I met your grandfather. I couldn't believe it when I read his name on the list of casualties – Prince Jan Poniatowski. You can't imagine how perfect, noble and handsome he was. Just the sound of that aristocratic name sent my heart fluttering.'

The photograph showed the Prince sitting up in bed with a large bandage wrapped round his head covering one eye. His other eye stared straight at the camera. Standing next to him, fingers folded together in front of her and wearing a white nurse's uniform with a huge cross on the bib stood a young and beautiful woman. Both she and her husband-to-be looked thoroughly miserable.

'You look so sad. I suppose people are sad when there's a war. Were you a nurse then?' asked Zosia.

'Yes, it was my patriotic duty to help all the poor soldiers who were wounded in battle. That's why I volunteered at the hospital.'

'Why does grandfather have that bandage on?'

'He was wounded by the Bolsheviks. They invaded Poland in 1920 trying to get us back into their empire after we had gained independence. But our brave Polish soldiers and all the Polish people of every class fought them off and sent them packing.'

Babcia looked lovingly at the pictures.

'I cared for all the soldiers but The Prince was special. We married later but he never recovered properly from his war wounds. So you see the Russians killed him in the end.'

Babcia stared at the photograph. The stench and heat of

that hospital came back to her. She could almost see again that young boy screaming for his mother as they amputated his leg even though they had run out of anaesthetic. A boy, only 15 or 16 years old ... 'Nurse, will you help me, get in here and help me,' the doctor had turned his blood-spattered face to her while she had clung in terror to the white curtains. But the young Babcia had panicked, she'd backed away and fled, her white veil flapping down the corridor as she ran.

'How was he hurt?' said Zosia.

'Who? The boy?'

'Grandfather.'

'He was a cavalry officer and he was wounded while trying to defend an important bridge from the Russians. His horse was killed beneath him and he was left ...'

'Oh, the poor horse, I hate it when animals are hurt.'

'Your grandfather fell to the ground and was hit in the head by a Russian bullet. But as he lay there, a miracle happened. The Black Madonna, whose icon you see on the wall there, appeared in the clouds over Warsaw. Your grandfather saw her holy face – the Russian cowards and pigs fled when they saw it too. They call that the Miracle of the Vistula.'

'The Black Madonna must be very powerful,' said Zosia looking at the portrait.

Babcia slowly turned the page of the album. Another photograph of The Prince as a little boy dressed in a sailor suit was placed all alone on the next page. A smile dimpled his cheeks and a halo of blond curls circled his head. He carried a hoop in his hand. Next to the picture, a small white envelope was stuck to the page. Inside it, wrapped in tissue paper, there nestled one tiny blond curl. Babcia took it out.

'My mother-in-law gave me this lock of hair which she had saved from The Prince's head when he was a little boy. I've kept it safe all through the years. His hair was blond, just like yours was when you were little, and it turned brown later as yours has.'

Babcia gently handled the holy relic. It was crisp and dry and she feared it might turn to dust in her fingers and disappear. Zosia put out one pink finger and carefully stroked the golden curl before her grandmother replaced it in its packet.

Babcia dabbed her eyes with her white lacy handkerchief and turned the page to a picture of her wedding. The Prince wore a black suit and stiff white shirt; Babcia, dressed in a flowing wedding dress, was holding a long bouquet of lilies.

'Ivory silk that dress was. And it took two people four hours to create that bouquet. Our wedding was the social event in Warsaw of 1924. We were a golden couple – everyone said so. My parents-in-law provided such a beautiful banquet, there was a string quartet and so many important people there. Unfortunately, The Prince was still unwell when we married but he absolutely insisted we go ahead with the ceremony. You see he wanted to marry me so much. The doctors said he had a nervous disease called neurasthenia. These days they would call it shell shock.'

'Were you sad?'

'Yes, *moja kochana*, I was terribly sad but the good thing is that although The Prince died so long ago he still lives on in you.'

Babcia stroked her granddaughter's thick soft plait. She saw Zosia glance up at Tadek and Helena's wedding picture standing by the clock on the mantelpiece. Tadek stood short and squat, wearing a bad suit with the jacket button pulled tight over his fat stomach. He had more hair in those days but otherwise looked much the same. Helena had her arm through Tadek's and was wearing a neat, fitted suit and small hat – she looked slim and elegant. She stood at least six inches taller than her husband. He was smiling but she wasn't.

'I wish my parents had had a wedding like yours,' said Zosia.

Babcia glanced briefly up the photo. 'Ah, well that was

just after the war and everything was in short supply – clothes, food, men. You had to take whatever you could get.'

Chapter 3

Standing beneath the image of the Black Madonna, slit-eyed, golden-brown, hanging on the wall, Pan Nowak began his usual lecture.

'No other country has suffered so much and achieved so little as Poland. We were partitioned between our greedy neighbours and disappeared from the map of Europe for centuries. Polish children were beaten for speaking their native language – Marek! Sit back on your chair right now – we came from under the Russian imperialist yoke after the First World War and became a free nation again. But only for less than 20 years. Then we endured the Nazi invasion and the Germans and Soviets again carved up our country between them. How could the British celebrate Victory in Europe when the whole point of the war was lost, freedom for Poland. When will we ever be free?'

Pan Nowak had tears in his eyes as his speech reached a crescendo while the children in his Saturday morning Polish class continued to chat, fight or flick bits of paper to each other.

Wanda Baran sat looking out of the window. A grey pall hung over the wet streets of Derby yet even they seemed more welcoming than sitting in an upstairs room of the Polish Club among the stale smells of bigos and cigarettes. At 14, she felt large and out of place in a classroom surrounded by much younger children. The teacher, Pan Nowak, was now talking about grammatical declensions and relating them to some obscure Polish poet. Wanda drew a little heart on her exercise book, she picked some old nail varnish off her thumb and then rested her head on her arms. She had to go to school all week so why, when all her friends were out in town shopping and meeting in cafes, did she have to go to another school on Saturdays? Zosia sat behind her, constantly putting her hand up to answer every question and diligently learning the stupid poem off by heart.

'Why do they always live in the past?' Wanda thought as she drew a flower on her exercise book. The future was the only thing that mattered to her. She didn't care about these old people, old wars, old quarrels. It was history that caused wars – if people didn't know about the past, they wouldn't fight over it.

Wanda didn't care about the past because there was something in her immediate future that interested her so much more. That afternoon, Wanda and her two best friends were going to the ABC cinema in Victoria Street to see *A Hard Day's Night*. And the thought of that film was the only thing that was keeping her going all through this boring, boring lesson.

When Pan Nowak finally dismissed the class, Wanda grabbed her books, raced downstairs, out of the Polish Club and down the street. She left Zosia talking to the teacher and helping him tidy up the class. Zosia would have to bring Janek home, she thought.

She had just enough time to get back, have something to eat, put on her make-up, new top and skirt then run out to meet Pam and Sue outside the cinema.

It took 20 minutes to get home to 16 Porton Crescent. This semi-detached house in a quiet residential street full of quiet residential neighbours had been the Baran family home since 1961, a definite step up in the world, another rung on the social ladder. Wanda ran up the front drive and let herself in.

'Hello,' she called but wasn't surprised there was no reply. Her father was probably still working – Saturdays were one of his busiest for painting and decorating. Helena was food shopping and Babcia was, no doubt, having a lie down.

Up in her bedroom, Wanda changed quickly, then bent towards the mirror to apply her make-up. She hated her nose, long and punctuated by a series of bumps and dips. It cast a shadow over her face, reminding her of a sundial. Her lips were very, very thin, her eyes were brown like her father's, her hair was blonde and one ear was rather cauliflower shaped. She was short and she was tubby. Her large hips were crushed into her new green denim skirt. Her bosom wobbled in her tie-dye red top as she pulled on creamy yellow half-length boots. She had painted her chewed fingernails red and applied green eyeshadow to her eyelids. After considering her reflection, Wanda grabbed an old headscarf and draped it over the mirror to obscure the image.

Zosia and Janek were entering the house as Wanda was leaving.

'What are you all dressed up for?' asked Zosia.

'I'm going to the flicks with Pam and Sue.'

'So what are you all dressed up for? Oh, didn't you realise – the cinema only works one way. You can see them but they can't see you.'

'Sod off,' retorted Wanda.

'Excellent argument,' yelled Zosia as her sister ran down the drive, 'you should have been a lawyer. Anyway, those colours don't match – you look like a traffic light.'

'Traffic light, traffic light,' taunted Janek.

As Wanda ran towards the bus stop she looked down and saw her sister was right. Never mind, too late to change now, the bus was coming. Wanda got off at Victoria Street, and saw Pam and Sue waiting for her outside the cinema. They'd managed to steal a few cigarettes from their parents and were practising lighting up. She saw them look at her and say something to each other. They were probably commenting on her clothes and make-up. She suspected they laughed at her behind her back but today, Wanda really didn't care.

'Hiya, kids,' she shouted happily. 'Are we ready to rock and roll?'

Pam and Sue were both dressed in knee-length boots, short sleeveless dresses and their hair was tied up with chiffon headscarves. Wanda knew they played around with their cigarettes to feel adult and sophisticated and she also knew it helped Pam and Sue's confidence to hang around with her as the boys' glances quickly passed over her and on to them. But friends, any friends, were a vital part of social success.

Anyway, today all rivalries would be forgotten. Today all three of them were excited – they giggled, bought popcorn, and checked their make-up in little pocket mirrors. Girls packed the cinema – the noise and excitement hung stiff in the air. Wanda and her friends found their seats and spent the next two hours bouncing up and down, chewing their handkerchiefs and screaming at the top of their voices. They could hardly hear a word of the film.

When Wanda came out of the cinema, everything was different, she felt different, the world was different. The shops, cafes, even the pavement and lampposts in Victoria Street were lovely, the world glowed – she was in love. She bought the LP, a huge poster and a T-shirt. She went home, put the record on her small box record player, hung the poster on her side of the bedroom wall and lay on her bed. She buried her face in her pillow, hugged it in her arms and sobbed, 'Paul, Paul'.

She wrote him letter after letter. And received a black and white photograph from the fan club with his signature across it. Zosia said it was just a facsimile and they printed millions of them for idiots like her, but Wanda knew he had actually signed it and she pressed the photo to her bosom and kissed the image's lips with her own thin lips. Eventually the picture became rather soggy, the edges dog eared and there was a deep crease in the corner.

But the photo provided her with some comfort when news came that Zosia had passed the 11-plus exam and would be going up to Pinecrest Grammar School for girls. There was much family celebration and Babcia smiled with obvious delight.

'You're just like I was at your age,' she soothed. 'Beauty and brains – a winning combination.'

Tadek patted Wanda's hand comfortingly.

'Don't worry, sweetheart. I don't mind that you didn't pass it. You're still my number one girl.'

'Well we have a lot in common, don't we? We're both thick and fat and ugly and failures, aren't we?' And Wanda ran from the room, slamming the door.

Chapter 4

Christmas 1964 was destined to be the last one the Baran family would all spend together. It began like any other. On Christmas Eve, Tadek went out to buy the tree and he, Zosia and Janek helped decorate it. Candles held on with little metal fastenings were attached to the branches, pine cones which the children has decorated with rolled up balls of coloured foil inserted between the spines were placed round the base of the tree and numerous little nativity scenes decorated the sitting room. Babcia had been cooking for days and preparing marble cake, poppy seed cake, katarzynki and other sweet offerings. Helena was busy making repairs and alterations to the children's Polish costumes, to be worn at the Christmas Eve supper.

Wanda hung back, angry. Christmas Eve was far too late to put up the tree, she thought. Most of her friends' families had had theirs up for at least two weeks.

'If you only put it up on Christmas Eve, you don't get time to enjoy it,' they said. Wanda was inclined to agree with them. She, in contrast, had to attend the Christmas Eve supper at the Polish Club and come back to open the presents before going to bed. Then go to mass on Christmas morning. Wanda's friends opened their presents on Christmas Day, then spent the rest of the day eating and waiting for the Queen's speech and the *Morecambe and Wise Show*.

Wanda didn't want to go to the Polish Club Christmas Eve supper but at least, now that she had nearly turned 15, she didn't have to wear her Polish costume. The previous year she'd felt a fool wearing that richly sequined black velvet waistcoat with a stream of four brightly coloured ribbons descending from the shoulder, the stiff striped skirt in orange and black, the dainty white apron and little black boots. Zosia gladly wore hers and Janek, in red trousers tucked into knee-high black boots with embroidered white shirt, was too young to object.

Wanda went to the supper wearing a leather mini skirt and red polo-neck sweater. When the Baran family arrived at the club, the large hall was arranged with rows of tables. The supper was the same one that had been served for centuries in Poland. There was barszcz (beetroot soup) to start, then pickled herring, followed by breaded fried carp, sauerkraut and potato and finished off with poppy seed cake and coffee.

Wanda groaned inwardly when she found herself seated next to Pani Turek who immediately began her usual speech, half joking, half serious.

'Oh, Wanda, my daughter-in-law. Why don't you sit over there with Piotr? You know your mother and I decided back in 1950, when you and Piotr were born, that you were destined to marry each other.'

Wanda smiled thinly, having heard this story for so many years, it was now nothing but an annoyance.

'And you know what a good husband Piotr would make,' continued Pani Turek, ' he will be going to a good university one day.' She squeezed Wanda's hand.

Wanda glanced over at the pale, short bespectacled Piotr and thought, 'Over my cold dead body.'

As Pani Turek droned on, Wanda watched her mother handing out plates of food, filling coffee cups and wine glasses. Helena's wavy brown hair was tied in a bun but a strand kept falling down over her forehead. She brushed it away with the back of her hand. Zosia helped, receiving pats on the head and kisses from admiring guests. Once she caught Wanda's eye from behind her mother's back and stuck her tongue out at her. Wanda looked away. Her father sat at the bar drinking beer with a friend. They were talking loudly and both waving their arms around in excitement at the conversation. Babcia, at the other end of the table, was complaining loudly to her nodding table companion about the decline in children's behaviour and spoken Polish while Janek tried to drive his little toy car across her bosom.

By 10 o'clock, they all sat waiting for the appearance of St Nicholas. Unlike the red and white version, the Coca Cola version her grandmother called it, he came dressed all in white, wearing a bishop's mitre and holding a crozier. The younger children would go up to him and receive their present. Zosia and Janek still qualified for a gift – Zosia received a book, *British Garden Birds*, and Janek was given a plastic boat for use in the bath, which he proceeded to dismantle immediately. Wanda would really have liked one too but was far too proud to say anything.

The next day, Christmas morning, dawned cold but sunny. Wanda squeezed into the back seat of the family's blue Ford Anglia. Zosia, wearing her new red coat trimmed with white fake fur, sat next to her on one side with Helena, wearing her dark green dress with large black spots and black coat, on the other. Babcia sat in the front passenger seat with Janek on her knee. Tadek drove.

Wanda felt Zosia poke her with her elbow.

'You're creasing my new dress. If you weren't so fat...' said Zosia irritable through lack of sleep.

'Get lost, idiot.'

'Wanda, don't use language like that. Be quiet.'

End of discussion – Babcia had spoken. Wanda looked to her mother for support but she was studiously gazing out of the window. Why did she never defend her? Wanda looked sulkily at the streets of her hometown. The familiarity depressed her. She'd walked this same route countless times all the years she'd been at St Joseph's primary school. That school had been dominated by hard-as-nails Irish nuns who hit first and asked questions later. Sisters of Mercy they were called. How ironic, thought Wanda.

In those days, the family had lived in shabby Agard Street in a rented Victorian terrace with a front door that opened straight into the living room and an outside toilet in the yard. Wanda felt, if she looked carefully enough, she could almost see her young self skipping along wearing her blue gabardine and red bobble hat, Zosia running along behind, identically dressed. Wanda thought about the time a little girl from school, who was walking with them, had bluntly asked Zosia, with the innocence of a six-year-old, why she was so pretty and her sister was so ugly. The truth had hit nine-year-old Wanda hard, like one of Sister Bernadette's slaps. She'd turned round to look at Zosia and saw immediately that it was obviously, glaringly, appallingly true. Why had she never noticed before?

Wanda stared out of the car window, forcing back tears and feeling the overwhelming weight of injustice. They drove over the bridge past Babcock's Mill where Helena worked, eight hours a day, hunched over a sewing machine. The river Derwent, which had once powered the mill, flowed past its red brick walls, glittering in the weak winter sun. Iridescent against the black lower walls of the mill, a solitary pure white swan glided downstream.

The car approached St Joseph's church. Across the road was St Wystan's – the two holy towers battling for supremacy. Wanda had been inside St Wystan's once when invited to a friend's family Christening. Feeling a little thrilled at the 'sin' of being in a Protestant church, she had been rather shocked by its interior – plain and dark with mouldy, disintegrating union jack flags hanging from the walls and large statues of the long-dead decorating the walls. St Joseph's, with its ornate statues, religious paintings and brightly coloured ceiling, could hardly be in greater contrast.

The Baran family went through the heavy wooden doors. Mass had already started. It was conducted by the Polish community's very own priest, Father Kantor. This little bald man barked out the service with a Teutonic air (he had seen active service in the German army – and not even under duress according to Pan Nowak). Wanda saw

Fr Kantor give the family a pained look as they arrived in the packed church, late as usual. They crept stealthily into the adjacent Lady Chapel where there was room to sit. It was dark and quiet and the service only just audible.

Wanda sat at the back on a pew by herself. She looked at Babcia dressed in a brown coat, stout brown shoes, and sable fur hat. As it was Christmas Day, she also wore her fox fur – the fox's head peeping over one shoulder and its little feet dangling over the other. Babcia's amber jewellery and dark brown walking stick finished off the effect. Wanda thought she looked ridiculously over-dressed for a provincial church at midday.

She watched as Janek crashed around the pews playing with his action man doll while Babcia tried to keep him quiet with sweets and threats. Wanda smiled despite herself as Janek tried to press a sweet into the mouth of Babcia's ornamental fox. Her smile faded, though, as she looked at Zosia, sitting bolt upright following the service in her book. Wanda noticed how Zosia would look up at the statue of the Virgin Mary – a beautiful lady wearing a white dress and blue veil with roses at her feet and stars by her head. She knew Zosia fantasised that she would be the next St Bernadette and the Virgin Mary might appear to her in the waste ground next to Queen Street Swimming Baths or near the climbing bars in Babcock Park. Knowing her luck, Wanda thought, it probably would happen. She imagined the scene with the Pope dressed in white flanked by two red-robed cardinals, seated on the little sofa in their front room while he went through the sequence of events as to how exactly the Virgin appeared and what she had said. Meanwhile, the world's press would be trampling on her father's carefully manicured flower bed at the front of the house, hammering on the windows to take pictures of the pious and oh so correct Zosia and her mother would be trying to offer everyone tea and cake.

After the service, Wanda stood silently behind her parents while they chatted to friends. Janek was racing up and down the aisle with his arms outstretched shouting, 'I'm a Spitfire.' Babcia and Zosia were kneeling on the bench in front of the little shrine to the Black Madonna.

'You know the real portrait was painted by St Luke himself,' Wanda heard Babcia whispering while making the sign of the cross. 'It is therefore an exact likeness of the Holy Virgin because St Luke knew her personally. He painted it on a piece of the door from the actual home of the Holy Family. Now it is kept at the monastery in Jasna Gora in the south of Poland and is covered with gold and jewels. Do you see those marks on the face of the Madonna? Those were made by the sword of a MuslimTurk centuries ago. They tried to banish Christianity but failed when Poland threw the heathen back. In this way, Poland saved the whole of Europe from Islam.'

Wanda looked at the icon. The face was dark brown, the eyes narrow and grim. The slash on the cheek formed the letter 'A'. An abused woman alone, caring for a child. The picture suddenly reminded Wanda of someone – a photograph she'd seen in the family album of Babcia as a young widow. The same hollow eyes and straight mouth. She was even holding her baby in the same casual fashion, staring straight ahead, numb with shock.

Zosia and Babcia lit a candle. Wanda read the bronze plaque screwed to the wall beneath the icon.

This portrait of the Madonna was given as a gift to the people of Great Britain by the Polish Community in exile. It is a token of our gratitude for their generosity in granting us a safe haven during and after the Second World War.

Chapter 5

Fab Fashions is an exciting new chain of clothing stores. We aim our designs at young, fashion-conscious girls who yearn for that sophisticated look yet want clothes that are reasonably priced. We have stores in Birmingham, Coventry, Derby, Glasgow, London and Manchester. Fab Fashions has the backing of a major international design corporation. We are really going places!

Wanda read the brochure again and again. The most exciting part was that there was a branch of the store just off Oxford Street – London.

After she'd turned 15 that January, Wanda had left school. There seemed little point in staying and no one made any effort to persuade her. She'd managed to land herself a job at Fab Fashions, which had just opened near Derby Cathedral in Irongate. The economy was booming and jobs were abundant. Art shops, bookshops, cafes, restaurants, jewellery and ceramics shops were opening all over town. Royal Crown Derby Pottery was churning out crockery, the aero-engine makers, famous for having helped win the war, were producing engines for the world's first supersonic plane and the football team, Derby County, were at the top of the league. Optimism was in the air.

On her first day at Fab Fashions, Wanda was kitted out in a purple jacket and black trousers (after a little difficulty finding a pair that would fit round her hips) by Fab Fashions management. This was the uniform all the assistants wore. She was entitled to receive a 15 per cent staff discount and she could help herself to free tea or coffee in the little kitchen. She would meet all the trendy people in Derby and she would get four weeks paid holiday.

For six months Wanda waited, hoped, agonised, feared rejection and finally wrote asking to be transferred to the London branch. Two weeks later, her request was accepted.

'Of course, you can't go to London,' said her father. 'Where will you live? It's dangerous. Children end up on the streets there with no job, no money, no house.'

'I'm not a child and I will have a job,' insisted Wanda. 'I've been offered one at Fab Fashions just off Oxford Street and I'll arrange a room in a house before I go. In fact, Pam's aunt and uncle live in London and they have a room for rent in their place. I've already written to them to see if it's available. I'm waiting to hear.'

'But we don't know these people. Who are they?' asked her mother.

'Pam's uncle is a vicar, OK? Her aunt is his wife, OK? They live somewhere called Croydon in a vicarage, OK?'

Sick of the arguments, Wanda stormed out of the house and went round to Pam's house. Mrs Haines opened the door.

'Hello, Wanda.' She pronounced the name like Wan-der rather than Van-da. 'Pam is watching *Juke Box Jury*. You can go and join her. Would you like to stay for tea? It'll be ready in half an hour.'

Wanda joined Pam, who was sitting on the floor in front of the TV.

'What a boring panel this week and they're judging Ken Dodd *Tears for Souvenirs*,' said Pam with a groan.

'It's not like when the Beatles were on it. And they were right in nearly all their predictions,' replied Wanda.

'I saw Mick Jagger on *Top of the Pops* on Thursday. He's so gorgeous.'

'He's ok,' said Wanda unenthusiastically. 'Not a patch on Paul, of course.' And she gazed distractedly towards the kitchen.

Half an hour later, Mrs Haines called them to the dining

table. Wanda looked at the food. There was soft white bread and butter and a kipper on each plate, served with a cup of tea. Thick slices of Marks & Spencer Battenberg cake were stacked on a large willow pattern plate in the centre of the table.

Wanda thought about the Haines family. Mrs Haines always wore flowered aprons, she didn't go out to work – in fact she rarely left the house. She was supposed to be suffering from postnatal depression even though Pam was almost 16 and an only child. Mr Haines was an English teacher at the boy's grammar school and he smoked a pipe. Their Christian names were Liz and Ron. They ate shop-bought food, there were no little white mats and ornaments everywhere – just a few ceramic statuettes of dogs. And there were no religious pictures or icons either, just a few pictures of pastoral scenes. Their house was plain, their food was plain, their names were plain – they were English, totally, 100 per cent English. Their ancestors had lived in this country for hundreds and hundreds of years. They never had to explain their name or spell it to people in shops, they didn't speak another language at home, they were just ordinary, ordinary English. Wanda envied them more than she could say.

'Have you heard anything from my sister about renting a room in her house yet, Wander?' said Mrs Haines.

Wanda had just taken a slurp of milky tea. She wiped her mouth.

'Yes, she said it would be available as soon as they've finished decorating it.'

'That's good. We did give you a positive recommenda-tion you know. That's why Val said you could rent the room. She's rather fussy about who she has in the house, naturally. Her husband, Dave, is a vicar and he collects all sorts of people and brings them back home. Val has to watch him like a hawk.'

'Val watches everyone like a hawk,' said Mr Haines. 'In less charitable terms it would be called snooping.'

'Nonsense, she just has to make sure Dave is under

control. He's liable to do the most impulsive things like spontaneously invite the whole congregation to the house for dinner, or give away his car to someone who just asks him for it.'

'I suppose that makes him a Christian, then,' said Ron.

'It makes him a nutter,' said Pam.

Wanda thought about the conversation they normally had at her family's dinner table. Babcia would control events telling the children to sit properly and correcting their Polish or enquiring about Helena's job and health. Unlike Mr Haines, Tadek rarely said a word.

There was an uneasy silence broken by the clatter of the cups and saucers and laughter from the television.

'What do your parents think about you taking a job in London, Wander?' asked Mrs Haines.

'They are a little nervous but they know I've arranged everything properly and they're quite happy now.' Wanda gabbled this sentence out in embarrassment. It was a blatant lie but there seemed little point going into the acrimonious details of the frequent arguments she was having at home.

'I'm really looking forward to going,' she continued in a more measured tone. 'Actually, my sister will be glad as she'll have the bedroom to herself then. My grandmother is also leaving so they'll have loads more space.'

'Where's your grandmother going?' asked Mr Haines.

'She plans to go back to Poland. She wants to spend her remaining years there with her family and she wants to be buried with my grandfather.'

'Really? It was such a struggle getting her over here in the first place. I remember your mother saying your granny was living all alone in a gloomy, crowded block of flats and was having trouble getting enough to eat. I wrote a few letters to the British Embassy for her. How odd that she wants to go back now. They were all so happy when they got her out,' said Mr Haines.

'I remember those Polish pilots during the war,' his wife said. 'They were really handsome and exciting. I went out with a few Yanks and Canadians. Actually there were even German and Italian prisoners of war kept in a camp just outside town. They used to come and mend the roads and things like that. We girls would hang around watching them.'

'Mum, that's yucky,' said Pam.

'But the Poles were really special. They were tall and well turned out. Was your father a pilot, Wanda?'

'No, he came after the war. He was just a farmer. Nothing special.'

'I used to think Poland was near the North Pole,' said Pam. 'Do you remember I once asked you if there were Eskimos there?'

Wanda smiled and shifted uncomfortably in her seat as the rest of the family laughed.

'During the war, I always thought I'd marry someone glamorous afterwards and go and live abroad,' said Mrs Haines.

'But you ended up with Ron Haines,' said Pam

'Yes, I don't know how that happened.' Wanda watched Ron pick some tiny kipper bones out of his mouth. At least he didn't pour his tea into his saucer as her father did.

She looked round at the rest of the Haines family and wondered why they all had monosyllabic names, Liz, Ron, Pam, Val, Dave. She presumed they liked to keep things short and sweet with no frills – just like their house. How simple, how plain, how ordinary. That was the way she liked it.

* * *

That morning Zosia had been listening intently to Pan Nowak in her Polish lesson. She was relieved Wanda no longer came. Her heavy sighs and groans of boredom had become a source of huge embarrassment. Now Zosia could relax and pay full attention to the lessons. She had asked her teacher if he had any historical information about her grandfather and his family.

'Of course Poniatowski is a very aristocratic name,' Pan

Nowak told her. 'The last king of Poland was Stanislaw Poniatowski. He was an elected king in the 18th Century. Perhaps your mother's family is descended from him.'

Afterwards, Zosia walked home from the Polish Club considering what Pan Novak had said. Janek ran around in front of her, picking up sticks to fight imaginary foes.

As soon as she reached home, Zosia took down the precious photograph album and examined some pictures of The Prince as a teenager taken when he was at military school. She had borrowed a Russian dictionary from the library and used it to decipher the script engraved at the bottom of the photographs. The first word was the name of the photographer she worked out, followed by the place where the picture was taken – the Imperial Palace near St Petersburg called Tsarskoe Selo. Zosia went to find Babcia, who was making golabki, stuffed cabbage, in the kitchen.

'What did The Prince do when the revolution happened in Russia?' she asked.

'He was in Petersburg but escaped,' replied Babcia tasting some of the meat and rice mixture. 'Of course, they were shooting aristocrats then. But he was clever – he knew how stupid and illiterate those Russians were. When they stopped him at the border, he told them he was a Bolshevik commissar and showed the guard a bit of newspaper telling him it was a passport. This needs a little more salt, pass it here, *kochana*. Anyway, the man held it upside down, pretended to read it then let him through.'

'Did you see much of The Prince's parents or his sister, Maria?'

Babcia stirred the soup in a large tureen and thought for a while.

'No, his parents both died in the 1930s. I didn't see them very often after the Prince died, it took them a long time to get over his death. His sister is still alive but she is a rather strange woman. Funny political ideas – she was a communist even before Lenin, the family always said. Being a princess I suppose it was just her way of getting attention – well that's what my mother thought. She married a ghastly Jewish fellow. They didn't have any children and he didn't survive the German occupation.'

'Do you think she would reply if I wrote to her?' asked Zosia.

'I think she is rather odd in the head. It's probably better not to disturb her at this late stage in her life. But you could write to my niece Irena – she is dear Witold's daughter. She has a son called Pawel who was sweet when he was a little boy. They would welcome a letter, I'm sure.'

At that moment Tadek came into the kitchen from the garden, thick slices of black mud under his fingernails from working in his fruit and vegetable patch. A basket of sour green gooseberries hung over his arm. The previous day he'd picked a large punnet of strawberries. Tadek pickled any produce they didn't eat so jars of onions, green tomatoes, gherkins, and cucumbers were lined up in regimented rows on the shelves of the understairs cupboard. Tadek also made jam with the cherries, plums and strawberries and a sweet wine with the elderberries. There were large sacks of potatoes in the pantry and baskets of onions, carrots, parsnips and beans in the kitchen. Tomatoes had ripened in the greenhouse and there were pots filled with herbs – dill, marjoram, thyme and parsley.

'Look what I found when I was digging my potatoes.' Tadek held an object out to Zosia – a coin. She found a duster and rubbed it carefully. It lay large and heavy in her hand. She could just make out the monarch's head on the front – a young Queen Victoria. There was Britannia on the back and the date – 1842. Zosia squeezed the coin tight, knowing the last person to have touched it must have been a Victorian gent or lady. This area had been fields back then so maybe it had fallen out of a young gentleman's pocket while he relaxed on a picnic, or perhaps a dairymaid from a nearby farm had lost it on her way to market. Zosia placed the coin carefully in her little box of treasures. History was all that really mattered, thought Zosia. If we don't know who we are and where we came from, we are nothing.

Inspired, Zosia put on her apron and went out into the garden. She took a trowel, crouched on a patch of bare earth and started to dig. She found lots of stones of different shapes and sizes. Then she came across something white and angular. She pulled it out and rubbed it clean with her fingers. It was white on one side and had small blue flowers on the other – a piece of Victorian pot, perhaps a teacup shard. Zosia put her finds carefully in a pile. She found another piece of pot that was just white and a piece of old glass which may have come from a medicine bottle. Finally, she stood up and looked round her patch of garden. There were little holes all around where she'd made her earlier archaeological excavations. It was only a matter of time before she found an Anglo-Saxon sword, or a gold sovereign or a jewel dropped by Bonnie Prince Charlie (son of the Polish princess Maria Klementina Sobieska) who had stayed for a few days in Derby before turning round and going all the way back to Scotland again.

Chapter 6

'Good posture is the key to a healthy mind in a strong body,' or so Babcia's deportment teacher at the Smolny Institute had always said. Now Babcia stood stiff and silent, staring at her reflection in the wardrobe's full-length mirror. It seemed to be her mother's face that looked back at her now. She drew herself up proudly, laced her fingers together in front and raised her chin, just as she remembered her own mother doing. Barbara's once-brown hair was now white, but it was still shiny and thick, always carefully pinned up in a bun. Her skin was very pale, almost transparent and her green eyes shone out like two bright jade gems. Her teeth, still her own, were firm and yellow and she had kept her slim figure. Well, her body was healthy and her mind was made up, her course was set – she was definitely going home.

Alone at Porton Crescent every day until the children came back from school at half past four, Babcia had had plenty of time to think over the past year. Her advanced years preyed constantly on her mind. She'd been born long ago, when all official forms printed 18 – for the date. Death would certainly be the next hurdle but she wanted it to be played out in her own country. She imagined the funeral cortege, the procession to the cemetery, the gravediggers hauling out the earth above Jan's casket, lowering her coffin on the cords into the vacant spot.

Babcia had already written to her niece, Irena, asking if she could live with her until the time came to make that great journey to heaven. The reply came expressing what she took to be enthusiasm. She would return to the land of her birth, visit all the places of her youth, see all her relations who were still living and then join her dead ones in Poland's sacred soil.

But first there was something to do before leaving Derby. She wanted to make sure her departure was an event to remember. Babcia enjoyed speaking to an audience so she felt calm as she called the family into the sitting room that evening to explain her plan. They all sat around waiting for her to speak.

'As you all know I have a flight booked to Warsaw next month. But before I go I want to have a special party to celebrate my seven years in Derby. The event will be held on Saturday 24 June and will start with a memorial service at St Joseph's for my beloved husband on the occasion of his name day.'

'Ooh, that'll be fun,' said Wanda.

'Then we will proceed to the Polish Club where I have already booked the hall. We'll have speeches, music, food and perhaps some dancing for you young ones. I just want to thank you, my dear family, for the time we have spent together. I have been so happy to know my dear daughter is safe and has her family around her. You cannot imagine my distress when she was taken from me, or my joy when I eventually received her letter to tell me she was safe in England. But now is the time for me to return home to die.'

Babcia looked expectantly round the room.

'If your mind is made up, Mama, I know we cannot stop you. I just hope you are doing the right thing. I suppose we could make this a joint party as Wanda is leaving to work in London.' Helena twisted her handkerchief round and round her fingers.

'Good idea, all my friends would love to come to a memorial mass,' said Wanda.

'Will you come and visit me in Warsaw, Helenka?' said Babcia.

'No, Mama, there is no way I will ever go back there again.'

June 24 was a clear day with a light breeze. Babcia was

dressed in black, mourning for her dead husband. Helena wore black in remembrance of the father she never knew and Tadek wore his one and only dark suit. Zosia wore her grey dress trimmed with white lace and Janek wore grey trousers and a black jacket. Wanda wore a pink T-shirt, blue jeans and a red bandana. When the Baran family arrived at the church to pray for their dead husband, father, father-in-law and grandfather, a large picture of The Prince draped in red and white ribbons (the colours of the Polish flag) had already been placed before the altar rail. Babcia had written a special eulogy describing The Prince's noble life and sacrifice for country and family, which Father Kantor read out in a slow monotone.

Babcia sat in the front pew listening to the speech, nodding sagely. Yes, Jan had sacrificed his life for Poland and for her. He was a brave soldier, a noble aristocrat, a scholar, a gentleman... She looked at his photograph, enlarged to four times its original size and framed in gold. His face seemed close, looming large in front of her. She could see his magnificent moustache. She remembered how bits of tobacco adhered to strands of the hair, staining them yellow-brown. The smell came back to her, it was always the smell that came first – cigarettes on his breath, constant, constant cigarettes, the sharp aroma of morphine, dulling and deadening the pain. She felt a sudden surge of panic. It was like her nightmares when Jan's face loomed large in front of her. In those grim night terrors, he would start to scream and his face would crack and shatter like porcelain. Babcia gripped her seat and looked at Father Kantor – should she make her confession to him? No – he would recognise her voice through the confessional screen. She must go to another priest. Babcia closed her eyes and forced her breathing to regulate, her composure to return – all was well, she had nothing to confess, her life was blameless...

'Pani Poniatowska? Would you like to lead the way out?' Father Kantor's words seemed to come from the end of a long tunnel. There was a long pause while everyone's eyes were upon her.

'Yes, of course, thank you Father. Thank you so much,' and she handed him a small brown envelope, her contribution to church funds.

It was then off to the Polish club for the big farewell party with selected members of the Polish community. There were kanapki, marble cake and coffee followed by vodka. Babcia made a very long speech of farewell. All the while, The Prince's portrait, complete with ribbons, sat in prime position on a table so he could enjoy the party given on his behalf.

Babcia's final farewell gesture was to have professional photographs taken to commemorate the event. She also wanted something she could show the family in Warsaw. Pan Nowak, whose usual occupation when he wasn't teaching Polish Saturday school was running a photographic studio in Green Lane, had been commissioned to take the pictures.

He arrived with his equipment and positioned the Baran family in 16 Porton Crescent's cluttered sitting room. For the first picture, Babcia sat in the middle of the sofa with Janek on her knee, Helena to her right and Tadek to her left. Wanda, her blonde hair a frizz of ill-discipline, sat on one arm of the sofa to the left and Zosia, her brown hair tied in two neat plaits, on the other arm to the right. A painting of Christ pointing to his glowing red heart hung on the wall above Babcia's head. Pan Nowak then arranged a picture of just the children. A grinning Janek, making machine gun noises, stood in the middle with a large sullen Wanda to the right of him and a shy smiling Zosia to the left. As Pan Nowak's flash went off and his camera clicked, a black and white image of the Baran family was locked for posterity on a bright summer day in June 1965.

Babcia was pleased with how the leaving party had gone. The service for Jan was respectful and dignified. The food at the Polish club had been adequate and she felt she had been able to show her appreciation of her family in her speech. The only problem was Zosia. The child looked pale and upset. Barbara drew her onto her lap in the quiet of her bedroom.

'Sometimes, Zosia, sometimes people have to do what is right,' she explained. 'Sometimes people have to do their duty rather than what they would like to do. I feel it is my duty to be with my people, to be in my country, to be buried with my husband. Do you understand that?'

'No, I just want you to stay here with me. The people there don't need you.'

'I have spent a long time with you and I am grateful that I could do that, but the pull of home is too strong. You'll understand that when you're an old lady, like me.'

'I'll never be an old lady, I'll always be young.'

'No, one day you will be old and when you are I want you to look at this picture and remember me.'

Babcia took a small white envelope from her dressing table and handed it to her granddaughter. The little girl opened it. Inside was a picture of the Black Madonna. The dark, grim face, the decorated shawl, the small child vulnerable, powerless in his mother's arms.

'The Madonna represents the suffering of people, the suffering of Poland,' said Babcia. 'She feels what you feel, she flinches at your pain, she is sad in your loneliness. Tell her your problems, she is listening.'

Babcia watched Zosia stare at the card and turn it over. On the back she had written,

Kochana Zosia, always remember the Madonna is watching over you, just as I am always watching over you. All my love, Babcia.'

Chapter 7

Warsaw, 1965

'Name?'
  'Barbara Karolina Poniatowska.'
  'Age?'
  'I am 70 years old.'
  'Where will you be staying?'
  'Sympatyczna Street, Flat 35a.'
Babcia could feel the antipathy, the narrow-eyed hatred directed towards her. The woman at airport immigration control stared at her and then ordered her to open one of her suitcases. She pulled out all the clothes, searched the pockets, hems, cuffs, and all round the inside of the suitcase, ripping the lining. The woman was middle aged, her hair scraped back in a severe bun, her bosom and stomach straining at the buttons on her uniform. Babcia knew what was happening – she was being subjected to a trial by humiliation, kept standing for ages, having her belongings searched, making everyone wonder what crime she had committed.

'So you've come running back. The West is not such a hot bed of luxury after all,' the official barked, closing the suitcase with the clothes half tumbling out.

At least there petty officials know their station in life and are polite and respectful to their elders and betters, Babcia muttered to herself.

She felt tears pricking at her eyes. Full of enthusiasm, she had boarded a Lot Polish Airlines plane at East Midlands airport earlier that day and arrived in Warsaw two hours later. Flying for the first time at the age of 70 had proved to be an exhilarating experience. Stepping onto Polish soil in a state of high excitement, Babcia was quickly brought down to earth again by this dog-faced official. The woman had obviously taken a dislike to Babcia's face, her coat with the sable fur collar, her elegant amber jewellery.

When, two hours later, she was finally allowed out of the airport, Barbara felt deflated, disappointed, let down. She approached a taxi whose surly-looking driver was leaning against the cab smoking a cigarette. Babcia's proffered pound note changed his attitude immediately. He busied around putting her cases in the boot, opening the door for her and addressing her politely. She told him her niece Irena's address.

'Do you know this place?'

'Yes, lady, those are the old flats in the south-west. They were going to knock them down but they ran out of money as usual.' He revved up the engine and screeched out of the airport car park. 'They did knock down plenty of flats to make way for that thing, though.' He gestured towards the tall pointed building in the distance. 'The Palace of Culture. They say Stalin was jealous of the skyscrapers in Manhattan so he built that thing. Look at it there poking up into the sky. Stalin's prick I call it. Stalin may be dead but he's still sticking it in us, if you understand me. Oh, sorry, Lady, excuse my language.'

Babcia nodded at his apology and settled back into the seat of his taxi, before lurching forward as the driver crashed the gears and stamped on the accelerator. The familiar smell of cheap-grade petrol assaulted her nose.

'How is life in Warsaw these days? I've been abroad for seven years now,' she called above the engine's roar.

'What on earth did you come back for, Pani? They finished rebuilding the Old Town but everything else is the same – no tea, no lemon, no meat, queuing and queuing for hours for every damn thing. My son and daughter-in-law have been living with us in our flat for 10 years now. Their names are down for a place of their own but there's a 15-year waiting list. 15 years! You could die in that time.'

The taxi sped along the grey streets of Warsaw. Babcia looked out of the window in dismay. Nothing, absolutely nothing had changed.

'Look at that,' she mused, 'they still haven't cleared away those bomb sites from the war. How ridiculous. It's 20 years and the rubble is still there.'

'Don't remind me. I don't know what keeps people going – it's probably just religion and vodka.'

Babcia gazed at the huge, grey buildings and wide boulevards bisected by tram tracks that characterised her home city. The multitudes of flats built quickly and cheaply after the war stood squarely as the enemies of elegance and good taste. Huge red and black posters depicting the so-called heroes of the revolution glared down at the population to show who was in charge.

The driver steered the filthy, rusting taxi at high speed, smoking and swearing at other road users out of his open window. He swung the car round violently at every turn flinging Babcia around in the back seat.

She was grateful to arrive at her niece's block of flats and escape the rancid car. She extricated herself from the red plastic seat and gazed up at the large brownstone building while the driver went to get her cases. These old blocks looked better than the cheap flats put up just after the war but they were still dark and forbidding, often pock marked with bullet holes – a reminder, as if one were ever needed, of Warsaw's violent past. Washing hung from windows and somewhere a baby was crying.

Babcia's attention was suddenly drawn up to a second-storey balcony. A young man stood there, something in his arms, a white bundle of some sort. He reached out and held it out over the edge of the balcony. Babcia's heart surged and she swallowed back the nausea in her throat. She almost felt her 29-year-old self, rushing to the door and racing up the stairs, panicstricken that she might be too late. Panting, leaping three steps at a time, chemical-soaked desperation. The man on the balcony stared down at her for a moment then shook out the tablecloth he was holding, crumbs falling to the ground. He turned and went back inside the flat. Babcia closed her eyes and allowed her panic to subside.

The taxi driver carried her bags to the lift and wished her a very pleasant stay. He gave her his card in case she had need of a taxi again and even kissed her hand.

All at once, Babcia felt elated. She looked out of the window while waiting for the lift. In the central courtyard below, some blond-haired, nut-brown boys were playing football. Once on the third floor, Babcia struggled along the corridor with her bags and rang the bell of Irena's flat. The smell of cabbage and dill wafted down the corridor, the shouts in Polish of the children outside brought a surge of joy to her heart. She was once more in a country where she understood everything that was said. The smells, the architecture, the wide streets were all familiar. Babcia relaxed. She would manage just fine.

She waited, hoping Irena would answer the door and not Irena's mother Mira Ostrowska, who lived there, too. Irena's son, Pawel, was away on military service and her husband had long since disappeared with a woman and a bottle of vodka.

The door was opened by a tired-looking, middle-aged woman. Her greying hair was cut short and her clothes were worn and old-fashioned. But her face lit up at the sight of her aunt, showing the beauty that had once been there. Babcia smiled. There was an unmistakable resemblance to her brother, Witold, in his daughter's eyes. Irena kissed and hugged her enthusiastically.

'Auntie, come in, come in. How lovely to see you. Let me get your bags.' Barbara felt delighted with the reception. Then she noticed her sister-in-law, Mira, hovering sullenly in the background. Ah, well it was time to made amends.

'Mira, my dear, how are you?'

'I'm well, Barbara,' said Mira stiffly.

The two women kissed without warmth and Mira went back to her seat in the armchair. Babcia looked at her stony face. It brought back a memory – standing in the kitchen of her parent's house, the smell of dill, a salad called *Mizeria*. Babcia had been preparing it for Witold. She'd proudly carried the plate towards the dining table to present it to him. But Mira had intercepted her and grabbed the plate. The two women had struggled inelegantly until the cucumber and yogurt shot off onto the floor.

'He's my husband,' Mira had yelled. 'Just because you've lost yours, you can't have mine.'

'A man can have many wives,' Babcia had snapped, 'but Witold only has one sister.' Witold had sat, his napkin tucked into his collar, gazing helplessly from his wife to his sister while the two cousins, four-year-old Helena and Irena, had burst into tears. That had been in 1929.

But Babcia was here to wipe the slate clean. She accepted a glass of tea from Irena and settled down on the sofa.

'So, what did you think of flying, auntie? What an experience. I should love to try it,' Irena said.

'Oh, it wasn't too bad at all. The flight was only two hours. Can you imagine? When I think of how long it took me to get to England seven years ago. I had to go all the way up to Gdansk and then get the passenger ship to England. I was at sea for two days. No, the plane was fine – it was some rude official at the airport who annoyed me, and the bad driving of the taxi driver. Do you have any lemon for the tea, Irenka my dear?'

'No, auntie.'

'We haven't seen lemon for about a year, nor ham or butter,' Mira snapped. Babcia bit her lip. She disliked her tea without lemon.

'How is Helenka?' inquired Irena.

'Oh, she's well. Tired and overworked but healthy. The factory seems to be doing well and she has so much paid overtime to do.'

'She's a machinist in a clothes factory, isn't she? Well

she's had enough experience at doing that, hasn't she?'
Mira sounded more cheerful. 'Irena is very busy also. She
has been promoted to head of paediatrics at the Lenin
Hospital. A great honour, of course, but doctors are not
given the financial rewards they should get.'

Babcia stiffened her back. Helena had always been more
intelligent than Irena, their long-forgotten school reports
had indicated that.

'No, well that's communism,' said Babcia. 'They pay
doctors nothing and miners get a king's ransom. Poor
Helena missed out on so much education because of the
war but her job at the factory is well paid. She has a two-
storey house with four bedrooms and its own private
garden.' Babcia looked round the tiny flat. 'And her
children are a delight especially my little Zosia. She is the
image of my husband – it's incredible, the similarity. I
always tell her how like her grandfather she is.'

Barbara saw Mira pulling a face.

'Have some cheese cake, auntie,' said Irena.

'Thank you, darling. I had hopes for little Janek, but I
think he rather takes after his father's side, as does
Wanda.'

'Oh, that reminds me – do you know who I saw on
the tram the other day?' Mira said. 'That strange sister
of Jan's. I still see her around from time to time. I never
speak to her of course because she wouldn't remember
me from a bar of soap. She's quite a local character. Goes
around talking to herself and wearing the strangest,
brightly coloured clothes. Sometimes children poke fun
or throw things at her. Anyway, she was on the tram
having an argument with the driver – shouting and
waving her arms around, beating the poor man with her
umbrella.'

'Princess Maria was always rather …' began Babcia.

'You know Pawel is still away on military service,'
interrupted Irena, changing the subject. 'My little boy
a soldier – just think of that. He won't be home for at
least six months. I wrote and told him you were coming.

And do you know what – he's so anxious to see his cousins in England. Could they send him an invitation so we can start the passport application? It takes months to come through, you know. But he will need the invitation.'

'Oh, that would be no problem. Helena would be delighted to see him.' Babcia sounded confident.

Mira pulled a face. 'He wants to go there, you want to come here.' She wandered off into the kitchen muttering to herself.

'How is Pawel?' inquired Babcia. 'I looked at the photos you sent to try to see any resemblance to my dear Witold but I don't know if it was too obvious. Is he enjoying military service?'

'No of course not, he hates it. Western music and Western clothes are his only interests.' She reached over to the sideboard and picked up a photo. 'Here is his latest picture taken in uniform. Look at that, Private P. Lato. He absolutely detests having his hair so short.'

Babcia took the picture. The boy didn't look up to much, probably took after Irena's feckless husband – Alex? Alexei? whatever his name was. He looked puny and his hair was far too long for the military cap he was wearing.

'Yes,' Babcia handed back the picture, 'I'm sure Helena would be delighted to have him to stay. She is so happily married. She and Tadek celebrated their 20th wedding anniversary this year. What do you give for that anniversary, ceramics, isn't it?

'I don't know, auntie.'

Babcia paused and looked out of the window. The tree in the courtyard swayed in the breeze.

'And I am commemorating 40 years of being a widow,' she murmured. 'What anniversary is that, do you think – a wilted flower, a silver thorn, a broken heart?'

'Well, you make yourself at home, auntie, and I'll help mother prepare lunch,' Irena soothed.

Babcia watched the steam rise from her glass of weak,

sugarless, lemonless tea and settled back onto the shabby sofa that would become her bed for that night and all the nights to come.

Chapter 8

London, 1966

Wanda stepped down from the train on to the platform at St Pancras. As she did so, one of her new, white high-heeled slip-on shoes slipped off. She watched in horror as the shoe bounced on the edge of the platform and then fell down onto the track under the train. She gasped, standing on the platform teetering on one white shoe. Crouching down and peering below the step of the train, Wanda could see her shoe lying sadly on its side, heel up on the track, the toe resting among the splashes of diesel and litter of the sleepers. She stood up and looked up and down the platform in desperation. Fighting back tears, she hopped and limped towards the ticket office.

'My shoe fell down under the train,' she told the man in the ticket office.

'What?' shouted the man above the station announcements and the roar of a newly arrived train.

'How can I get my shoe back? It fell under the train.'

'I'll get the pole when I have a minute,' he said, as if he'd heard it all before.

Wanda waited on a nearby bench, people glanced at her single, shoeless foot. One woman was staring so persistently, Wanda said, 'It's the latest fashion in Derby, you know,' and the woman looked quickly away.

Wanda looked up at the high, vaulted ceiling, the iron construction, the glass panels blackened with age. This place was really old and really shabby. Unintelligible messages were being broadcast over the loudspeakers, bits of newspaper were wafting around the platforms, and pigeons were flying around the roof splattering their white deposits down the grimy, black walls. A tramp slept full length on a bench just underneath a hole in the glass ceiling. The snow was gently falling onto his ragged coat.

Wanda turned away and saw the guard approaching carrying a long pole with a hook on the end. She hopped and hobbled after him to show him where her shoe was.

'Soon get that out,' he said. 'I'm always having to get things off the track – bags, glasses, coats, someone's false teeth once.' He hoiked it up. 'There you are, love. No harm done. Just a bit of diesel,' and he rubbed the white shoe with his sleeve, smearing the black stuff all over it.

As she tottered towards the station exit, Wanda realised that the shoes were really hurting and her case seemed much heavier than before. She had not gone very far when her ankle twisted over. Wanda winced in pain. It was only 4 o'clock but already twilight had fallen on the leaden January sky. She looked at the address on the slip of paper in her purse. It read: Rev D Greenhalge, The Vicarage, St Mary's Road, East Croydon. She asked a porter which tube she should take to East Croydon.

'There's no tube,' he replied, 'You can get a bus from outside here but it will take about two hours to get there. Or you can take the tube to London Bridge station then get another train from there. That will only take an hour, maybe less.'

Wanda plumped for the bus as she decided there was less chance of getting lost that way. As she waited in the cold and dark, she fought back tears of pain from her ankle and from disappointment. Two hours! East Croydon was nowhere near the centre of London.

But as she sat on the bus, Wanda felt a tug of excitement as it drove over Waterloo Bridge, Big Ben and the Houses of Parliament on one side and St Paul's on the other. All lit up, their splendid light reflected in the water. She felt safe – these monuments were solid, powerful, immovable. Wanda wondered if she would ever be able to grab a tiny piece of that power.

To while away the time, she took out some paper and a pen and began practising her new signature – Tracey

Thompson? No, too common. Patricia Osborne-King? She'd never remember it and it was too posh. She needed something plain. Maybe, Jean Stapleton. Yes, that was perfect.

The pain from her ankle was getting worse so she slipped off her shoe and bent down to massage the swelling. A short, bald man boarded the bus. For half a second Wanda's heart lurched and she nearly blurted out, 'Daddy'. As she had left home that morning, Tadek had embraced her with tears in his eyes. He told her she must phone when she arrived, she must write every week, she mustn't open the door to strangers. As soon as she was ready to come home he would come to fetch her in the car. Why couldn't he take her down in the car and see where she would be living? But Wanda had been adamant – she was doing this on her own.

She was almost asleep when the conductor told her they had reached East Croydon and gave her directions to St Mary's Road. A thin layer of snow had fallen and Wanda slipped a little on the pavement, her ankle still hurting. She saw the church first, the thin black spire rising up in the gloom. An illuminated sign outside read, CHRISTian, hope and joy. The vicarage was opposite the church. It was a large, Victorian house with a balcony over the front door and dead Virginia creeper hanging about the façade. There was a brass doorknocker in the shape of a fox. To be on the safe side, Wanda rang the bell and knocked the knocker. A tiny yellow child's tricycle stood in the garden covered in snow.

A youngish man opened the door dressed in a navy blue sweater and jeans.

'Hello, I'm Jean,' said Wanda. 'I'm the new lodger.'
The man stared at her.

'I went to school with Pam Haines, your niece. She told you I was coming and I wrote to you.'

'Yes, of course, I'm sorry,' said the man. 'Pleased to meet you,' and he held out his hand in greeting. 'Do come in. You must be freezing. Let me get your bag.'

Wanda entered the hall. She looked down and noticed the man was wearing blue socks with brown sandals. The warmth of the house was comforting.

'Is the vicar in?'

'Yes, that's me, Dave the Vicar,' he laughed. 'Dave Greenhalge – that's green as in the colour and halge pronounced to rhyme with bilge. Well, not rhyme exactly but you know what I mean. People always have trouble with it – I suppose I should change it to Smith or something but it seems rather deceptive to change one's name. As if you're ashamed of something. It would make life easier for me, though. I always have to spell it out for people.'

Wanda smiled. She'd introduced herself as Jean but Mrs Haines would have told them her name was Wanda. He hadn't seemed to notice. Perhaps she'd just say she wanted to be called Jean, and leave it at that. Dave picked up her bag and began carrying it upstairs.

'Anyway, I'll show you your room first,' continued Dave. 'It's at the top of the house, quite nice. My wife, Val, will be back later and you can talk to her about what you want to do with meals and that.' Wanda followed him upstairs. The house smelled of furniture polish and long-cooked vegetables. Dave paused, 'the bathroom is here on the first floor and that's my little girl's room, Sarah, she's asleep now. She's nearly three. I hope you don't mind kids. She makes rather a lot of noise early in the morning but at least she's in bed early.' He walked up another small flight of stairs and Wanda followed. They entered a door at the top and Dave put on the light.

'Here it is, let me close the curtains. I'll put your case on the bed and you can unpack later. Now, come down and meet some young people from my youth club, I say my youth club but it's affiliated to the church, that's All Saints over the road there, and I run it along with many other helpers, of course.' Wanda quickly slipped off her tight shoes with a sigh of relief and followed Dave downstairs again.

In the kitchen sat a group of young people. 'Here we are, everyone, this is Jean our new lodger. Jean is from Derby – isn't that where they made those planes in the war? – and I'm sure she'll want to get involved in the youth club. Jean this is Paul, Rachel, Mark and Peter. Say hello to Jean everyone.' They all murmured a greeting. Wanda smiled and gave a feeble wave.

'Aah, I hear a key in the door, that must be Val,' continued Dave. 'What excellent timing! Yes, it is – Val, come and meet Jean our new lodger. Jean, this is my wife, Val.'

Wanda turned to see a woman with short black hair and a very red face enter the hall. Wanda hung shyly back.

Val whispered something in a very small voice.

'What?' said Wanda.

'Welcome, sorry, I thought my sister said your name was Wanda,' whispered Val a little louder.

Wanda moved closer, straining to hear.

'Erm, yes but I like to be called Jean.' Val's eyes narrowed as she looked at her.

'Anyway, Jean,' said Dave the Vicar, 'I bet you'd love a nice cup of tea, let me put the kettle on. Now Jean, when do you start your new job? You know the station is only a 10-minute walk from here and that will whiz you up to London Bridge in about 15 minutes then you get the tube. You'll probably have to get the Northern Line and then change to the Central Line.' Dave filled the kettle, lit the gas and plopped it on the stove with a clatter. 'If you start work at 9 o'clock on Monday you'll probably need to catch the 8.09 train so you'll need to leave the house by 10 minutes to 8 to be on the safe side. I'll get you a map and ticket prices. You know you can always make sandwiches to take which will save so much money. Shall I show you the train timetable?'

Wanda smiled. 'Perhaps tomorrow we could do that. I think I'll get an early night. I had some food on the train so I'm not too hungry.'

'Just wait a minute for your tea,' said Dave as the kettle began to whistle. He poured the steaming water in a large, brown teapot and brought out a yellow and green chipped mug. 'Here, we are – a nice cup of Rosie Lee.'

Wanda took the mug. The strap of her handbag, which she still had over the shoulder, suddenly slipped down her arm, jerking the cup in her hand and spilling some of its boiling hot contents on her hand. She gave a little scream and hurriedly put the mug down and brought her hand up to her mouth.

'Oh, quick, quick' said Dave, 'get your hand under the tap, here put it under the cold water straight away.' Dave grabbed Wanda's hand and propelled her over to the sink. He turned the tap on so violently the water splashed all over Wanda's dress.

'Don't worry, it's ok, I'm fine,' said Wanda pulling her hand from his grasp. She disliked him touching her, the feel of his clammy hand. 'You know, um, Dave, I think I'll take my tea upstairs and get an early night if you don't mind. I'm really tired after that long journey.' The pain from her twisted ankle was getting worse.

'Oh, of course, you do that. Make yourself at home,' said Dave the Vicar.

'Goodnight,' she called to the teenagers sitting round the dining room table. They were all reading from *The Good News Bible* with pictures of happy, smiley, wholesome youths on the front cover.

'God bless,' they called looking up from their orange juice and Bourbon biscuits.

Wanda made her way up the two flights of stairs, into her room and shut the door with relief. The only window looked out onto the street with a view of the church. There was a chest of drawers, a dressing table with a mirror, a single bed, a chair and a bedside table, as well as a small wardrobe with a full front mirror and a Victorian fireplace which had been painted all over in white. The pictures on the wall were of flowers or fruit.

Wanda opened her case and took out her little radio, sponge bag and night things. Folded neatly in the bottom of her case was her poster of Paul. She looked round for the best place to stick it to. Above the bed would be ideal so he could watch over her. Wanda climbed onto the bed to attach the poster with the bits of Sellotape that still adhered to the back. She was trying to position it when she heard scratching and whispering from the door. Did the Greenhalges have a dog, she wondered. The door opened and Val walked in.

'Jean – oh please don't put posters on the wall. We've just had the room decorated and it will pull off the wallpaper,' whispered Val. Wanda froze, noticing how Val's face became redder as she spoke. The redness seemed to end at a definite line on her neck. 'Oh, and please don't put hot tea mugs on this bedside table without a mat. If you can avoid bringing hot drinks up here at all that would be best. Also that bed is not super strong so I think it's best not to stand on it. I just wanted to let you know that there isn't any hot water left now so perhaps you could have a bath tomorrow. Also, I'm afraid the hot water tank isn't very large so we have to confine ourselves to baths not more than 2-3 inches deep. I wanted to talk to you about meals. The price of the room doesn't include meals but they could be arranged for an extra fee. Anyway, we can talk about that tomorrow. Good night, oh and we don't like loud music,' she pointed at the radio, ' because of Sarah – she needs her sleep. Goodnight.'

Val walked out of the room and closed the door. Wanda still stood on the bed, back pressed against the wall. 'What?' she whispered.

Chapter 9

Derby, 1966

'Hello, Gorgeous!'

Helena wasn't quite sure if he was speaking to her. She was standing under the flickering fluorescent lights in the Co-op, Tom Jones's *It's Not Unusual* playing over the store sound system. As Helena examined a Vesta ready meal, reading the instructions that said you just had to add water and boil it for a few minutes, the young lad who stocked the shelves in the shop had grinned up at her with these words. She stared at him in astonishment restraining a small smile.

Outside, the January weather had made the steep pavement slippery and Helena had battled her way to the shop on her way home from work. Her green headscarf and brown coat covering her light blue factory overall weren't enough to keep out the chill and her thick-soled, black shoes only just managed to grip the slick paving stones. The warmth and bright lights in the shop were temporary relief. Helena didn't need to buy so much food anymore, not since Babcia and Wanda had both left. Looking in the basket, she'd also found herself buying more convenience meals now that Babcia was no longer there to cook. She knew standards were slipping and was feeling rather depressed until the boy's comment had caused some amusement and satisfaction.

Helena never really concerned herself with her appearance. She tended to wear dowdy clothes and flat shoes for work and that evening her hair was wet from the sleet, but the cold had reddened her cheeks to a healthy glow and nothing could hide the fact that Helena was beautiful. She had been an exquisite baby, a sweet little girl, a glamorous teenager and a beautiful woman. She knew this to be true but somehow she had forgotten to think about it. The boy's comment brought the thoughts back. She must be beautiful still – she was tall and slim with a perfect complexion. She stood out like an orchid among the ragwort at Babcock's Hosiery Works.

It had been a long shift that day at the factory. Her overlock machine had kept breaking down so she'd had to wait for the engineer to mend it and then make up the work later. Fortunately, she was a fast and accurate machinist.

As she walked towards her house, weighed down by two string shopping bags, Helena considered the words 'fast and accurate machinist'. These had been the exact terms she'd used to describe herself to the manager during her initial interview at Babcock's 15 years earlier. It had been a hot day, an Indian summer and Helena had walked up to the entrance feeling miserable because she'd had to leave her nine-month-old baby with a neighbour. The clatter of the sewing machines had been audible from the street outside. Helena had stood for a while rooted to the spot – the sound hammered in her head and made her feel sick with fear. Above the entrance to the mill was an enormous statue of Britannia with her spear and shield. Helena looked up at it, wishing she never again had to enter a clothing factory, sit at a sewing machine, push the fabric beneath that juddering needle. But she had to get a job, her family needed to eat, so she braced herself and walked into the tiled foyer.

There was the bust of the mill's founder Mr Babcock (1820-1888) taking pride of place in the entrance hall. Feeling miserable, sick and frightened, Helena walked up to the office.

'Have you any experience of being a machinist?' the oily manager had inquired. 'We make knickers, stockings, trousers and jackets. I want someone fast, who don't natter all day long and can sew a fine seam.'

Helena looked through the office window at the

machine room. Scores of women hunched over their machines, large reels of coloured thread spun round on their pivots, machinery clattered and hammered, fabric dust filled the air. She swallowed the nausea in her throat. The thought of sitting down at a sewing machine again in the company of dozens of other women made her want to scream in panic.

'Yes, I have four years experience of machine sewing. I'm extremely fast and accurate machinist. Take me on and I show you it.' Helena had to force the words out. Her right hand shook with fear and she held it tightly in her left, trying to disguise the tremor.

He had eyed her suspiciously. Her clothes marked her out as a foreigner even before she opened her mouth and spoke her heavily accented English.

But he'd taken her on for a three-month probation period.

Helena made sure he didn't regret it. She was the fastest machinist in the company – she had had plenty of practice. She caused the other girls some concern.

'Ere, Helen. Slow down. Nobody's got a gun to yer 'ead,' they said.

But Helena let her fingers fly across the fabric and her basket of completed work filled at a rapid rate. She didn't find it difficult to imagine that someone did indeed have a gun to her head.

Helena had been pleased when the oily manager made her supervisor with increased responsibility and a pay rise. And with her quiet manner and gentle ways, she caused little resentment among the other workers. Helena was used to soothing violent outbursts and mollifying aggressive natures. She had had many years of practice at that too.

At the very moment when Helena was being called 'gorgeous' by a 16-year-old boy in the Co-op, her husband, Tadek, was flushing the toilet in the downstairs cloakroom of the Polish Club, *Dom Polski*. He had spent all afternoon fixing a leak and unblocking the cistern. Finally, it was working as he proudly demonstrated to the club manager, Jerzy Batorowicz. The plumbing in the building was old and cranky and Tadek was often called to see to its various faults and temperamental problems.

'Excellent, Tadek. I also need you to put up some more coat pegs in the hall, a new handle on the front door and…'

'I'm afraid I won't be able to do it for a few days, Pan Batorowicz,' Tadek interrupted. 'Tomorrow I'm doing some painting and decorating for Pani Zawada. That will take me about a week. Then I can come back and finish here after that.'

'Fine. I have a list of several jobs I need doing. Actually I also need some painting done at my own house. I'll let you know about that.'

'Certainly, Pan Batorowicz'. Tadek stood still, silently waiting.

'I've already put the petty cash box away. I'll pay you next week, Remind me.'

'Yes, sir,' Tadek sighed.

'Oh Tadek – are you coming to the dance this Saturday? The Airforce Association is putting on a really good event. We want everyone in the community to support it. The proceeds will go to a charity that helps the elderly in Poland.'

Tadek thought about his mother-in-law.

'We might well be there, Pan Batorowicz. See you later.'

Tadek packed up his tools and made his way out past a large banner in the dance hall proclaiming, 'The Battle of Britain.' Beneath it a large aircraft propellor was fixed to the wall. The room was adorned with black and white photographs of smiling young fighter pilots sitting and standing next to their planes. Tadek glanced at them. Were they smiling because they had lived through another day? Those who had survived formed the Polish Airforce Association in 1951 and their headquarters was at this club. They were an elite group, a happy band of brothers who held the reins of power. Tadek was not one of them. His grimy hands clutched his tool box, his navy blue all-in-one overall rustled as he walked, and his paint-spattered working boots stomped heavily over the polished wooden floor.

Tadek got into his old car and headed back to Porton Crescent. Since his mother-in-law had gone, he knew the house and family were not running too well. He actually missed her home cooking and he knew Helena was getting over tired. He worried about Wanda all alone in London, realised Zosia was looking very thin and miserable these days and knew that, left to his own devices, Janek would grow wild and forget his Polish heritage. Tadek realised he should spend more time with the boy but he was always so busy working trying to keep up the mortgage payments on the house they could only just afford.

He kept his worries to himself, never sharing them with his wife. Their marriage had always been one of quiet resignation. They never argued, never even had strong words, but she was the boss. She had lowered herself to marry him and he hadn't been able to believe his luck. In every relationship, there is the one who loves and the one who is loved. Tadek was the one who loved and he would never do anything to jeopardise his position.

He wanted to keep Helena in a suitable manner for a lady of her birth and early upbringing. Life had been hard at first in England, but after years of living in rented accommodation, feigning indifference to the *No Poles* signs he saw on properties just after the war, and the time spent living in a slum terrace house, Tadek was determined to keep hold of their middle-class house. It was his pride and joy and his foothold in the new society.

Chapter 10

Babcia woke to the sounds of Mira banging pots in the kitchen. It was All Soul's Day, 1 November, and outside drizzle fell from a glowering sky. Babcia had plans for that day. She'd put it off for a few months, but now she was grasping the nettle, taking her chance, being courageous.

She sat up, her back aching from the unyielding metal ridge across the middle of the bed – the trials of life in this country. She had become accustomed to a higher standard of living after seven years in England, and was having problems in Warsaw. There was no privacy – every morning Babcia had to fold up her bed to serve as the daytime sofa. The shortage of space with three people in such a small flat meant there was nowhere for her to store her clothes. And the noise – Warsaw howled like a wounded monster. The trams starting rattling and clanging around 4 in the morning, neighbours in the flats above, below and either side shouted and argued with each other interminably, the pipes and heating system hissed and squeaked all day. And she was lonely. Irena worked long hours and Mira had refused the olive branch of friendship. Babcia would even have welcomed the company of a television, but Irena didn't have one.

She got out of bed, walked to the tiny bathroom and turned on the taps. The green, chlorine-stinking water filling the chipped and stained tub. Lying back in the bath, she thought about her recent excursions.

She sometimes went down to the Old Town and bought herself an ice cream while sitting in the market square. Babcia remembered the original medieval market square from before the war. Every merchant house, every gable, every window, every doorway had been meticulously recreated. Babcia herself had spent time during the 1950s in helping to rebuild the structures. During that time, there had been even less food, poorer housing, shabbier infrastructure, yet they had spent precious energy putting the past back in place again. It had felt futile at the time – like sending the Polish Cavalry to fight the German tanks – but futility, honour and pride were all vices and virtues of the Polish character.

Babcia also whiled away the days visiting the museums, and she would attend as many operas, plays and films as she could at the Palace of Culture. At least such entertainment only cost a couple of zlotys. She even went up to the viewing galley at the top. Everyone said it was the best view in Warsaw because it was the only place from where the pointed palace could not be seen.

Lying in the bath that morning, Babcia thought about her plans for the day. It was one of the reasons she had returned to Warsaw and she had already put it off for too long. She had to go and make her peace before it was too late.

Curiosity had finally overcome fear. Her sister-in-law, Maria, was her social superior but memories of her hard and caustic manner were still strong – even though they hadn't seen each other since 1926. It was at Jan's funeral that they had last met face-to-face. Babcia thought back to that freezing cold January day. The ground had been iron hard and there had been considerable trouble digging the grave through the unyielding soil. Babcia had left baby Helena with her parents and walked into the church on the arm of her brother, Witold. She remembered pausing at the door waiting for everyone to notice her.

Mira had been there as were some people from the Technical Institute but otherwise the church was almost empty. Babcia's parents-in-law arrived swathed in black but curiously unemotional. They hardly glanced in her direction.

But it was Maria, Jan's elder sister, who had made the

most dramatic entrance. She arrived (late) with Nathan –
her husband or at least the man she lived with, no one
remembered her ever having a wedding – and to everyone's astonishment she came dressed in a bright scarlet
dress complete with plunging neckline, jet jewellery and a
large green hat with an ostrich feather in it. She laughed
loudly, sat reading a novel and even smoked in church.
Babcia remembered staring at her in silent fury. Even at
her own brother's funeral she had to be the centre
of attention. Dr Nathan sat beside her, seemingly
unembarrassed. He was a small, neat man with curly
black hair and a little beard. He had dressed respectfully
in a black coat and hat. After the funeral his dark eyes
looked with compassion at Babcia and she turned away to
avoid his pity.

'Dear Barbara – I understand what you went through,'
he'd said to her sympathetically. She had looked at the
ground without replying.

Afterwards all the talk had been of Maria's behaviour
and not of Babcia's quiet dignity. It was the final straw –
the relationship was ended. All through the 1930s and
during the war, Babcia had avoided Maria. Her anger
lingered and fear of Dr Weinberg's knowing eyes struck
deep.

But that was all so long ago. Babcia had come back to
Poland to start making peace with the world and going to
see her sister-in-law was part of that. She wasn't making
much progress with Mira, so if one sister-in-law wouldn't
take the bait, try the other one, she thought.

Despite the passage of time, Babcia knew where Maria
would be living. Flats were allocated and people stayed in
them for the rest of their lives. Maria had lived in the same
place since 1924.

Without saying anything to Mira who would only scoff,
Babcia made her way outside and walked along to the
tram stop. There seemed to be a man following her. How
ridiculous – the secret police were still keeping tabs on her.
No wonder everyone supposedly had a job when people

were employed following old ladies around the street. Babcia stopped and waved cheerfully to the man who turned away and made great play of reading his newspaper.

A short tram ride later and Babcia alighted, her stomach shaky with nerves but knowing she'd feel better after the ordeal was over. Deep breaths, straight back, imagine a piece of string is attached to your head and it is pulling you upwards – the words of her deportment teacher at the Smolny Institute, uttered about 60 years ago, came back to her.

It was here that she would need to change trams. She felt a little better until she glanced up casually at the sign on the side of the building – Senatorska Street. The street sign lurched alarmingly in and out of focus. She looked at the gutter and seemed to see a wicker shopping basket rolling down towards the drain. A sickness came to Babcia's stomach and rising panic to her throat. Her heart raced and sweat ran down her back. On the pavement, there was a roadside shrine with flowers and small black and white photographs of smiling men and women. Babcia knew who they were – the faces of those who'd been shot that day in 1942.

'Helena, Helena' she mumbled and bent her head against the wall, leaning on it for support. A stranger came up and asked if she was all right. Babcia looked up.

'Yes, yes, thank you,' she gasped. 'I'm sorry – I was just remembering a round-up in this street during the war – a *lapanka*. I hadn't thought about it for a long time.'

'It's best not to think about it, Pani,' replied the stranger. 'Where are you going? Do you need help?'

'Could you just help me on to the right tram please? I need to go to Piekna.'

Recovering her composure, Babcia boarded the correct tram which rattled down the wide boulevards. A young boy stood up and allowed her to have his seat. Babcia smiled graciously. The tram approached Piekna. She knew this street very well. She checked the address written on her piece of paper and found the door to the correct apartment block. Making her way up to the second floor, she paused for breath every now and then. This was the flat. On a yellowing card by the door bell an ancient spidery hand had written *Maria Poniatowska*.

Babcia waited a moment before ringing the bell. How did one restart a conversation after 40 years? The only option was to be as cheerful and dignified as possible. Anyway, at their advanced ages did it really matter anymore? No, one of the good things about being old was that many things ceased to matter. Babcia took the plunge and pressed the button.

Eventually there came the sound of a terrible hacking cough, mumbling and panting and an indication that someone was fumbling with the locks. A croaked voice said, 'Who is it?' but Babcia said nothing and waited for the door to open. When it eventually did, it revealed a tiny figure dressed in black with vibrant orange hair, a brown, wrinkled little face with two small black eyes and bright red lipstick. A long, deep scar cut itself down her cheek from her left eye almost to her mouth. Throughout all the fumbling, Babcia noticed, the woman had managed to retain a long length of ash on her cigarette. The small eyes stared at her.

'What?' she said.

'Good morning, Maria. Such a long absence. I hope you don't mind my calling on you. I have recently returned to Warsaw and decided now was the time for us to meet. I hope we can be friends, life is short ...'

Maria continued to stare. Babcia continued.

'I'm sorry I didn't telephone. I thought I'd just come and see you. Is it a convenient time? I hope so.'

'I have absolutely no idea who you are,' squawked the little old woman.

'Forgive me, forgive me. Dear Maria, I'm Barbara, Jan's widow.'

'Jan's widow? Ostrowska is it? I remember you. Miss New Money. Your father made hats didn't he?'

'Actually, he imported high-quality fashion accessories from Paris ... but never mind, what I was ...'

'Well, you'd better come in, I suppose,' and the little woman turned round and walked back into the flat, leaving Babcia to close the door.

Once in the hall, Babcia took off her thick brown coat and hung it on a peg. Then she followed her sister-in-law into the main room of the flat. The door to the balcony was slightly ajar and the area was filled with pot plants and flowers. The net curtains floated gently in the cold breeze and a pale winter sun caught on the gold top of the Palace of Culture in the distance and twinkled into the flat.

'Tea?' enquired Maria curtly.

'Oh, yes please. That would be lovely, dear Maria.'

Maria shuffled off into the kitchen. Babcia glanced round the room. There were a few nice pieces she recognised from the Poniatowski estate – the gold clock on the mantelpiece, the portrait of an ancestor on the wall. There was also a black and white photograph of Nathan next to the clock. Those knowing eyes – Babcia looked quickly away.

'Actually, I had a bit of a panic on the way here,' said Babcia loudly so she could be heard in the kitchen. 'I came down Senatorska and remembered the *lapanka* in '42. One of those coded whistles came into my head and I nearly fainted. A kind gentleman helped me. I don't know why I had a panic attack now. I never had one during the war. I suppose as you get older, emotional incidents from the past return to haunt you.'

Maria returned carrying a tray with tea and cake. Perhaps this meeting wasn't going to be as awful as Babcia had anticipated.

'Senatorska? That street always makes me laugh. I remember walking down there – I think it was May 1940 – carrying detailed plans of the sewers to pass on to the resistance. Did you know our sewers were designed by an Englishman called Lindley? I know a lot about them.' She placed the tray down on the small coffee table in front of the sofa and settled herself into an armchair. 'I had on my prettiest dress, my hair was done nicely and the day was so sunny one could almost pretend to be happy. Suddenly I heard a German soldier shouting behind me, '*Fraulein, fraulein*'. I stopped and had to make an instant decision. Should I go to him or make a run for it. I decided to turn and go back. He came hurrying up to me with one of the rolled up maps in his hand. He bowed and said, 'Excuse me miss, but you dropped your piece of paper!"

At this Maria cackled with delight, started coughing violently and lit another cigarette. Babcia smiled thinly.

'How did you manage to be so brave, Maria?' said Babcia settling herself on the sofa despite the fact she had not been invited to sit.

'It wasn't bravery,' Maria leant back in her chair, 'I wanted to get caught. They had taken Nathan by then.'

Babcia wondered whether to ask about Maria's scar (she certainly didn't have it in 1926) but she decided to say nothing and wait for Maria to break the silence.

'Why did you say you'd come back to Warsaw? Where were you?' asked Maria.

'In England. Back in '57, I went to live in England with Helena. She has a lovely house and three beautiful children.'

'Ah, Helena. So you found her again. I heard she'd been taken.'

'Well, she found me. A year after the war I suddenly had a letter from her. After she was taken in the *lapanka*, I didn't know where she was or even if she was still alive.' Babcia thought back to the unspeakable joy of the day that letter had arrived. She still had it safe among her most treasured possession, the ink smeared with tears. 'Helena told me she was living in Derby in England. I was so happy I cried for days. My life had lost all meaning and now it all came back. Children and grandchildren are the only meaning in life.'

'Well, I wouldn't know.'

Babcia looked down at her tea. Maria had no children

and therefore no grandchildren. Her line was ended, her genes wouldn't continue. Biologically she had failed, she was finished.

Babcia picked up her handbag and began searching inside. 'Look I have pictures of the children, Wanda, Zosia and Janek. This was taken just before I left to come here. And here is a picture of us all taken at Zosia's First Holy Communion.' She handed them to her sister-in-law.

Princess Maria fumbled with her spectacles and looked at the pictures.

'The eldest girl could do with losing some weight. When I was that age I was slim as a poker. I was much prettier than that, too. And who is that funny little peasant man. He looks just like the gardener we used to have on the estate.'

Maria started laughing until her mirth turned to coughs. Babcia pressed on with her pictures.

'Look at little Zosia in her lovely white dress. Isn't she a beauty? Who does she remind you of? Oh here is a picture of the house, four bedrooms, can you see the garden? Look at little Janek – what a precious boy.'

'So why did you come back? What could there possibly be for you here,' said Maria looking up from the pictures.

Babcia shrugged. 'I'm sure my time is nearly up. I want to be buried with Jan. I'm staying with my niece, Irena – Witold's daughter. Do you remember Witold? How he danced on the table at my wedding?'

'Buried with Jan? In Powazki cemetery? Father had to pull enough strings to get Jan buried there. How are you going to manage it?'

'As his wife I have a right to be buried with him.'

'Do you think they'll let me be buried with my husband? Will I get my ashes strewn across the fields of Auschwitz?'

'I do realise how lucky I am to have a grave at which to grieve. I wish you had the same for Nathan. I always admired him, Jan told me how clever he was and what a skilled doctor he was. I'll never forget his kindness to Jan and to me. Nathan was a good man.'

'A good Jew, eh?'

Babcia tried to keep her patience. Maria had always been like this, always spoiling for a fight, trying to put words into other people's mouths.

'I said a good man. He was understanding, kind, he took an interest in Jan. Of course, the family were all rather upset when you married him. It's only natural. He wasn't one of us, was he? Different race, different religion, different class, different customs. At first Jan was a bit concerned about your honour. It seems silly now but that was how he felt. He hit Nathan once, did you know?'

Maria's eyes lit up with an evil little glint.

'Jan hit everyone once. Don't tell me he never knocked you about. One time he attacked mother with a fish knife and the servants had to pull him off. Another time Father had to bash him on the head with a great big heavy candlestick when he'd run amok. That was why he was in the hospital when you met him. Father told them he'd been in a fight. I'm sure Jan was the only patient in that military hospital with a candlestick injury.' Maria began to laugh again. Babcia thought she was just like a little witch, crowing with a witch's cackle. 'And once, I remembered this again only the other day, we had a grand reception at my parent's country home for the composer, Paderewski. Everyone who was anyone was there, the prime minister, the British ambassador, some pompous French official. Anyway, my parents had told Jan to stay in his room for the evening but half way through, just as Paderewski had finished a grand concerto and everyone was clapping, Jan walked elegantly down the grand staircase like a ballet dancer. He lifted one hand and announced, 'Ladies and gentlemen, you may not realise this but I am God.' Everyone turned to look, women screamed, my father grabbed a tablecloth sending a vase of flowers shattering to the floor and threw it round my brother. You see, apart from his black polished shoes and a German pickelhaub helmet, he was completely naked.'

The evil witch's cackle came back again. Babcia felt she

couldn't stand much more of this. The heat of anger and resentment she had felt for so many years when she'd lived in Warsaw before was all coming back. So much for making amends – she was only succeeding in reopening old wounds.

'Nathan was really interested in Jan, though,' Maria continued, her laughter suddenly ending. 'Psychology was his hobby. It was all new and exciting then. He was getting a little bored of ears, noses and throats and was starting to write a book. He was planning to call it *The Fragmented Mind*. Jan was one of his case studies. He conducted long interviews with him. I was supposed to type them up but I never got around to it.'

Babcia looked up in alarm. 'He took notes? What kind of notes? Where are they now?'

'Here, somewhere. Helena should see them, you know. The condition is probably hereditary. It could skip a generation and show itself in one of her children. My father's aunt was put in an asylum at the age of 17 and stayed there till she finally succeeded in killing herself. Set herself on fire and managed to take half the asylum and 15 nursing staff with her.'

'Helena is fine and so are all the children. She is a good, strong girl. Considering all she has been through,' said Babcia pulling her cardigan around her shoulders. Feeling the cold draught from the balcony, she got up and pulled the door shut with a snap.

'She still doesn't know about Jan, does she?' said Maria looking up at her with a smile. 'You should tell her.'

'There's nothing to tell. Jan had problems with his nerves but he was a good husband and father.'

'Huh, I don't know what upset my parents more – a daughter who lived openly with an intellectual Jewish Socialist or a son who was bonkers.'

Babcia remained standing, looking down at her sister-in-law. 'Excuse me, as it is All Saint's Day I'm going to put some flowers on my husband's grave'. She picked up her handbag.

'Good day, Maria. Perhaps we will meet again soon,' said Babcia and she walked out of the room, down the hall to the front door, taking her coat off the peg on the way. Glancing back, she saw Maria still sitting in her chair, lighting another cigarette despite having one still burning the ashtray.

It was dark by the time Babcia reached the cemetery. All Souls was the most important night in its year. Already crowds had gathered, chanting and praying. Almost every grave was covered in tiny white candles, each one representing a holy soul, a spirit now in heaven. Barbara looked around at each point of light twinkling in the gloom. Jan was one of them – he was now just a tiny spark, a dot, a very small chemical reaction.

Chapter 11

Contrary to her name, Eunice Small was tall, indeed some would say statuesque. She was also stylish, poised and efficient. During the working day at Fab Fashions, she could calm and charm angry customers on the phone, find items of stock that others had been seeking for ages and arrange the window display in a simple and elegant manner. In stark contrast, Wanda would lumber round the shop, knocking skirts off the rack with her hips and constantly getting in people's way. She felt shy about approaching customers and hated asking them if they needed help even though Leonard, the manager, specifically asked her to do that. She was conscious of her northern accent, she was worried in case she used the wrong word, or that she might pronounce it the wrong way. She feared she sounded like a bumpkin, a northern hick. She preferred to stand by the far wall gazing out of the window and it took her ages to respond if her colleagues called out 'Jean' to her. Leonard put her payroll through under the name Wanda, but she told everyone she wanted to be known as Jean.

Eunice lived in a little trendy flat in Camden Town with a friendly, handsome boyfriend who worked as a photographer. She told Wanda she was just filling in time before university by working at Fab Fashions 'as an ironic statement, of course'.

Eunice had been trusted with a key to the shop so she opened up in the mornings, put the lights and radio on and prepared a coffee for herself and Leonard. Wanda watched Eunice looking at herself in the changing room mirror, adjusting her tight black skirt and fixing her large white plastic earrings in place. Unlike the Derby branch, in London they didn't have to wear uniform. Eunice usually wore black relieved with dashes of white on her belt or shoes. She had short black hair cut in an angular style, an extremely slim, flatchested, almost boyish figure. 'I don't bother with a tape measure, I just use a spirit level for my bust,' she told Wanda. Eunice's height was in contrast to Leonard who could not have been more than 5ft 2in. What a strange trio they made, thought Wanda. Eunice tall, dark and elegant, Leonard very short and slight, and Wanda broad and heavy with flaxen hair.

Leonard always gave Wanda the shit jobs. Once he sent her to hand out leaflets in Oxford Street advertising the shop. As Fab Fashions was around a hidden corner in Poland Street, it was sometimes overlooked so Wanda was told to entice the customers in. She hated doing it – people either didn't want to take the leaflets or if they did they glanced at them before discarding them on the pavement. The old tramp, who always sat in a narrow doorway on the corner of Oxford Street and Poland Street either asleep in a pool of his own urine or awake singing and swearing, made loud comments from behind as Wanda distributed the leaflets.

'Big arse!' he shouted. 'Nice fat arse – I like that in a woman.'

Throngs of bored shoppers blanked Wanda out. A group of teenage boys headed towards her shouting, 'Hey Fatty, what have you got there?' A scruffy man shouted, 'Jesus loves even you' in her face and tried to force a leaflet about hell and damnation on her. Wanda took his leaflet but only after insisting he took one of hers. After standing on Oxford Street for about an hour, Wanda threw the rest of the leaflets into the bin and went back to tell Leonard she had handed them all out.

Most of the time, Wanda kept close to Eunice. She was an important link, a vital clue. Not only was she Wanda's role model, but she was something far more important. She had seen the Beatles play live, she had all the LPs, knew all the lyrics and, most importantly, she knew where Paul McCartney lived.

'Let's go together and maybe we can see him,' Wanda urged one day.

'I can't go this weekend. Roger is taking me to Paris. He's going on a photographic shoot and I'm going with him.' Eunice leafed through a copy of *Vogue*.

'Well, we'll go after work tonight,' Wanda urged.

Eunice shut the magazine. 'Ok, tonight. But we probably won't see him because we can't stay too late and he doesn't usually come home until well after midnight.'

'Well, you never know. We could stay a couple of hours just in case. Please ...'

'Off groupying tonight?' called Leonard as the girls left the shop.

'He's just jealous because girls don't hang around outside his flat,' said Wanda.

'Oh, I'm not interested in girls,' replied Leonard. 'I'd rather have gangs of Paul McCartneys outside my house. Isn't he gorgeous?'

They left the shop and headed for the Tube. Turning the corner, Wanda tripped over the old tramp's outstretched leg as he lay drunk in his usual doorway.

'Poor old sod,' said Eunice. 'He used to be in the Army he told me. Fought for Queen and country – now look at him.'

Wanda looked at the man's thick matted hair, filthy old coat and grimy black hands. She knew she ought to feel pity, but all she really felt was disgust.

The girls took the tube from Oxford Circus. Wanda still wasn't used to the incredible crush and power of the crowds. She was shocked by the heat and wind down in the tube platform and the almighty roar the trains made when they arrived in the stations. When she first arrived in London, she had stood back to let others on but was surprised the way everyone else pushed on first. She soon realised there was no decorum – it was everyone for themselves. Eunice and Wanda squeezed on. Eunice managed to get a seat while Wanda stood up by the doors. Everyone was tightly packed together in an intimate way and yet no one spoke a word. Wanda was constantly apologising for touching people but she noticed no one apologised back as they would in Derby.

At the next station a very elegantly dressed man in white tie and tails came running up to the doors as they were about to close. He just managed to leap on board but the edge of the door must have touched his face because a long strip of black grease carved its way right down his cheek. People stared at him but no one said a word. Eventually Wanda ventured,

'I think you should check your face in the mirror when you can.'

The man stared at her uncomprehendingly then he and everyone else looked away.

At St John's Wood station Eunice motioned to Wanda that they were getting off. On the street, Wanda looked around in astonishment at the huge, beautiful white houses – a demi paradise. They walked a while and, as they turned the corner, Wanda was amazed to see a group of about 20 girls sitting on the pavement outside high, wooden gates. They had blankets, sleeping bags, flasks of hot drinks, playing cards, bags of sandwiches, small radios. Did they live here all day and night? A couple of them greeted Eunice who in turn introduced Wanda. The girls nodded and went back to their own conversation.

'Who are these people?' whispered Wanda.

'You didn't think you'd be alone out here, did you? These girls practically live here, rain or shine. That's dedication, isn't it? I think some of them have even managed to get inside. They say they've pinched a few things as souvenirs.' She nodded towards the house.

Wanda and Eunice sat on the grass verge under a tree. The evening was warm with a light breeze. Sticky burs and pollen fell on Wanda's face and dark skirt. She sat looking up at the swaying trees and breathing in the sweet smells of an English spring day. The road was quiet, the only people who walked down it were those who lived there – and, of course, the devoted fans. Wanda leaned against the gate and thought, 'The centre of the universe is where you are.' She looked around at the houses. Large white detached mansions with gates and intercoms, big cars in the driveways. Look at this, a world of peace, greenery, wide roads and money. How could anyone not think it would be heaven to live here? How could anyone believe that money would not buy happiness?

Eunice lit a cigarette and looked sidelong at Wanda with a small smile. 'So how do you like working at Fab Fashions? Leonard's a weird character, isn't he?'

Wanda laughed. 'He's so tiny – he can't be much more than 5ft. You're tall and slim and I'm fat. We could start a pop group – Titchy, Lanky and Pudge.'

'Yes, or The Three Freaks. Do you miss home?'

'I miss my dad and mum. I've a younger sister and brother and I'm glad to see the back of them. My sister is the one with the beauty and brains, I got the child-bearing hips and the preposterous nose. She goes to grammar school. I went to a secondary modern where they taught us how to make apple charlotte, knit vests and apply for secretarial jobs. How about you?'

'I went to a boarding school in Hampshire. It was horrible.' Eunice picked at her lips with her thumb and little finger, her cigarette clenched between her index and middle fingers. 'I'm an only child so you'd think my parents would have wanted me at home but they couldn't wait to get rid of me to school. At least your parents wanted you. Anyway, there's nothing wrong with your nose. Don't put yourself down. Actually, you have really beautiful skin, it's so fresh and clear. I'd do anything for a complexion like that.'

Wanda blushed with pleasure.

'And what do your parents do?' asked Eunice.

'My dad is a painter and decorator and my mum works in a clothing factory as a machinist. Do you know Derby? It's a dump – I'm so glad to be out of that hole.'

'I went through it once on the train. They make those little ceramic ornaments there, don't they?' Eunice looked at Wanda with a suspicious air. 'You didn't come to London because of him, did you?' said Eunice gesturing towards the house.

'No, I came to get away. I had to escape from my family – they had me in an arm lock.'

'In what way?'

'It was just such a rigid, narrow community with fixed ideas about everything. The world is changing but they don't seem to realise it – they live in the past.'

'Well, old people always do. Perhaps we'll still be sitting here when we're 64.'

'I don't even want to think about old age – I'd sooner die young.'

Eunice laughed and stubbed her cigarette end out aggressively on the pavement.

By nine o'clock it was getting dark and rather cold. The girls had been waiting two hours.

'I'll wait just a few more minutes and then I must go,' said Eunice in a bored voice. 'Anyway, I've nearly finished all my ciggies.'

'I think I'll stay a little longer,' said Wanda. 'I'm just so excited by everything. This is a brilliant time to be alive, don't you think?'

Eunice laughed. 'Look I'm off now. It's work tomorrow and I need my beauty sleep. Don't stay too late, my dear.' She stood up, dropped her cigarette end on the pavement and squashed it flat with a deft movement of her slim ankle.

Wanda watched. Eunice had even managed to get up from sitting on the pavement in a chic manner. Her hair was always in perfect condition, her clothes were clean, neat and stylish. Bits of dirt, twigs, grass never seemed to adhere to Eunice as they did to lesser mortals. Eunice always said the right thing, did the right thing, wore the right thing. She even put cigarettes out in style.

Wanda watched her heading off toward the tube. She was slightly apprehensive about being left with these tough girls. But she also couldn't help feeling a little pleased that there was one less person waiting. No man would ever look at her when Eunice was around.

Tonight Wanda felt she was going to be lucky. The hardened campaigners began getting out their sleeping bags. By 11 o'clock most girls had either gone home or were getting ready to sleep. Still Wanda waited. 'If I go now,' she thought, 'he'll come home just after I leave.' By midnight she had fallen asleep under a borrowed blanket. She dreamt her father was coming up the stairs at home and was getting an extra blanket out of the airing cupboard. He was spreading the blanket lovingly over her and bending down to kiss her goodnight.

Wanda woke stiff, cold and aching next morning with her hair full of twigs. She looked up blinking, trying to remember where she was. Then she saw the other girls were packing up their sleeping bags.

'Did he come back?' she called desperately.

'Yeah, around 2 o'clock,' said a hard-faced girl with a Yorkshire accent.

'Oh, what did he say?'

'He said hello and asked us to keep the noise down in the morning. Anyway, we're off down the High Street for our brekkie. He won't wake up till midday so we'll be back then to see him come out. Are you coming?'

'No, I've got to go to work.'

So off Wanda ran without breakfast, without a wash and with no chance of seeing her idol.

She arrived at the shop red in the face and sweating copiously. Leonard eyed her.

'Through whose hedge were you pulled?'

'Sorry, I'm late. I was groupying all night'

'Did you see him?'

'Well, you could say that.'

'I hope he was worth it. Right, I've got a really important job for you. We're having an exclusive evening for select clientele here next week.' He rubbed his little hands together. 'It's to celebrate our first anniversary and there'll be Champagne and cheesy bits. We're offering the guests a 20 per cent discount on anything they buy. We need to send out invitations with reply slips to let us know if they are coming.

Leonard told Wanda she had to put the invitations and the return envelope for the reply inside some envelopes and then stick on the address labels which have already been printed. She was to take money from petty cash and stick stamps on all of them and get them posted. There was a sponge thing she could use to moisten the stamps so she didn't have to lick each one. He told her to send out 150 invitations.

'Will you get 150 people in the shop?' asked Wanda.

'Oh, we'll be lucky if even a third turn up. It's best to send out more, not less,' said Leonard.

Wanda sat in the back office stuffing envelopes. Eunice and Leonard were chatting in the front of the shop and Wanda could hear gales of laughter. They were discussing the Champagne evening. Apparently Eunice's boyfriend, Roger, was bringing in huge black and white copies of his portrait photos and they were going to be hung from chains around the store. Eunice had come up with a black and white theme with checks, stripes, large black squares, large white squares. Wanda could hear the discussions and arrangements going on around her. Leonard was ordering the food and drink. When Wanda had finished the envelopes, she took them to the post office on the way home and sent them all off.

She arrived back in Croydon as Val was washing up after dinner.

'Ah, there you are, Jean,' whispered Val. 'We were wondering where you were last night. I notice your bed wasn't slept in. I was listening for you last night. I'm a very light sleeper so I thought I would stay awake rather than be woken by you coming in.' She paused. 'Oh, your father rang. I told him you hadn't come home all night. He'll ring again this evening. I told him I had no idea where you were.'

'Thanks, thanks very much. I'll phone him.'

'And will you be wanting meals in the future? We need to decide if you want me to cook for you.'

Wanda looked at the remains of the fish pie on the table.

'No, thanks. Don't worry, I'll make my own arrangements.'

'Well, your father did ask if you were eating your meals here. I think he would prefer it if you did. But as you wish.'

'Hi, Jean,' called Dave from the dining room as she walked past. The members of his youth club were sniggering, 'I just wanted you to meet Rachel, Rob and Jeff. They've been really helpful at the youth club. Everyone, this is Jean who rents our upstairs room. I'm sure Jean will be coming along to our youth club before long, once she gets settled down here.'

'Hello, there,' said Wanda. 'I won't keep you, I'm just going up to my room. Maybe see you later,' and she made her escape. She spent enough of her life at religious school and going to church – she didn't have to get involved with that any more.

Upstairs, Wanda lay on the bed. She noticed her make up bag, which she had left on the bedside table, was on the dressing table and a little talc was spilled on the carpet nearby. Also a brand new packet of tissues had been opened and some were missing. Wanda really wanted a bath after her night on the pavement but she could hear Val bathing Sarah so she waited for her to finish but fell fast asleep before she knew what was happening.

She woke next morning still in the same clothes. There was no time again for a bath so she quickly got dressed and went downstairs. In the kitchen she made tea and toast and went to catch her train.

It took a good hour to get into work and by the time she arrived, late as usual, Leonard was holding a bundle of envelopes and looking incredulous.

'These are all the reply envelopes,' he said. 'How could all the punters have sent them back so quickly – and how come they have all arrived at the same time?'

Wanda's face changed from red to purple as the awful truth dawned on her. Leonard opened one envelope. Inside it was the invitation, the return slip and the envelope addressed to the customer.

'Oh, for Christ's sake,' yelled Leonard. 'You idiot. Now you'll have to do them all over again. I don't know if they'll get there in time. Fuck, shit, fuck, shit,' and he beat his little fist on the counter in time to each curse.

Chapter 12

Derby, 1967

Pinecrest pigs
Snobby little tarts
Only get O levels in
Smelling their own farts

A gang of girls from the Secondary Modern had spotted
Zosia's grammar school uniform on the upper deck of the
bus and started their predictable chant. Zosia usually sat
downstairs among the old age pensioners and young
mums, but today the lower deck was full and the
conductor ordered her up top. Zosia reluctantly took a
seat near the stairs and sat still staring straight ahead,
gripping her tennis racquet. She felt a yank at her scarf
and half looked round with a frown. Then her hat was
snatched from her head and thrown round the bus. Zosia
knew it would be pointless and undignified to try to
retrieve it so she did nothing. After a while the girls threw
the hat on the floor and kicked it down the aisle before
getting off the bus. One of them elbowed her in the head
as she went past. Zosia took up the hat and brushed the
dust from its dark felt crown.

Once off the bus, she ran back home and let herself in.
Relief flooded through her as she stepped through the
door. Although she'd had some trouble on the bus, things
at school had not been as bad as usual. Was it possible her
tormentors were losing interest? She had managed to
avoid them during break and lunch time. She had cleverly
found a new place to sit, round the back of the science
block – a cold, windy strip of grass shielded from the sun.
As it was inhospitable, no one ever sat there even though

there was a bench. Zosia decided to make it her special place and escaped to it as often as she could. There she could read her book in peace or get on with her homework.

But her relief at entering the house soon turned to depression. The place was cold and felt a little damp. Her father was supposed to be installing central heating but because of the disruption it would cause as well as the cost, he had put it off for the time being. So, unlike almost everyone else in their street, they still had to make up coal fires in the little grates. The house was empty and silent. Zosia's parents were both at work and Janek spent his time after school at a friend's house.

The breakfast things had still not been cleared off the table so Zosia put on rubber gloves, took the pots to the kitchen and washed them up and wiped down the surfaces with a little bleach. She took the bleach bottle upstairs and squirted some in the toilet before going to the bathroom and using some washing up liquid to remove the black ring around the bath. Washing was hanging up to dry over the bath. The washing machine had broken down, her father had not had time to mend it yet and they couldn't afford a new one. Her father's shirt, Jan's football top and her mother's stockings hung from the rack above the bath. Zosia took the legs of the stockings in her hand and held them against her cheek for a while. She had been wearing the same school shirt for three days now because her spare one hadn't been washed. Her mother had too much work to do without hand washing as well.

Zosia went to her bedroom and took out the letter to read again.

Warsaw, 15 March

Kochana Zosia
   I miss you so much and every day I wonder what you are doing. How are things at home? I hope you are able to help your mother with the cooking and cleaning. Is Janek well?

Give them both my special love. Things remain difficult
here. My back is really hurting because the sofa I sleep on
is so unyielding. Irena is such a dear like her father, but she
works too hard. I met the no-good son Pawel briefly at
Christmas but he didn't have much to say for himself.
Helena sent him an invitation to visit you all but there is
some problem with his passport. He has now gone back to
his military service, although I don't hold out much hope
for the Polish army if he is the standard recruit.

I went to see the Prince's sister Maria again last week. It
is hard to believe they are brother and sister as they are so
unalike. I think poor Maria is losing her mind but that is
only to be expected in someone her age. She kept asking me
who I was and she seemed to think her long-dead husband
was coming home soon. How sad!

I went to put flowers and candles on The Prince's grave
again today. White roses were his favourites. You know he
is buried in Powazki cemetery. He has the largest
monument and all the men from his regiment are buried
around him in smaller graves. I remember his funeral as if
it were yesterday. All his comrades carried his coffin to the
grave. The church was full to overflowing. My parents-in-
law had ordered this magnificent black marble headstone
and they had chosen a wonderful photograph of The Prince
to be set in the stone alongside the inscription. I sat by the
grave and told him all about you and how much I was
missing my little family.

And it's true. I miss you so much, darling Zosia.
All my love
Babcia

Zosia loved the phrase, 'Things remain difficult here.'
Excellent news. Perhaps Babcia would come back, the
signs were good. She didn't seem to be getting on with the
family, the flat was small and the bed uncomfortable.
Zosia decided she would write back emphasising the good
things at home but making it clear Babcia was really
needed. She would suggest Babcia come back for a

holiday and then they would persuade her to stay. She would also be sure to say there was more room now as Wanda had gone and didn't seem to be coming back. Zosia knew Babcia never liked Wanda. Nothing was ever said, of course, but Zosia could tell Wanda was never her favourite, never her ideal grandchild.

That was one good thing – Zosia now had the bedroom to herself and there was no more stupid music, pointless posters and make-up. Since Wanda had left more than a year ago, she had been back for just a week at Christmas and that was it. She had spent the time boring everyone senseless with tales of what a wonderful time she was having in London. She talked about her trendy new friend, Eunice, some stick-like model of fashion excellence, and Eunice's photographer boyfriend, Roger, who took pictures of celebrities. Or she went on and on about a party she been to at her boss's place or whatever. Somehow, though, Zosia got the impression Wanda wasn't having quite as much fun as she made out.

At primary school, Zosia had felt quite close to her sister. They had walked home together, made up stories about fairies and goblins, held hands. The 11-plus exam had separated them. Perhaps it was going to that awful Secondary Modern that ruined their relationship. There were always thugs and bullies there. Maybe Wanda had been part of that gang of girls who bullied people on the bus. Zosia wouldn't be surprised. Wanda had no imagination, no soul, no romance. She was welcome to her trivial life in London. Zosia realised her relationship with Wanda had deteriorated after Babcia came to live with them. Her grandmother had somehow driven a wedge between the sisters but she hadn't done it on purpose – had she? Zosia dismissed the notion as ridiculous and tipped the contents of her satchel on the bed. No, the problem was that they were completely opposite characters and had nothing in common.

Hunger pains stabbed in Zosia's stomach but she ignored them. As she stared at her bed, a little black seed of fear sprouted. Among her textbooks were two more notes. Zosia sighed, took a deep breath and unfolded them. One read *Roses are red, violets are blue, stale sweat smells, just like you.* The other said, *Little Miss Lah-di-dah, spots all over your face, you think you're something special but you're just a waste of space.*

Like all the other notes they were unsigned but she knew who had put them in her bag. She took the notes and placed them with the others in a box in her drawer. Catching sight of herself in the mirror, she stared at the long line of brown moles that ran across her lower cheek and made their way down her neck. She brushed them gently with her finger. Then she took her pair of compasses from her pencil case and poked a little of the point into her arm. The pain was sharp but it caused relief to spread over her body. There were other tiny pricks on her arm where she had sought the same relief.

Zosia looked out of her window onto the garden. Most of the lawn had been dug up to make way for her father's vegetables. The potatoes, cabbages and carrots were neatly laid out in long rows. By summer, there would be straw-berries under little frames, gooseberries and raspberries. There were apple and peach trees, and a greenhouse with a vine carrying small, green bitter grapes. At the end of the garden was a noisy, smelly chicken run. Her father collected the eggs every day and sometimes he expertly grabbed a chicken and twisted its neck to provide Sunday dinner. The vegetable garden annoyed Zosia. Why couldn't they have an elegant lawn with flowers and a fountain instead of growing food as if there was going to be a shortage any minute? It was such a peasant mentality. She imagined the large house, sweeping lawns, flower-beds and large cars she would have when she grew up. And she knew that to achieve that lifestyle she would have to work and work hard.

She heard her mother come home with Janek who immediately put the television on. The banging of pots meant her mother was making dinner. Then she heard her father's car draw up and the clatter as he brought his tools into the house. Eventually, Janek yelled up the stairs, 'Dinner'. After a while, she heard him shout again, 'Zosia, dinner'. She still didn't move. Ten minutes later her mother's head appeared round the door.

'What's the matter?' she demanded. 'Why aren't you coming down for dinner?'

'I have a migraine headache. I don't want any dinner.'

You're always getting headaches these days. It's probably because you're hungry. You only make yourself one small sandwich for your lunch. That's not enough for a growing girl. Why have you stopped eating?'

'I've been sick so I don't want any food.'

Helena tutted and left the room, snapping the door shut behind her.

Chapter 13

Warsaw, 1968

'I think I'll go back, Jan,' Babcia whispered. 'Just for a holiday, just to see my babies. It's a good idea isn't it? A few weeks there will refresh me and then I'll come back. The problem is I feel so well, so healthy, so very unlike dying.'

She stood beside her Prince's grave. His photograph in the headstone showed a handsome, unsmiling face whose unlit eyes seemed confused and full of sorrow. Barbara threw out the old flowers and arranged the new roses in the metal pot by his tombstone. The Prince watched without emotion.

She tried to listen for his reply but it was hard to bring back the sound of his voice. It had been deep, she remembered, but became high and child-like when he had his episodes. And he had a speech impediment, a strange way of saying his Rs. But it was too long ago and the memory faded.

Babcia returned slowly to Irena's flat. As she opened the door, she heard Mira complaining about her, that she spread herself out in the flat as if it was her property.

Babcia walked in.

'I went to Jan's grave again today to put some flowers there. Do you remember how wonderful his funeral was? There were so many people they couldn't all get in the church,' she said.

Irena and Mira looked at each other.

'I remember that funny little Jewish fellow your sister-in-law was married to,' said Mira. 'What was his name? And Maria wore red. Can you believe it? Wearing red to her brother's funeral. And she smoked cigarettes in one of those long holders. Witold said she looked like a tart. Was she trying to make some kind of protest?'

'It was a beautiful funeral. I want to be buried next to Jan. I don't suppose it will be long now.'

'Mmm,' agreed Mira and trotted off to the kitchen.

'Auntie, you'll be with us for some time yet,' said Irena soothingly. 'Look! I've got some butter. I was so lucky today – I just happened to be passing the shop when a delivery was being made.'

Babcia sat down on her usual seat in the sitting room. She could hear Irena and Mira talking in the kitchen even though they were doing their best to keep their voices low. It was hard not to hear everything in such a small flat. Babcia pretended to be a little deaf but in actual fact her hearing was as sharp as a knife.

'If she mentions that lunatic husband of hers one more time, I'll scream,' Mira was saying in a whisper.

'Have some patience,' said Irena. 'She has led a disappointing life.'

'She's been here for more than two years and it's all she ever talks about. The husband was mad and his sister is quite potty, too. I heard the parents were first cousins – it was well known in Warsaw at the time'.

'Daddy told me Jan had a mental condition. I suppose it was schizophrenia – the poor man. At least he avoided the electric shock treatments they're inflicting on schizophrenics now. Anyway, leave poor auntie to her delusions. It's probably the only way she can cope with reality. She has never faced up to his suicide and it's too late to do it now'.

'It was all a big cover up,' sniffed Mira.

'What do you mean?'

'Well, how did he get a Church funeral when he was a suicide and how come he was buried with full military honours when he never went near a battle field? His family pulled so many strings. It's so unfair when I think of my poor Witold lying in some unmarked grave in a foreign country.'

Irena sighed. 'Life is very unfair, Mama. But would you like to have been married to a schizophrenic? Suicide is very common in people with that condition. The doctors probably prescribed him morphine. I suppose he took an overdose. I remember she and Helena came to live with us for a while, didn't she? It is one of my first memories.'

'Well, she could never have stayed with that mad man. Witold told me that one day Barbara was coming home from shopping when she looked up at their second-storey flat and saw Jan standing on the balcony. He was holding poor tiny baby Helena out in mid air as if he were going to dash her to the ground. Apparently, Barbara raced up stairs, grabbed the baby from him just in time.'

'Oh, how awful. Poor auntie. But he probably didn't realise what he was doing. It's actually rare for schizo-phrenics to harm other people, it's almost always themselves they destroy.'

'Well, after that incident Barbara came with the baby to stay with us. It was Jan's sister, Maria, and her odd husband, Nathan, who found Jan's body when they went round the next day. And it was Nathan who wrote the death certificate. There was no inquest – it was all very hush, hush.'

'Probably his parents wanted to keep the whole thing quiet. His mental illness and his suicide.'

'Then we were landed with Barbara for years – just like we are now. We always seem to be bailing her out, one way or another.'

'I remember them coming on holiday with us, to the Lakes. At one time Helena and I were more like sisters than cousins. It's funny – there were always so many pictures of Helena's father around her flat. They seemed to hero worship him. In the pictures he didn't look like a violent man – he looked so solemn and peaceful.'

'He wasn't peaceful at all – he was extremely peculiar. He would suddenly start laughing during at a serious music concert or in church or somewhere like that. And other times he would talk loudly as if answering questions from someone who wasn't there. Actually, Witold said his parents didn't want Barbara to marry him but she was carried away by his title. And I suppose he was handsome. But it really wasn't worth it.'

'Helena wrote to me asking how auntie was. I must write back. Pawel keeps nagging me about going to stay there.'

'I wish the old woman would go back. Witold always said she was a social climber – actually not so much a climber as a mountaineer,' said Mira.

Babcia sat in the armchair hugging a cushion to her chest. The tears poured down her cheeks. Then she wiped her eyes, got up and strode in to the kitchen.

'I want to book a telephone call. I need to speak to my daughter. I shall be going to stay with her and the family this summer for a holiday.'

Chapter 14

'Delighted to meet you, Jean,' said Roger with a broad smile.

Wanda had seen Roger before at a distance but this was the first time she'd been properly introduced to him. He had collar-length, curly hair, an unshaven face, and beautiful blue eyes and wore blue jeans, black T-shirt, blue denim jacket and brown desert boots. He was friendly, cool and casual – the type of person who used your name a great deal when he spoke to you. Wanda had never met such an amiable, laid-back person, so handsome, such a brilliant smile. And what's more he seemed to be genuinely friendly towards her. She detected no mockery or amusement. She looked at Eunice standing by his side. They made a perfect, golden couple.

The pictures Roger had provided for the Champagne evening were enormous, about four feet by three pasted to large wooden backings, and they hung on long chains from the ceiling. It had taken the combined efforts of two carpenters to hang the chains then Roger and Eunice together attached the pictures.

A large sign proclaimed, *Pictures by Roger Elliott* and each one was priced for sale. In the centre of the room was an enormous black and white photo of Eunice. She looked spectacular, dressed in a mini dress of large black and white checks. In the photo, she wore knee-length white boots and large loopy white earrings. Her short black hair was sleek and glossy and the black make up round her eyes emphasised her clear white skin. She stood in an aggressive stance with her feet apart and her hands on her hips.

Once the Champagne evening began, Wanda sat, round and lumpy, sipping rum and coke in the back room. She was responsible for changing the records, washing the used glasses, and re-filling the nut dishes. She watched through the curtain. Roger and Eunice were greeting the guests – they seemed to know everyone personally. Many exclaimed at the beauty of Roger's pictures, they admired Eunice's dress in the photo and asked to try on the same style. (Leonard had cleverly had an extra consignment of them bought in.) Roger handed out leaflets about his forthcoming photographic exhibition at the South Bank. Leonard was busy directing people to the latest British, American and Italian designs. Eunice flattered the chubby women who were trying to squeeze into dresses a few sizes too small for them. They worked as an efficient team and Wanda was not part of it.

She sat in the back room, watching and knocking back drinks with increasing abandon feeling like the outsider again. As she peered out, she noticed the old tramp standing outside the main window. He was holding up a bottle of cider, grinning and gesturing. Wanda smiled – he looked so incongruous standing there with a dirty knitted cap and his heavy black coat. Leonard spotted him at the same moment.

'Excuse me,' he said to the large, Italian-looking woman he'd been speaking to and he rushed to the front door and stepped outside.

'Hey, you get out of it. Go on – on yer bike. You're putting people off.'

'Fuck off, fuck off,' the tramp slurred, taking a swig from his bottle and wandering off down the street.

Wanda watched him go then turned to look at Eunice and Roger who were standing together in the middle of the room. Eunice nestled her dark head against his shoulder and he lifted her chin and kissed her lips. They gazed into each other's eyes, their fingers intertwining.

Wanda poured another rum and Coke. She sang along with the records. Conscious of her weight, she had eaten almost nothing all day. She thought she'd better munch a few peanuts to wash down the alcohol. At that point her head began to spin. When she changed the record she scratched the needle across the first track. She saw Leonard look crossly in her direction as the screech was amplified around the shop.

Cut off from the laughter and the buzz of chatter from the shop, Wanda began to feel lonely and bored. She found another bottle of rum, poured herself a large one and took a swig. Suddenly a powerful pain gripped her stomach and she realised nature was determined to take its course. She needed the toilet, she really desperately needed the toilet but it could only be reached through the shop. Wanda waited as long as she could but with increasing alarm decided to make a dash for it. She fled across the shop floor knocking against one of Roger's huge, heavy pictures which swung violently to one side. It hit some posh woman hard on the shoulder and she shrieked. Wanda apologised profusely, turned, tripped over a waste paper bin and fell against the light switch on the wall, plunging the room into darkness. As she staggered into the toilet, she heard Roger laughing and loudly declaring, 'That was brilliant.'

Then she heard a woman's voice say, 'Who on earth was that, Leonard?'

Leonard replied, 'I may as well start selling Royal Doulton – I'll have my very own bull in a china shop then.'

Chapter 15

Roll of Honour

Pamela Green,	*1903*
Gladys Smallwood,	*1904*
Frances Rivers,	*1905*
Lavinia Roberts,	*1906 …*

Zosia spent every morning in school assembly reading the names, etched in gold on the pale wooden plaques that hung around the hall. They listed in chronological order all the head girls that Pinecrest had appointed since its founding. Zosia knew most of the names off by heart. There was Janet Parmeter who, in 1921, had written the school song – a tuneless dirge they were required to sing each morning. Rosalind Thomas, who went on to write a popular children's book in the 1950s and of course one day there would be *Zofia Baran, 1971* who would go on to present history programmes on television, or write biographies of the great and good or... Zosia felt a sharp prod in her back. She reached behind and pulled off a piece of paper with the words 'freak lesbo' written on it. Zosia tried to move along the line, but Heather simply moved to stay behind her. Another girl began spitting little balls of paper in to her hair. Zosia fought back the tears and forced a smile onto her face as she looked up at the head mistress making her usual speech about behaviour and good manners to the assembled girls.

There had been such celebrations at home when Zosia passed the 11-plus. Her best friend from primary school, Lydia Batorowich, daughter of the Polish club manager, went up to Pinecrest with her. Lydia couldn't speak much Polish as her mother was English and her parents had only made a half-hearted effort to send her to Polish

Saturday school. Pan Batorowicz, the influential leader of the Polish community, an ex-Battle of Britain pilot, a man of independent wealth and means, was also a frequent employer of Zosia's own father in his painting and decorating capacity.

At first, Zosia and Lydia sat together, played together, and visited each other's houses. Lydia's parents could afford for her to have piano lessons, dance lessons and riding lessons. The family often went abroad for their holidays – Spain, France and sometimes Poland. Once Pan Batorowicz mentioned in passing that Zosia could come on holiday with them to keep Lydia company. Zosia kept hoping but he never mentioned it again. Zosia begged her parents for riding lessons and for trips abroad but the answer was always the same – they couldn't afford it. They had extended themselves as much as they could to buy the house and that meant no extra frills.

Zosia turned her imagination to her projects. She'd buy a cheap scrapbook and decide on her subject. It might be Derby's local artist, Joseph Wright, or King Henry VIII, or Guy Fawkes or it might be the history of furniture or houses. Zosia would write the text from history books borrowed from the library, draw pictures, cut illustrations from magazines and stick in postcards. Sometimes she would write stories of her own – perhaps the history of the piece of pottery she had found in the garden (who had made it, who had owned it, who had drunk from it), or she would mount the coloured stones she often found in the garden or on the walk home on stiff pieces of card and write a small note of geological information.

During their first year together at Pinecrest, Zosia would persuade Lydia to walk through the Derby portrait gallery or read the inscriptions on the tombs in the cathedral or take walks along the old disused railway line.

Once Zosia asked Lydia to come with her to a talk at the Municipal Museum entitled, *2000 years of immigration to Derby*. A local historian led the group through the museum display cases commenting on the contents.

The historian had pointed to a first-century Roman brooch found at Chester Green area of Derby during archaeological excavations five earlier. 'Could a young soldier, fresh from Sardinia or southern Spain have dropped it as he was coming out of his barracks?' he asked. 'Can you imagine what the native British population of Derby, although we don't know what the town was called back then, made of the Romans? This super-efficient army of short, dark-haired soldiers.'

'Bloody foreigners, is what they thought,' said one man in the group and everyone laughed.

'Maybe,' said the historian, 'but within a hundred years the native people of this area were happily making marital alliances with their conquerors.' He moved on to a sixth-century Anglo-Saxon gaming piece. Perhaps dropped by a little girl whose grandparents had been born in north Germany, he suggested. A little blue-eyed pagan girl playing a game. How had the Christian Romano British population reacted to her people? Did they consider them to be too barbaric, too uncivilised, too blonde? 'We know they named this town Northworthy,' he said. 'The thing is, though, after a couple of hundred years no one could tell the two groups apart any more – the original British population had now become the English.'

They moved onto another display case. Lydia looked at her watch and adjusted her collar. Zosia was paying rapt attention.

The historian pointed out a tenth-century Viking belt buckle found when a new office block was built in the Corn Market. 'The man who wore this had perhaps been born in Sweden but had come to England ...'

'To rape and pillage,' said the same man in the group. 'Bloody foreigners!'

'Maybe,' the guide continued, 'but look at the delicate metalwork on this piece. Does it suggest a people who only knew violence and destruction? No, the Vikings brought crafts, farming methods and some useful words to our language. And they gave Northworthy the current name of

Derby. And here,' the said moving on, 'we have a French coin perhaps brought by one of William the Conqueror's men when they came to Derby to evaluate the city for the Domesday Book. They said it was worth £30.'

'That much, eh? Bloody foreigners,' said the man again.

By the time Zosia and Lydia reached the third year at Pinecrest, Lydia changed. She began to take a great interest in clothes and make-up, she wanted to go out to discos all the time and she became close friends with another girl who was an acknowledged expert on these matters. When she addressed Zosia she began to call her by the anglicised Sophie. Zosia didn't understand, she wasn't interested in discos. She wanted to do school work, she loved doing her projects and writing her stories. She was determined to go to university.

Then one day Zosia found herself alone at lunchtime. She wandered over to the vending machine to get a cup of hot soup. A tall girl, who Zosia had never taken much notice of before, was lounging nearby. Zosia looked at her.

'What do you think you're looking at?' the girl demanded.

'Nothing,' replied Zosia.

She pressed the buttons on the machine and took out the soup. The other girl barged into her spilling the soup over her hand and on the floor.

'Oops, sorry.' She and her two friends walked off laughing while Zosia stared miserably after them and looked around to see if anyone had noticed. 'Why did she do that?' thought Zosia.

After that, the tall girl began staring at Zosia all the time. If she was with Lydia, she left her alone but increasingly Lydia was off talking to her new friend. Zosia gave up trying to join in with them – she could see they didn't really want her.

So Zosia had been pleased to find a cold, windswept corner behind the science block where no one else sat. Despite it being cold and inhospitable, she found solace in this secret place.

So that was here, one lunch time, Zosia, alone with her cheese sandwich, was reading *Tess of the D'Urbervilles* on her designated bench. She was lost in the world of Thomas Hardy when she heard giggling and sniggering. She put her book down in alarm.

'So, this is where you hide, is it?' sneered her tormentor. Her two companions laughed.

'What's it to you?' Zosia said, a tremble in her voice.

'Don't speak to me like that, you little shit,' shrieked the tall girl.

She lunged for Zosia. One of her friends grabbed Zosia's arms behind her back and the other held her head in a tight grip while kicking Zosia's legs. Zosia's book went flying across the grass. The ringleader laughed and pulled a blue ballpoint pen from her pocket.

'It's time for some art. Do you like art, Dotty?'

She started drawing on Zosia's face. Zosia struggled but the others held her down.

'Can you see what it is yet?' the girl spat, stepping on Zosia's book.

'A dog,' suggested one.

'A chicken,' volunteered the other.

'I think you're right – it's definitely a chicken,' roared the tall girl. 'There you are,' she pushed Zosia back against the wall, 'you look much better now.'

The group went off, laughing, one of them tripping over Zosia's book lying on the ground as she went.

Zosia was shaking and crying. She picked up her book. The picture of the Black Madonna had landed in the mud, and a shoe had ground part of the image into the soil. Zosia picked it up, carefully wiping the mud from it. Tears poured down her cheeks as she murmured, 'Babcia, Babcia.'

Zosia managed to get to the toilets without too many people noticing her by holding a hanky to her face and pretending to blow her nose.

Once in the toilets she stood by the washbasins and looked in the mirror. A blue line linked up all the small brown moles that ran across Zosia's cheek and down her neck on one side of her face. It looked like some crazy dot-to-dot picture. Zosia stared at her face and realised the pattern did indeed look rather like a chicken. She took some toilet paper, moistened it, added soap and began scrubbing. She scrubbed until her face was red and raw but still the outline of the chicken could clearly be seen. She looked at her watch. It was one o'clock and she would be late for the next lesson.

Zosia opened the biology room door and went in to the classroom. The bullies started making clucking noises. Everyone else looked up. Zosia sat down, her eyes red and swollen, her cheeks aflame, the image of the chicken still imprinted on her face and neck.

'Be quiet,' snapped the teacher, 'Get on with your work.' Zosia slowly took out her textbook. As she did so, she momentarily caught Lydia's eye. The two looked at each other for a few seconds, then Lydia looked away and carried on with her work. Zosia opened her textbook and looked straight ahead. The granddaughter of Jan Poniatowski, Prince of Poland, sat in her biology class with the outline drawing of a chicken on her face. She took out her compasses and pushed the sharp point into the fleshy part of her thumb.

Chapter 16

Derby, 1968

Babcia was back in Derby! Of course this was just a visit, she told herself, and soon she would be going back to Warsaw. But in the deepest corner of her heart, her spirits sank at the thought of returning. She was already making herself at home again in Porton Crescent, sitting in the garden, enjoying the warm sun. A bee lazily bobbed at the purple buddleia and in the distance there was the tinkling of an ice cream van. But there was no other noise – no clatter of trams, no roar of traffic, no noisy shouts from too many people living on top of each other. Babcia looked at Tadek's carefully tended rosebushes. She really didn't want to go back to the tiny flat and live with Mira's black moods, the claustrophobic room or the lack of everyday necessities.

For now, though, she would put it out of her mind. She turned her attention to her jewellery box, cradled in her lap. It was a fine large box, made from walnut wood and decorated with silver hinges and clasps. It had been a present from her father to her mother in 1900 and Babcia still had the memory of sitting at their breakfast table while her papa handed her mother the birthday gift.

She opened the heavy lid and touched the red satin lining. She had decided to distribute the contents among her family now, while she was still alive.

Helena would have the gold and diamond necklace that Tatiana had given her so long ago. Tatiana … vain, proud, mocking. That night heading for the ball in Moscow. Her voice, it was back again …

'Papa, I can't wait to get to the dance,' she had shrilled in her squeaky little voice.

'Yes, my dear. Dance away. We are all dancing to the edge of the precipice.'

'Feodor, don't spoil the child's fun,' said his wife. 'Anyway, the Tsar's brother will be there, perhaps you could have a word with him. Get him to speak to the Tsar.'

'It's too late I fear. You know what they say? The most important person in Russia is the Tsar and the person he last spoke to. Nothing I say will make any long-term difference.'

Babcia had stared at her delicate white slippers and wondered what on earth he'd been talking about. She was to find out soon enough.

But she had managed to keep the necklace safe all through the Russian revolution and the war and occupation. Now the precious object would go to her daughter.

Babcia held it in her hands, letting the sun dance off its edged prisms. She could see it on Tatiana's white neck.

'You poor girl,' she murmured.

Babcia had met a Russian aristocrat, who'd fled after the revolution, to Warsaw. She spoke to him about her friends in Moscow and when she mentioned the Bessov family, the man tutted. He'd known the family very well. They had all been massacred by the Bolsheviks and their magnificent residence looted. He'd heard that Tatiana had tried to run away as her family were being killed. She'd managed to get to the front steps of the house before a Bolshevik soldier speared her through with his bayonet then kicked her body down the steps. He then started ripping through her clothing looking for the jewels that he guessed were sewn into the hems. Tatiana, so privileged, so elegant, a favourite at court, dancing partner to the Tsar's brother – had ended her life howling in mortal terror.

Babcia looked at the diamond necklace. Well, the Bolsheviks didn't get this anyway, she thought. Next to the diamond necklace were her amber bracelet, necklace and earrings that had been passed down in her mother's family. Babcia planned to give them to Zosia as the colour of the amber complemented her green eyes.

She wanted to give Janek something that had been his grandfather's. She had The Prince's silver cigarette case and hip flask. Of course, she would have preferred something military but that couldn't be helped. These objects gave the impression The Prince sat around smoking and drinking vodka from his flask. Although this was true, Babcia worried that this would be a bad influence on little Janek. However, the objects were made of good-quality silver and were embellished with Jan's initials and his family crest, a double-headed axe topped with a crown. They would have to do. Actually, she had some military buttons that had belonged to Witold. She could give them to Janek and tell him they were from his grandfather.

What should she give Wanda? The silly girl was off in London selling clothes. Imagine – The Prince's granddaughter was a shop girl. Babcia had a white linen tablecloth that her mother had embroidered for her as a wedding gift. Babcia decided she would leave it for Wanda to have at a later date.

Babcia heard Helena arrive back from work and the clattering of pots in the kitchen indicated she had started cooking. She insisted that Babcia not cook on her first evening back home. She made zurek soup, pierogi, cucumber salad and fruit compote. When dinner was served, Babcia once more felt she was the centre of attention where she belonged. Zosia sat next to her – beautiful, slim and elegant. At 15 Zosia was a lovely creature ('just like I was at that age,' Babcia told Helena.) Nine-year-old Janek, although blond haired and good looking, was silly in his behaviour and badly brought up, Babcia thought. He started to eat before everyone else, he sang loudly and tunelessly, shifted around in his seat and after a few mouthfuls went back to playing with his toy soldiers. Babcia frowned at Helena who made no effort to reprimand him.

Zosia made a point of telling Babcia all about the courses she was doing at school, the books she was reading, the 'O' levels she would be taking and the 'A' levels she hoped to take.

'I want to take Polish language and literature at university. I'll probably apply to the School of East European and Slavonic Studies in London.'

'I didn't you know you wanted to do that?' said Helena looking at her daughter in amazement.

'Well, you never asked,' replied Zosia.

'You hardly ever speak to me – you just sit around looking miserable.'

'It's not surprising is it?' Zosia dropped her fork on her plate with a clatter.

'She isn't usually so talkative and enthusiastic, Mama,' said Helena, trying to lighten the atmosphere. 'It must be because you're here.'

Babcia felt sure that was the case. How could she ever return to Poland now? It was clear she was needed here. Babcia turned her attention to Janek and asked him, in Polish, if he was enjoying school at St Joseph's.

'Dunno,' Janek replied in English.

Babcia looked critically at her daughter.

'I'm afraid he doesn't hear Polish too often now,' said Helena apologetically. 'He refuses to go to Polish school and it's easier for us to speak to him in English. He uses it all day at school and now he won't speak anything else. At least now you're back he will have to speak Polish again.'

'That was a delicious meal, thank you very much, Helenka,' said Babcia ignoring the reference to her staying permanently. 'I hope you don't mind if I go to my room now. I think I will get some rest after my journey. Zosia, my darling, would you bring me a glass of tea in about half an hour?'

When Zosia knocked on her grandmother's door and brought the tea in, she saw with a shock that Babcia was lying on the bed with her hair down and flowing over her shoulders. She couldn't remember ever seeing her grandmother with her hair loose – she had always worn it in a neat bun.

'I've brought your tea, Babcia,' she said.

'Thank you, my darling. Come and sit on the bed next to me.'

'Look, Babcia, I still have the picture of the Black Madonna you gave me when you left.'

'But look at the state of it – it's dirty and torn. Here, let me give you another one, I have plenty of them.' She reached over to the small compartment in the chest of drawers.

'No Babcia, I like this one. It's special to me, it keeps me safe.'

'Yes, darling, if you want. But I have something I do want to give you.' The jewellery box was placed on the chair next to the bed. Babcia picked it up and opened it. 'You see this amber necklace, bracelet and these earrings? They belonged to my grandmother and now they are yours.'

She took the jewellery out of the box and placed it in Zosia's lap.

'I wanted to give them to you personally,' she continued 'rather than for you just to have a note in my will'.

Zosia leaned her head against her grandmother's shoulder. She fingered the yellow crocheted shawl.

'Please, don't go, Babcia. I need you here. It's been horrible since you've been away. The food is awful, the house isn't clean, my clothes and sheets are never washed. Janek is a nasty, rude, badly behaved brat. Mummy is always too tired to talk to me so I can't tell her anything. Life is terrible, just terrible. There are some mean people at school. Can you talk to mummy about it? If I tried she would say she was too busy to do anything about it and I had to sort it out myself. She never comes to the school, she never asks if I have any friends. She never wants to know about my school work.'

Babcia glowed with pleasure and stroked her granddaughter's hair.

'I'll speak to your mummy and see what can be done. At least you have a bedroom to yourself now that Wanda is away. Imagine what it is like in Warsaw where we all have to live in one room, practically.'

'But I really want to see what it's like there,' said Zosia. 'I want to see The Prince's grave and see the buildings where you lived. Are they still standing?'

'The flat we first lived in is still standing, riddled with bullet holes from the Warsaw uprising. The Prince's family home was destroyed, though. My parent's estate near Tarnow is now a museum, so I hear, dedicated to the People's Struggle to Build a Better Poland or some such nonsense. Perhaps next year you can come and visit me but it is difficult as the apartment is so tiny.'

'Did you visit Princess Maria a lot?'

'Yes, but as I told you, she is a little strange in the head. It's no surprise after all she has been through. She was an eccentric girl when she was young but she is definitely very odd now.'

'I would still like to meet her. It would be the closest I'll ever get to meeting The Prince.'

Babcia kissed her granddaughter's head and wished her good night. Zosia went to bed happy. Everything was going to be all right.

It was half past three in the morning. Babcia could make out the numbers on the luminous clock on her mantelpiece. Although her mind was alert, she was unable to locate the exact source of a strange feeling somewhere in the room. She managed to bring up her left hand and clutched at the frilly top of her nightdress but her right hand and arm were completely dead. Tears raced down her cheeks. She was afraid. She had been meaning to speak to the priest for a while but had not got around to doing it. She wanted to explain, she wanted to put her side of the story. She wanted to place her sins in context, to explain the mitigating circumstances, to show she had acted in everyone's best interest.

Her mouth felt strange, her voice was mute.

In her mind she began to explain. She saw the dark judge, she viewed the shadowy jury. She began her evidence, swearing to tell the truth, the whole truth and nothing but the truth.

Chapter 17

Helena waited while Dr Kowalski bent over her mother. Eventually, he straightened.

'Thank you, Pani Poniatowska,' he said, then turned to Helena. 'Pani Baran, could I have a word with you downstairs?'

Helena looked at her mother slumped in bed; the right side of her face hung at an unnatural angle, her right arm was curved like a claw across her chest, her eyes were wide and frightened. She appeared small, foetus-like and she quivered like a bird.

Helena and the doctor went downstairs and joined Tadek in the sitting room.

'How is she?' asked Tadek.

'She's had a severe stroke,' said the doctor. 'It's affected the whole right side of her body so she won't be able to walk or speak again. She will find any movement difficult, but remember her hearing is perfect and she understands completely what is happening. So be careful what you say in front of her and you don't need to shout at her. Her brain and hearing are fine.'

'But she will need a great deal of looking after, won't she?' said Tadek.

'Yes, she'll need everything to be done for her – feeding and washing, dressing. I will be able to get you some nursing help but you'll have to manage alone to begin with. I'm very sorry – she was such a determined lady. She will find life very hard now. I'm afraid, at her age, it's extremely unlikely she will recover. To be honest, she's unlikely to live for long.'

After the doctor left, Helena and Tadak sat alone together.

'Poor mama. She wanted so much to be buried with my father and now she will be buried in Derby after all. Just another disappointment to add to all the others,' said Helena blowing her nose.

'No, no – many good things happened to her. She survived to see her grandchildren. How can that be a disappointment? Many others didn't,' said Tadek.

'She was a good mother, you know. She brought me up alone, never married again. She was a good and faithful wife, mother and grandmother. She did her best for me until I was taken.'

'I know she did.'

'There were just two of us for all my childhood – alone.' Helena twisted her handkerchief tightly round her fingers until they turned white. 'We lived in the flat that had belonged to my father. After he died, we never saw any of his family. My grandparents were still alive but we never saw them nor my aunt Maria. I used to ask mama why that was but she said they never got over their grief about my father and I reminded them of him too much. Do you think that makes sense? Mama's parents and Uncle Witold and Aunt Mira were very kind to us though. I was supposed to be going to university. Mama wanted me to be a doctor. That's what would have happened if I hadn't been taken.'

'What happened? I mean during the *lapanka*? Can you talk about it?'

'I was 14 when the Germans invaded. At first things weren't so bad for us. We had an allotment so we were able to grow some fruit and vegetables for ourselves and earn some money by selling the surplus. That allotment was peaceful and I used to sit in the little summer house there and read books and daydream.'

Helena thought about the day when she was reading a romance novel instead of studying for a maths exam. She remembered the insistent heat of the sun on the tin roof of that little house, a wasp stuck by the window, buzzing to get out.

'But there were some things we had to buy, such as tea and bread,' continued Helena. 'We had heard there was some for a sale in a shop on Senatorska Street and we rushed out to try to be near the front of the queue. You had to be quick to get anything in those days. I was 16 by then. Mama and I went out together – it was summer and I remember I was wearing a dress with blue flowers on it. Mama was carrying the shopping basket. We were approaching the main road when mama stopped to say hello to someone. It was no one I knew well so I carried on walking into Senatorska Street. I was daydreaming and didn't realise what was happening at first. The street was being cordoned off – it was a *lapanka*. The previous night, the resistance had killed a German soldier and this was the retaliation. The street was cut off at both ends by hundreds of soldiers. I turned around and a soldier pushed me back. I looked for mama and I couldn't see her. She wasn't in the street. There were scores of people around me, they started to scream and shout when they realised what was happening'

Helena held her handkerchief to her mouth to stop herself screaming. Tadek held her in his arms and rocked her gently.

'There used to be a system of whistles that warned us of round-ups but this one happened so quickly we had no idea. I heard gunfire at the other end of the street. They were already shooting some people. Then, just for one second, I saw mummy's face peeping between the solder's arms. Her eyes were wide and her face was white. She mouthed my name. Some trucks screeched to a halt in front of us and the soldiers pushed us inside. We were driven away – all I had was the dress with blue flowers on and a small bag with some money in it and a photograph of my parents which I always carried with me.'

Helena's face was streaming with tears, her handkerchief wet with grief.

'It was better that your mother wasn't in the street. She wouldn't have survived being taken away,' said Tadek.

'We were only separated by the width of one soldier. She was just behind him, I was just in front. We were so close but a universe apart.'

'War is full of small chances. A few seconds here or there or a metre here or there makes all the difference in the world.'

They sat in silence. Helena's body was racked by sobs, Tadek struggling to take in these events which he had never heard about until that moment. After minutes had passed and Helena ceased to cry, Tadek kissed her and stood up to turn on the television.

It was the news from the BBC. They were reporting events from Czechoslovakia where Soviet tanks were starting to roll through Prague to suppress the uprising. The Czech radio was calling in vain for Western help and a young man, Jan Palach, had set himself on fire.

Helena stared at the screen in horror. 'It's happening again. Thank God Mama came back – perhaps Warsaw is going to be next on the Soviet list. At least we can look after her here,' said Helena watching the tanks crushing small cars on the streets of the Czech capital.

Chapter 18

Wanda was sitting on her bed at the Vicarage. She had definite evidence that Val was going into her room when she wasn't there. She had smelled an unusual perfume on her pillow one day. Another time there was a bright pink button lying in the middle of the floor. Wanda kept trying to see if Val wore anything pink that the button may have come from. And there were little things, such as the bedclothes being slightly rumpled or the curtains being closed when she was sure she had opened them that morning. Wanda hated the thought of Val being in her room. What on earth was she doing in there? What was she doing in Wanda's bed? Was she trying to find something incriminating? Well, there wasn't anything. Wanda didn't smoke in the room, take drugs, or bring men home (unfortunately) so there was nothing for Val to find.

Just the previous day she had carefully placed her make-up bag on the dressing table. Inside she had put a little tub of face power with the lid left off. If someone opened the bag, the powder would go everywhere and she would have proof that Val had been in her room. But the bag and powder were untouched. Wanda would have to find another trap.

She was roused from her thoughts by Dave calling from downstairs, telling her that her father was on the telephone. As she came down, he handed her the receiver.

'Here you are Jean. What is it your dad calls you?'

'Wanda – it's my nickname. Thanks.'

'Oh, Jean after you've finished your phone call come into the sitting room and meet Simon, Lydia, Rachel and Jen. They are great fun. You'll love them.'

'Yeah, ok, I'll see you in a minute.'

Wanda paused waiting for Dave to go back into the sitting room.

'Hello, Dad, how are you?'

'Wanda, listen, I have bad news. Your grandmother has had a very serious stroke. She can't speak or move and is completely helpless. The doctor doesn't know how long she will live.'

'I'm sorry. How is Mummy?'

'As well as can be expected. Zosia is terribly upset of course.'

'I'm sorry,' mumbled Wanda.

'But I was ringing to ask you to come home and see her. Can you get the train and I'll pick you up at the station?'

Wanda said nothing but bit at the nail on her left thumb. Eventually she spoke.

'No, I'm not coming.'

'What? What do you mean you're not coming? I said this could be the last time you'll see her. Of course you're coming.'

'No, I'm not dad.'

'Look, I'm sure you can get time off work if you explain the reasons. They will understand. Tell them your grandmother brought you up, for goodness' sake.'

'I don't want to take time off work, but that's not the reason anyway.'

'What is the reason?'

Wanda started to chew on her index finger nail. She took a deep breath and spoke.

'I don't want to come because I don't like her and she doesn't like me. You should understand, dad, because she doesn't like you either. We didn't match up to her expectations. She thought we were both fat, stupid and ugly. I remember the way she always looked at us. It would be hypocritical of me to come and see her now.'

'You're talking absolute nonsense. You have to come because it will hurt your mother if you don't.'

Wanda felt tears coming to her eyes. Her father was using emotional blackmail. She squeezed her eyes shut and her words started gushing out in a torrent of latent feelings.

'I don't mean to hurt Mummy, tell her that. My quarrel is with my grandmother. I couldn't help being the way I was but she always made it quite clear she thought I was rubbish. She had a mean streak, a vicious nature. When I was little I tried so hard, so damn hard to please her. I wanted the embroidery to be perfect, I wanted the cake to turn out well, I was desperate for her approval and for her attention. She rejected me and I always felt I had let her down. But I hadn't. It was she who let me down. I was only little, I couldn't help being clumsy or awkward.' Wanda choked back the sobs.

'You are just imagining things – none of that is true. Why do you think you were the centre of everything?' Tadek's voice rose with emotion. He never got angry but he was coming close to it. 'Do you think she spent her time trying to humiliate you? Of course she didn't. Just think about the kind of life she had, for God's sake. If she was tough or strict it was because events beyond her control had made her like that. Can't you have some under-standing and compassion? She lived through the First World War, lost her beloved husband after only a year of marriage, spent the rest of her life as a widow, cared for her daughter and had to suffer having that only daughter carted off by the Germans to God knows where to suffer God knows what fate. You have always had it easy, my girl. What do you know about suffering?'

Wanda couldn't believe her father was speaking to her like this. She felt angry, betrayed.

'Well I'm sorry I didn't have the good luck to have been born in a war torn country and then I could be so noble about my suffering. I suffered from being the eldest child and being a failure while my little sister gets all the glory for being thin, pretty and clever. And Janek gets praise for simply being male. Anyway, I want to look to the future,

I'm not interested in the past. *This* is my country and I love it here. I'm not coming so you'll just have to explain that to anyone who cares at all.'

'Wanda, please listen, I'm sorry…

Wanda put down the phone and stamped off upstairs. Dave put his head round the door and called out,

'Jean, come and meet the folks.'

'Fuck the folks,' mumbled Wanda under her breath as she continued upstairs. Once in her room she flung herself on the bed and burst into tears. No, she wasn't going to let her grandmother hurt her anymore. She was in London for a reason and she would continue with her plan.

The next day was a Sunday and Wanda decided to try again to see Paul. She came out of the tube station in St John's Wood, following the route Eunice had shown her. When she arrived outside his house, no one was there. This was surprising. Maybe everyone had decided to do something else – all at the same time. Wanda felt quite hopeful – this was a good sign. She placed her jacket on the ground and sat down on it. The street was very quiet, extremely quiet. Wanda imagined him arriving in a black cab. He would step out of the cab and see her, sitting on the ground. He'd say he was surprised she was the only one there today. He'd invite her inside the house, make her a cup of tea, ask her where she came from. Yeah, they had played a gig in Derby in the early days. He remembered it well. He'd ask her to sit down. She imagined lowering herself onto a brightly coloured beanbag. But as Wanda contemplated the scene, no matter how hard she tried she couldn't stop herself visualising her weight causing the bean bag to tip over, hurling her fat thighs backwards onto the floor. And he would stand there laughing and laughing.

Wanda pulled herself back to reality and looked down either end of the street. There was a man walking his dog and a boy riding past on his bike. She sat and waited for one hour, then got up and walked up and down a while.

She sat down again for another hour. She leant back against a tree and contemplated the sky. The swallows flew high round and round in circles, a squirrel ran down the trunk of the tree.

Then a black taxi came down the street. Wanda's heart pounded as she watched the car slow down as it approached the house. She stood up and shielded her eyes against the sun. The taxi was definitely slowing down near to her. Wanda was sure – she was absolutely certain. The window was down and the driver leaned out and yelled,

'He's in India, you daft git.'

Humiliated, Wanda ran down the street into St John's Wood High Street. She found a phone box and on impulse telephoned Eunice's home number. Roger answered.

'Hey, Jean. How are you doing?'

'Not great, actually. Is Eunice there?'

'She's just popped out to the shops. Where are you, love?'

'I'm in St John's Wood. I just wondered ...'

'Well, come over then. You're so close why don't you come and have dinner with us? You'd be more than welcome. Come on Jean – it'll be fun.'

Wanda suddenly felt elated, a glow of pleasure spread across her body.

Forty minutes later, she came out of Camden Town tube station and began walking. There was a market selling hippy clothes, houseboats on the canal and a woman leading a mongrel on a string while shouting loudly at everyone she passed.

Eunice and Roger's flat was situated above a record shop. Wanda pressed the button for the intercom and Eunice's voice told her to come up to the first floor. A push button light on a timer lit the way up a narrow flight of stairs. At the top, a sign by the bell read, *Eunice and Roger's Love Pad.* Eunice opened the door and gave Wanda a hug. Wanda felt like crying. Roger was standing by the stove, tasting something in a large pot.

'Jean,' he cried. 'It's great to see you.' He smiled broadly and winked at her. 'The *piece de resistance* of Leonard's poncy Champagne evening. I'll never forget that evening. You were brilliant.'

Though embarrassed, Wanda found herself smiling. Roger looked so happy and handsome. The room was painted dark purple. A mattress lay on the floor in the corner covered with a scarlet quilt and books about Buddhism, the Vietnam War and feline diseases were scattered round the room. Long purple curtains blew around the open window through which the sounds of Camden Market echoed. The kitchen was in one corner of the room. In another corner Roger's photography equipment was situated. Enormous black cameras, lights, large silver-coloured screens and bags of film. As well as pictures of Eunice on the walls, there were photos of beautiful Far-Eastern children.

'I'd had rather too many drinks that evening,' Wanda said. 'I'm really sorry I bounced your picture.'

'Oh, it was a great shot. Got that woman right on the arm. Well done. Dinner will be ready momentarily, as they say in the States.'

Wanda pointed to the pictures. 'Where were those taken?'

'In Vietnam. I was taking some photos of children there for *The Observer*. They wanted some images of the country that weren't just concerned with the war. It's a fantastic place – I can't believe what the US military machine is doing to it.'

'Roger works freelance for a number of papers and magazines,' interrupted Eunice. 'He has an assignment in Chile coming up soon. I'm really anxious about it. An American journalist was kidnapped and murdered there not so long ago.' She and Roger looked at each other.

'I want real work,' sighed Roger. 'You can understand that, Eunice. I don't want a job where I just go around taking pictures of Princess Margaret out on the piss or another hypocritical Beatle. I'm sick of celebrities. I want to take some pictures of real people in desperate situations.'

Wanda was a little confused. She thought everyone of her generation was a Beatle fan. She decided to change the subject.

'That smells nice, what is it?' Wanda said.

'Lentil stew, my speciality. I hope you don't mind sitting on bean bags. We never got round to getting a table and chairs.' Roger handed out some plates and forks.

'How's the trendy vicar these days,' said Eunice.

'Oh, he muddles on. Poor old Dave – him and his youth club. It's the evil Val I'm more worried about. She's full of whispered threats. She's one of these people who speak so quietly you can't hear what she's saying but you know it's unpleasant. I'm sure she's snooping around my room when I'm out. I find things moved around.'

'She sounds delightful. Maybe you should get a lock for your door,' said Roger.

'Yeah, but that would involve drilling holes and she'd want to know why I was doing it. So then I'd have to accuse her of snooping.'

'Hey, you'd better check there aren't any holes in the walls. Suppose they were both peeping at you,' said Roger. 'Perhaps when you were getting undressed.' He winked again. 'Maybe they are these Christian fundamentalist types who are really perverts.'

Wanda laughed but felt worried. She had never thought of something like that.

'Yeah, I really wish I could find somewhere else to live.'

'Actually, there is a bedsit upstairs and the bloke who rents it is never there. We could find out about it and see if you could take it over. It would be more expensive than where you are but probably safer,' said Roger.

'That would be brilliant if you could find out about it,' said Wanda blushing. 'I'd love to move from that place. Apart from anything else, it's such a long journey to get to work. I think Dave is quite nice actually. I feel sorry for him having such a mean wife. I really think she was hoping for a better catch than a vicar. She was moaning the other day about the house belonging to the church and if Dave fell under a bus she and their daughter would be thrown out in the street.'

'Oh, is that what happens with vicars?' said Eunice.

'Apparently. That's probably the reason why Catholic priests aren't allowed to marry. So the Church won't have to support their widows.'

'Is that so? Are you Catholic, then?'

'Yeah, well, I was brought up Catholic.'

'My friend, Siobhan, is Catholic. Are you Irish?'

'No, actually, Polish. But I was born and brought up in Derby so I'm English really.'

'Jean Stapleton doesn't sound like a Polish name.'

'It isn't. I just use that because it's so much easier. I don't have to explain it or spell it out to people. It's so difficult having a foreign name – you've no idea. People usually laugh or make some comment that they're glad you spelt it for them. It may seem romantic to you but it's just a nuisance in reality.'

'So, what is your real name?' asked Roger.

'Wanda Baran.'

'That's a lovely name,' said Roger. 'It's not very difficult at all. There are some English people I know with ridiculous names. I went to university with a bloke called Harris Pratsides.'

Wanda laughed and tried to shake off the feeling she was playing gooseberry.

'Actually, my name's not so bad when you say it in Polish.'

Eunice looked at her with renewed admiration.

'Do you speak Polish, then?'

'Yes.'

'You're bilingual. That's fantastic. Why did you never tell me? Let's hear you say something in Polish.'

Wanda paused and saw Roger looking at her with interest and admiration. She cleared her throat.

'I can sing a nursery rhyme if you like.' And she did, her

beautiful clear singing voice resounded round the tiny flat, bouncing off the walls, competing with the backdrop of jazz music and voices from Camden Lock market. When she had finished, Roger and Eunice both clapped.

'What's the song about?' asked Eunice.

'Oh, just some silly men in a wheat field,' replied Wanda and to her delight Roger roared with laughter. Wanda suddenly felt special and different – for the first time, her otherness was a cause of admiration instead of derision.

'I've always wanted to be able to speak another language,' he said. 'Have you ever been to Poland?'

'No, but from what I hear it's all tiny little flats, great long queues and food shortages.'

'Why are there food shortages? Don't they grow a lot of food in Poland?' asked Eunice.

'The Soviets rule everything there and they take Poland's food for themselves. They are always causing trouble in Poland.'

'Ah, just like the US does in Central and South America,' said Roger. 'The super powers are always shitting in their own back yards. I was at the Grosvenor Square demo outside the American Embassy last March. It was fantastic. I'd love to go to another one.' And he leaned over and kissed Eunice on the lips.

Chapter 19

Derby, 1970

The woman behind the counter at the Job Centre did not even look up when Helena sat in front of her.

'Name?' she snapped out.

As always, Helena said, 'I'll spell it for you, B.A.R.A.N Initial H.'

'Age?'

'45'

'Qualifications?'

'I'm a machinist. I don't have any formal qualifications because of the war. Before the war, I was confident of a place at Warsaw university to read medicine. But I was taken away by the Germans when I was 16 and put to forced labour in Germany. By the time I got to England I had to work and was never able to take up my education again. I was very well educated until the age of 16, though.' Helena was surprised she'd come out with this rush of personal information to a stranger. She felt embarrassed that she'd done the wrong thing.

However, the woman looked up and stared at Helena for a while with interest. When she spoke, her voice was softer, more sympathetic. 'I'm afraid I don't have any machinist jobs at the moment.'

'I know. I need to sign on for the Dole,' said Helena.

'I do have some other jobs that may be of interest. There are several cleaning jobs.'

'Yes, but at my age – I don't mean to sound arrogant – but I don't want to do cleaning now. I don't have any office skills and I don't suppose people would want me to answer the phone because of my accent.'

'I may be able to get you on a training course, if you want.'

'Don't you think I'm too old for that now? I don't think anyone would give me a job in an office anyway.'

The woman paused as if in thought.

'Actually, there is something. Wait here a minute.'

Helena sat waiting as the woman went through a back door. She looked around the office. A little wooden box calendar marked the day's date – March 20, 1970. The decade had turned and it was almost as if Nature knew it was time to turn as well. As if the arbitrary calendar invented by man was now firmly locked through men's minds into the universe itself. The penny ride was over, the machine had stopped.

The huge engineering works in Derby that had built the famous fighters in the war and employed most of the town's people had crashed out of business. The newspapers headlined the event – the company had been overmanned, was inefficient, too large and too cumbersome. The Government would rescue it but only if over half the workforce was made redundant, there was serious restructuring and the question of productivity was addressed. But nothing happens in isolation – the failure of such a huge company on a small town had serious knock-on effects. Not least at Babcock's Mill.

Helena, along with all the other workers, had been called to a meeting in the staff canteen by the factory manager. He came straight out with the bad news – Babcock's was going out of business, all the jobs were going where labour was cheap in the Far East and 755 people, mostly women, would be thrown on the Dole.

That evening, Helena had watched Zosia filling out her application form for university. She was applying for a four-year course that involved one year in Poland. Zosia's 'O' Level results had been excellent and her teacher had told an excited Helena and Tadek that Zosia was a prime candidate for university.

Helena had looked at her with a mixture of pride and regret. In contrast, working at Babcock's for 20 years, she found herself out of work with no training for anything except using a sewing machine.

'Perhaps it's for the best,' she said to Tadek. 'If I can find a job that doesn't have such long hours, I can spend more time with Mother. I leave the nurse to do so much and I feel guilty about it.'

At the job centre the following day, Helena had seen a few jobs listed on the board. There was one for a dinner lady at a school for a ludicrously small salary, there were cleaning jobs, a job in a solicitor's office that required shorthand and typing skills and a vacancy for a traffic warden. Helena had decided to speak to the counsellor who was now taking some time to come back to her desk.

'Sorry, I had trouble finding this.' The woman handed Helena a piece of paper with a name and telephone number on it.

'Have you heard of this man, Robert Kaminski?'

'No.'

'He's American, well Polish American and he's here writing a book about the war. There was an article about him in the *Evening Telegraph*. I met him at a party last week and he said he was looking for an assistant. I think he is doing some research about the old airforce base at Newly and that's why he's in Derby. I don't know exactly what his book is about but it won't hurt to call him.'

When Helena phoned, she discovered that not only did Robert Kaminski have a strange way of speaking Polish tinged with an American accent but also that he was a friend of Jerzy Batorowicz, the Polish Club manager. He was staying with Pan Batorowicz in his house in the smart suburb of Cheldon. When Helena arrived there, Pan Kaminski greeted her at the door. He thanked her for coming and offered her tea as his friend Jerzy had given him free run of the house.

Helena thanked him and expressed surprise that he wanted to see her as she had never done any research before. ' I thought you'd want someone younger with experience,' she said glancing into the kitchen. 'Oh, hello,

Lydia, didn't see you there. How are you? What have you been doing since you left school?'

Lydia looked up from the kitchen table where she was sitting. Her pale face was tired and drawn.

'Hi. Erm, I started doing A levels at the Tech but had to give up,' she said with halting words.

'Oh, why is that?' Helena felt Pan Kaminski nudge her in the back.

Lydia stood up.

'Well, as you can see I'm expecting a baby.'

Helena felt her face redden.

'Ah, yes. Well, take care of yourself Lydia. Zosia sends her love, I'm sure,' she stammered.

'What's she doing now?' asked Lydia.

'Hoping to go to London University to study Polish Language and Literature actually.' Helena's voice trailed away as she contrasted Lydia's situation, pregnant at 17, with that of the wonderful career Zosia would have.

'OK. Say hello to her for me and tell her, sorry.'

Helena looked confused as Lydia marched off upstairs.

Helena and Pan Kaminski looked at other.

'I didn't know about that. How embarrassing. Poor girl – how awful' said Helena

'It happens. Her father is pretty upset about it, I can tell you.' He gestured for her to sit down and took a seat himself in an armchair.

'Yes. Poor Pan Batorowicz. He must be very worried. I understand you knew him during the war?

'We were both fighter pilots. We became very close but he decided to stay in this country when I went to America. He said he was and always would be a European. I, on the other hand, decided to try a new and booming country. I haven't regretted my decision.'

He flicked a biro between his fingers and crossed his legs. 'Anyway, let's get down to business. I was very impressed by what you said and the way you spoke. You obviously come from a very good family. I heard that the factory you worked at had closed down so I wanted to help. You deserve better than working in a factory, you know. Unfortunately, this job is only for about three months but I hope you'll be interested in it.'

'What does it entail?'

Kaminski told her he had funds from the Polish-American Foundation in Chicago to write a book about the Polish Diaspora during and after the war. The book was to include information about the British-Polish experience. Help would be needed to record interviews, do translations, indexing, etc. Time was pressing because the fighter pilots were getting old.

'It sounds like interesting and useful work,' said Helena enthusiastically. 'I know most of the Poles in Derby and all have a story to tell although some are quite harrowing. The war did terrible things to many people, not just physically but more psychologically. There are many of them in mental homes. I thank God every day for the peace now. I never want a war again.'

'Actually, I enjoyed it.'

Helena stared at him in complete amazement.

'You enjoyed the war? How could you say that?'

Kaminski shrugged. 'I think most of the men in our RAF squadron enjoyed it as well. Why do you think they formed the Pilots' Association and the Polish Club? Not just to maintain the Polish community but to try and retain and recapture that spirit of comradeship and excitement that the war brought. It doesn't really work, though. Everything is a let down afterwards. You never again get that same adrenaline rush, that same feeling of purpose, that sense of being really alive.' He looked at Helena. 'But I realise the war was not the same for you. Tell me about your war.'

Helena looked down at her hands. She told him how she had worked for 16 hours a day in a clothing factory and there wasn't too much comradeship and certainly no excitement. She'd been born in Warsaw and her father had died when she was a baby. Her mother had brought her up alone. She'd been hoping to study medicine but in 1942 was taken away to work in Germany. She'd worked there until 1945 and then escaped and came to England She'd met and married her husband Tadek in 1948. They had three children. All she'd wanted to do after the death and destruction of the war was to have babies.

'What happened when the Germans took you away?' asked Kaminski.

Helena swallowed hard and gazed out of the window.

'I was just 16. I was lucky being young, strong and blonde haired. Others were not so lucky. We were taken to the outskirts of Hamburg to a textile factory. We made German army uniforms.'

'Really? So you've worked in clothing factories most of your life?' said Kaminski.

'Yes, I'm a very good machinist although that skill won't be of much use to you.'

'How did they treat you at the factory?'

'As well as you would expect of Nazis. We were given food, bunks to sleep in and we worked at the sewing machines. It's funny really – have you seen those advertising posters everywhere that show a young girl wearing jeans and little else? She has her arms crossed over her chest. It has the slogan, 'Goss Jeans – nothing else matters'

'Yes, I know about the company.'

That's who I worked for – Reinhard Goss. His son, Peter Goss, still runs the firm and I believe they are still in the same premises in Hamburg. I remember Peter Goss extremely well.' Helena stared out of the window, her face a picture of sorrow.

'That's incredible, Goss is a huge company – they have offices in the States. I had no idea they used to make German uniforms,' Robert Kaminski rubbed his hand together in glee. 'I'm not surprised, though. The Mengele family firm are still making tractors, aren't they? Ooh, this is really good news, it's going to be really good,' he said.

Helena stared at him, she suddenly felt terribly worried.

'Not many people know what Goss used to do. That's

how Reinhard escaped punishment. He's dead now, fortunately,' she explained.

'So, what was it like, working there?'

Helena told him how there was a huge warehouse where hundreds of girls worked night and day to make uniforms for all branches of the German army, navy and air force. They were hardly ever given a break. The girl next to her, a lovely person called Wanda, was so tired one day that she ran her finger under the needle of the machine. She was screaming and the blood was spurting all over a pile of clothes that had just been sewn. The other girls tried to help but the guards made them get back to their machines and they took Wanda away. Helena never saw her again. She was probably unable to work after that so they took her off to concentration camp. If anyone fell ill and couldn't work they are taken away. Helena was lucky, she said, she stayed healthy. She worked there for three years.'

'Tell me about Peter Goss,' said Kaminski. That would make a very interesting story for the book. He is running a big advertising campaign in the States at the moment as well.'

'He'll probably sue you if you write anything bad about him. I don't think you should mention him.' Helena shifted uncomfortably in her seat.

'If it's true then it isn't libel, is it? Did the Goss family take personal command of the factory?

'Well, Reinhard did. He was always strutting round the place. One time I remember him examining a jacket one girl was making. He said it was substandard and hit her across the face with this stick he always used to carry. He said substandard work was to be expected from sub-humans.'

'Did he say that? What nationalities worked there?'

'Many Poles, also Jews were there. They loaded the lorries with the finished uniforms. They never stayed long. The Germans treated them worse than us. After a couple of weeks they were sent to concentration camps and replaced with others. There were also some Czechs, Lithuanians, Hungarians and others.'

'This is fascinating. I think a history of the Reinhard Goss company would be of enormous interest – especially in the States.'

Chapter 20

London, 1971

Wanda was in the changing room at Fab Fashions trying to work out if her new jeans suited her. After a year of trying she had managed to lose some weight. Following advice from Eunice she stopped eating meat and ate salads, lentil stews, wholemeal bread and fruit. She had also taken up smoking. Her life had moved on. Paul McCartney was happily married with a child now and she was surprised how little it had hurt her. All the fans had been waiting for the sword to drop, agonising about it, crying about it. Now it had and suddenly they were free. Some woman had got him but she was no one they knew, she wasn't one of them so they didn't have to be jealous.

Anyway, he had been replaced in her affections by Roger Elliott. She just couldn't help it. She was sure Eunice could find someone else easily but she just had to have Roger. He often came round to the shop when they were closing to pick Eunice up and sometimes he invited Wanda to go for a drink with them. Apparently, the bedsit above their flat was not yet available. After Wanda complained about her boring train journey back to Croydon, he'd lent her books to read on the way, by authors such as Herman Hesse, James Joyce and Milan Kundera. Wanda struggled to get through them so she'd have something to discuss with him but often she had no idea what they were about. She found it hard to get through the first few pages. Just the words 'translated from the German' were enough to make her heart sink.

Wanda viewed her reflection in the changing room mirror. She wanted to look her best because she was meeting her sister for lunch and she was determined to look like a fashionable London sophisticate. Zosia might be going to university but Wanda was an independent, West End girl.

Eunice poked her head round the curtain.

'Hey, Jean, they look great. Are they the new Goss jeans?'

'Yeah, they just came in. I'm going to buy a Goss jacket as well.'

'Is it for anything special?'

Suddenly the words of that little girl as she spoke to Zosia came back to her – 'why is your sister so ugly while you are so pretty?'

'I'm meeting my sister for lunch. She's down here for an interview at London University,' said Wanda.

'Really? Which college? I keep putting off going to university because I keep changing my mind about which course to do. The trouble is I like earning money here and Roger is always on at me to do more modelling.'

'Zosia's wants to go to the School of Slavonic and East European Studies, to do Polish language and literature.'

'Well, she has a head start doesn't she? What's her name again?'

'It's Zosia, that's Sophie in English.'

'Oh, well, have a fab lunch,' said Eunice and wafted away in a cloud of sweet petuli.

Wanda left the shop on her way to meet Zosia. She felt a spring in her step – her figure was slimmer, she thought her new jeans looked good and her handbag matched her new sunglasses. Fancy wearing sunglasses – she felt like Jackie Kennedy. Wanda passed the tramp sitting in his doorway holding out a cup, begging as usual. She was feeling at peace, at one with the world. She searched in her purse and found half a crown, no it wasn't half a crown, it was now the new 10 pence. As she walked past, she dropped it into the tramp's cup. There was a splash.

'Hey, that was my fucking tea,' shouted the tramp looking down at his drink. 'What the fuck have you thrown in it?'

Wanda hurried off down the street towards the vegetarian restaurant in Soho Square where she'd arranged to meet Zosia. She took position outside looking up and down the street. Eventually Wanda saw her sister coming. She was shocked to see how tall, elegant and sophisticated her little sister looked. Her long dark hair, usually tied back in a thick plait, was flowing freely about her shoulders. She was wearing a stylish top decorated with geometric designs and slim-fitting dark trousers. She looked incredibly beautiful. Wanda's efforts had been to no avail – her sister was the beauty, the Jackie Kennedy lookalike, not her. Wanda took a deep breath and raised her hand in greeting.

'How did the interview go?' she asked her sister as they took their seats in the restaurant.

'I think it went very well,' replied Zosia confidently in Polish. 'They seemed to like me and were impressed by what I'd done so far. If they really want me, they'll make a low offer so I will only have to get two Es in my A levels or something like that. Easy!'

'Where will you live if you do go there?' Wanda continued to speak in English. 'It's really hard to find places here that you can afford. I've been living with Daft Dave and Evil Val for years now because it's cheap and nasty. I try to spend as little time there as possible but I just can't afford anything nearer town. Eunice, who I work with in the shop, was hoping I could move into the bedsit about their flat. She is going to let me know if it becomes free. It will be quite expensive on my salary but I had a pay rise recently.'

'Accommodation will be no problem because I'll get a full grant as mum and dad earn so little,' Zosia persisted in Polish. 'Then I'll just live in the student room provided. The student halls are in Bloomsbury round the corner from the college so I won't have any travel expenses. I had a look at them after the interview.'

A couple sitting at the next table heard Zosia speaking and the woman looked round, obviously trying to work out which unfamiliar language it was.

'Good for you. How are mum and dad and the brat?' Wanda continued in English.

'Mum is working for this awful man who's writing a book about the Polish Diaspora.'

'What does that mean?'

'When all the Poles were scattered around the world because of the war. Mum's doing research for him. He's paying for her to doing a typing evening class at the Further Education College. He keeps coming round to our house and mum has been telling him all about when she was taken to Germany during the war to work. They have these earnest discussions about her work in a clothing factory. I heard her telling him things I never even knew myself. It's all going in his book, apparently. Dad doesn't say much when this bloke is round but he is just the same. His hands are still always covered in either paint, soil or grease. Janek is hardly ever at home. He goes to his friend's house every day after school and spends most Saturdays playing football in a school team.'

'Doesn't he have to go to Polish school?'

A crash of plates as someone in the restaurant kitchen dropped a tray made everyone look round. There was slight cheer from a group of suited young men sitting in the corner.

'No, mum's given up – Janek refused to go,' said Zosia looking back her sister. 'He's only interested in football. He's so spoilt – he doesn't remember having to live in that disgusting house in Agard Terrace with an outside loo. He only remembers Porton Crescent. Also, he's forgotten how to speak Polish now. He never uses it anymore so it's gone out of his tiny little mind. Still, somehow he managed to pass the 11-plus so he'll be starting at Broughton Boys.'

Wanda stared at her plate. So, she was on the only one in the family to have failed that exam. Even Janek could pass it – how stupid must she be?

'Well, it's no great loss if he's forgotten how to speak Polish,' said Wanda, ' it never was of much use anyway.'

The waiter brought the pumpkin soup Wanda had

ordered and the vegetarian lasagne for Zosia. They started to eat, each sisters silent for a while, both in quiet offence. After only a few mouthfuls of soup, Wanda lit a cigarette. Zosia raised an eyebrow but said nothing. Eventually Zosia spoke, finally reverting to English.

'We've had another letter from cousin Pawel wanting to come and stay. He's desperate to visit but they keep turning down his passport application. He's having trouble apparently because he was involved in some student march so the police have marked his card. Actually, I'm thinking of spending the summer in Poland before I go to college so I'll probably stay with them.'

'That will help their space problems,' said Wanda pulling a face.

'You haven't asked about Babcia.'

Wanda was dreading hearing about her grandmother. There was a lingering guilt about not having been to see her and that awful conversation with her father.

'Well, how is she?'

Zosia shrugged. 'Just the same. The nurse comes in to bath and change her. We take it in turns to feed her. Daddy carries her downstairs sometimes but most of the time she stays in her bedroom. I read to her but I never know how much she really takes in. Sometimes she whimpers and sometimes she cries.'

'Whimper? Babcia? I can't imagine it.'

'Why do you never come home?' Zosia suddenly looked at her sister, her green eyes shining with an unfamiliar intensity.

'Because I am home.' Wanda asked the waiter for the bill. She felt the meal was pointless and tedious. Zosia was just the same as she had been at home – narrow-minded and rigid. Wanda had hardly touched her soup and she noticed Zosia left her lasagne half-finished.

Outside the restaurant, the sisters parted with the coolest of goodbyes. Wanda walked back to the shop leaving Zosia to make her way to St Pancras.

'If your sister goes to London University you'll see a lot

more of her, won't you. How did her interview go?' asked Eunice.

'Oh, I'm sure it went swimmingly. She'll get a place there, plus loads of money in a grant and somewhere to live in the middle of London. She always gets what she wants. She's always had everything so easy.'

'She probably envies you your independence,' said Eunice quietly.

'No, Zosia doesn't envy me one little bit. We don't get on, we don't speak the same language.'

Chapter 21

Warsaw, 1971

Pawel Lato sat at the dining table in the tiny Warsaw flat reading the letter that had just arrived from England. His aunt Helena wanted to know if it would be all right for her daughter, Zosia, to stay with them during the summer holidays before she went to college. He couldn't help feeling annoyed. He had been trying for so long to get a passport to go to England but had been rejected each time. It was true he took part in a student demonstration against the Soviet occupation, it was true he had a bit of a contretemps with a policeman and it's true he spent a little time in jail. But did they have to punish him by not giving him a passport? Apparently, yes.

Still, having his cousin to stay would be interesting although he would have to find somewhere else to sleep while she was there. It would give him an opportunity to practise his English and get some information about working in England. Who knows, perhaps the girl would turn out to be pretty. Perhaps he could make a pitch for her.

Pawel glanced down at *Tractor Maintenance*, the textbook he had borrowed from the students' library at Warsaw agricultural college where he was enrolled. He was forced to spend endless hours reading about the finer points of farm machinery, but his real interests were rock music, clothes, making money and above all, freedom and independence from this tiny flat with his mother and grandmother.

The sound of the key turning in the door meant his grandmother was back from shopping. He closed his eyes, wishing his solitude could have lasted longer. 'I'm 23 years old,' he thought. 'And I have to live with these old women.' Military service had given him a taste for freedom and now he felt trapped. He couldn't play his music, he couldn't have girls round, he couldn't do anything. It was driving him mad.

'I'm exhausted,' said Mira flopping into a chair. 'It's heartless at my age having to stand in a queue for two hours trying to buy the essentials for life. Pawel, make some tea while I sit down. I must take my shoes off.'

Pawel handed his grandmother the letter and told her cousin Zosia wanted to stay for the summer before studying Polish language and literature at London University in September. Auntie Helena had said Zosia wanted to find out about her grandfather, who she said was a prince, and wanted to write a biography of him.

'Oh, for goodness' sake not him again,' moaned Mira. 'You were lucky you were often away when Barbara stayed with us. She never stopped talking about her so-called prince. She's obviously passed on her obsession to this child.'

'Was her grandfather really a prince?'

'Of course he was a prince, everyone was a prince. About 90 per cent of the aristocracy called themselves prince in those days. It was nothing special but it impressed poor gullible Barbara no end.'

Later that evening Pawel left the flat. He made the short walk down the street to the flats where his friend, Bogdan, lived. But he didn't take the lift up to Bogdan's flat. This wasn't a social call. Pawel looked around carefully then slipped through a door on the ground floor marked, 'Private'. He ran down the stairs and knocked on another door at basement level. 'Yes?' said a voice. 'Four legs good, two legs bad' whispered Pawel. The door opened and he stepped into an underground room heavy with the heat from the boilers and noisy with the clatter of the presses.

'Where have you been?' Bogdan snapped annoyed. 'We've been waiting for you. We need help with these presses. I'm printing off more copies of *Animal Farm*. We also need to print more copies of the magazine. Can you do some distribution? I'm running out of paper and ink, too.'

Pawel told him that his cousin from England was coming to stay in August. 'She speaks fluent English and Polish,' he said. 'She might be able to help us.'

'Is she sympathetic?'

'I have absolutely no idea. She probably doesn't even know there is an underground press. People can read and write whatever they like in England so they probably don't understand what it's like for us. I suppose I could talk about it to her when she comes. From what I gather, she's more interested in the past than the present, but we'll see.'

'Well, that's a well-known Polish disease. Could we risk bringing her here, do you think?'

'I'll find out her views first. I don't think my mother would be too amused if I got the girl arrested so we'll have to be careful.'

'How old is she?'

'About 18, I think. She starts university in September. Her mother is my mother's cousin.'

Bodgan turned to the printing presses. There was a crunch of grinding metal as the machinery stopped.

'If you were any kind of engineer, you'd fix these stupid machines.'

'Yes, well I'm a twentieth century engineer. These presses last job was to print the Gutenberg Bible by the look of them.'

Through the window, Helena saw Robert Kaminski draw up outside her house in his pale blue Ford Zephyr car.

'Why does he need such a big car just for himself?' said Tadek.

'I suppose that's the way they do things in America,' said Helena.

Robert bounded from the car and rang the doorbell.

'Hello, Pani Helena, Tadek. I've something interesting

for you. I've been doing a little digging into the Reinhard Goss Empire. The Foundation in Chicago really thinks we can make something of this. Goss is a multi million dollar company basically built on slave labour – your labour. Don't you think you deserve some compensation?'

Helena looked at Tadek.

'I've never even considered it,' she said with a shrug.

Kaminski told them the Jews were getting huge sums of money in compensation from Germany. Didn't they think the Poles should get some for the work they were forced to do? Being taken away against their will, compelled to work until their health failed. What happened had blighted their lives and meant they didn't get the education they deserved. As a result many were not doing the kind the work or living the kind of life they should be doing according to their class and intelligence.

Helena saw Robert glance at Tadek.

'In fact, the whole experience has caused an enormous loss of earnings, wouldn't you say,' continued Kaminski. 'You should get compensation. And it's not just you. There must be hundreds of others. We are thinking, that is the Foundation and I, about a class action lawsuit against the Goss clothing empire. What do you think?'

'What does that mean?' asked Tadek.

'It means we sue Mr Peter Goss for every penny the bastard has. As we speak I am trying to make contact with all the others who worked in his factory of death. A few of them live now in the States and I'm flying back next week to try to take this whole action further. When I've collected all the relevant material, I'll be making contact with Mr Goss. His dirty little secret will come out in the end.'

Kaminski looked triumphant and Helena felt shocked and worried.

'But Reinhard Goss is dead now. Peter wasn't involved in any war crime. And anyway, I don't want to give evidence. I really don't want to do anything like that,' said Helena.

'Don't worry – it will be fine. He'll probably opt for an out-of-court settlement.'

Helena wished she'd never mentioned the Goss family to Kaminski. All this would drag up the past – a past Helena had been trying to avoid for 20 years. She twisted her white linen handkerchief round and round until it was a tight, taut knot in her hands.

Chapter 22

Early one morning before the shop was open, Wanda could hear little Leonard singing happily as he preened himself in front of the changing room. She knew he was pleased because his branch of Fab Fashions had been turning a healthy profit and was managing with fewer staff than many other branches. He had been commended for his efficiency and hard work and had been selected to attend a management training meeting at head office. The meeting would last two days and all expenses would be paid. He was going to leave Eunice in charge while he was away – something she would probably enjoy.

'Well, off jet-setting, is it?' Eunice bent down and straightened Leonard's tie.

'Jet-setting? You said this training course was at head office, didn't you? But that's only in Baker Street,' Wanda said.

'No, that's just Fab Fashions head office,' said Leonard. 'The Company head office is in Hamburg.'

'I didn't know that.'

'Yes, Fab Fashions is a very small part of the Reinhard Goss empire,' Leonard said, his small neat hands fastening the button on his striped blazer.

That evening Wanda sat nervously on the train heading for Croydon. She had made a decision to confront Val and accuse her of snooping. The thought made her feel sick. Before she left her room that morning, she had placed a length of black thread over her make-up bag and left it hanging down over the top drawer of the chest. If the thread had been moved that was conclusive proof that Val was a snoop. But obviously once Wanda had exposed her, she would have to leave the vicarage. She decided she would ring Eunice and tell her Val had thrown her out. Eunice, in the kindness of her heart, would be bound to invite Wanda to stay with her – until some suitable alternative accommodation could be found. Maybe the bedsit above their flat would be available at last. Wanda was determined to get it – she had to, absolutely had to be near Roger.

As she came through the front door, she saw Dave in the sitting room. He called to her.

'Hello, Jean. Good day at work? I'm just having a chat with Rachel here. She's one of the regulars at the youth club.'

Rachel turned to look at Jean, her white face full of fright as she nervously bit her bottom lip.

'Hold on Dave. I've just got to go upstairs for a moment. I'll see you soon,' Wanda said. She rushed up to her room. It was on the floor – the black thread was lying on the floor. Wanda picked it up. Oh, hell – what if it had just fallen? She thought she had fixed it round the make up bag but had she? Should she accuse Val of coming into her room anyway? Then Wanda noticed the thread wasn't lying in the place you would expect if it had just fallen. Could it have drifted over to one side? Only if there was a breeze in the room – which there wasn't.

Wanda went downstairs. Dave was at the front door showing Rachel out. It looked as though Rachel was crying.

'Ah, Jean,' said Dave closing the door. 'There you are. Would you like some coffee, or a meal or anything?' He ran his hands through his dishevelled hair. 'If there's anything you'd like…'

'That's kind of you, Dave, but there's something I want to discuss with you. Is Val here?'

'No, she isn't here, actually, she's out. She went with Sarah to stay at her mum's for a little while. Um, her mum's not well. She and Sarah left really early this morning. I'm sure they'll only be gone for a couple of days. What did you want to discuss?'

'Oh, nothing – it'll keep.' Wanda noticed Dave looked pale and had dark circles round his eyes. 'Is everything OK, Dave?'

He paused and looked nervously back towards the front door. 'Yes, of course, why wouldn't it be?'

Wanda felt puzzled but went back up to her room. This was worse. She had put the thread on the make-up bag this morning before going to work. Had Val already left by then? She didn't remember seeing her or Sarah in the morning, come to think of it.

She sat on the bed, a horrible, disturbing thought forcing its way into her mind. Val worked as a nursery nurse and so was out most of the day. Sarah went with her to the nursery. Dave spent a lot of time at home, writing sermons, chatting on the phone, entertaining kids from his youth club. Why was he always hanging round with teenagers, anyway? He was at home far more than Val was. Oh God, what if it was Dave who had been snooping in her room? Had she been distracted by his bluff and friendly manner? And why was that girl crying as she left this evening. Dave was certainly behaving strangely. And it was just the two of them in the house at the moment. Oh shit, there was no lock on her bedroom door. Wanda stared at the door in wild panic.

She started throwing her things into her bag. She would quietly leave the house then ring Eunice from the phone down the street. Wanda opened her bedroom door and looked around before creeping down the stairs. In the hall, she could hear Dave on the phone in his study. His voice sounded urgent, almost tearful. 'Please, Val, please Val,' he begged.

Wanda slipped out of the front door. She ran to the phone box and dialled Eunice's number.

Chapter 23

Warsaw, 1971

After the hustle and enormity of Heathrow, Zosia couldn't believe how tiny Warsaw airport looked. As the plane came to rest on the tarmac, Zosia placed her tattered postcard of the Black Madonna between the pages of her book as a bookmark and looked out of the window. She watched the steps being brought to the plane as a soldier with a gun slung over his shoulder took position at the bottom. Zosia had never seen a gun before.

Once inside the terminal, she collected her suitcase and looked for her relations. She spotted a young man of medium height with light brown hair holding a piece of card with her name on it. She studied him before he saw her. That must be Pawel, she thought, he doesn't look up to much. A middle-aged woman stood next to him. Zosia's heart felt a little pull – the woman reminded her of her mother. She was holding a bunch of red and white carnations tied with red ribbon and she looked so happy and excited.

Zosia went over and introduced herself. She was overwhelmed with hugs and kisses from her aunt, Irena, who thrust flowers into her hand. Pawel gave her a kiss on each cheek and took her bag.

'Did you have a good flight? Oh, darling, you look just like your grandmother,' Irena said. 'She told us how proud she was of you.'

'I'm really grateful you could put me up,' replied Zosia. 'I hope there will be room for me and this isn't causing too much trouble for you.'

Pawel told her it would be fine as he had a good friend who lived just round the corner where he could stay if necessary.

Zosia told them she hoped to repay their kindness when they visited England. She mentioned that because of the currency restrictions, she had brought some new clothes to sell to get Polish currency. She had jeans, shirts and jumpers – all from Marks & Spencer. She hoped she'd done the right thing.

Pawel watched her with growing interest.

In the taxi travelling towards the flat, Zosia looked out of the cab window at the huge grey buildings, the yellow trams, the little fruit and flower stalls. To come from Derby, with its small streets and modest municipal buildings, to this city of monolithic structures was quite a shock. They passed a massive war memorial depicting a grey stone woman with one huge, muscular arm out-stretched and the other holding a big ugly infant – a state memorial to a fierce mother. War memorials at home were usually of delicate white stone featuring a weeping angel or a simple obelisk adorned with names.

The taxi driver was talking in a surly fashion to her aunt – and she had never heard such bad Polish spoken before. Her aunt answered back in an equally rude and brusque a manner. How strange, Zosia, thought to encounter such kindness and such rudeness in the space of minutes.

Back at the flat Mira had prepared a splendid lunch that had taken hours of queuing to achieve. She greeted Zosia, anxious to make a good impression on the girl Barbara had boasted about so much.

'So, what do you want to see while you're here?' Mira patted Zosia's hand kindly.

'I want to visit Powazki cemetery, of course. And I'd like to visit my great aunt Maria but I know she is rather strange so she may not want to see me. I'd also like to do a little research because I'm thinking ahead about my undergraduate thesis. The war with the Russians in 1920 is of particular interest to me because you know my grandfather fought in it.'

Mira and Irena exchanged glances.

To change the direction of the conversation, Irena

inquired if Zosia wanted to find out more about her father's family. Zosia explained that her father had just two spinster sisters who lived on a little farm in a very remote area near the Russian border. She didn't think she would see them and anyway, what she was really interested in was the 1920s war with Russia. She wondered if there were any records still available or if they'd been destroyed. She presumed the Russians didn't want that little war talked about too much.

'That's right, they don't,' said Pawel. 'But I'm sure I'll be able to help you a little with that research.'

'Babcia always used to say that Poland saved Western Europe from communism by defeating the Russians at that time,' said Zosia.

'Yes, Poland saved Europe from communism but it couldn't save itself,' said Pawel.

Irena looked sharply at her son.

'But by stopping communism perhaps we paved the way for Hitler instead,' she said. 'Wouldn't a communist Europe have been better than a Fascist one?'

'Not really,' muttered Pawel.

Irena continued, 'I remember before the war once wandering onto the fields at the back of our estate in Tarnow and walking into a peasant's hut. There were four families living in one room, can you imagine that? I was only 10 but the horror of that remained with me. Things are so much better now. Did you know we have just had a whole new wing built at the hospital where I work – paid for by the Soviet Union? We get free health care here, available to everyone, as well as excellent education. And everyone here has a place to live, there are no homeless people and no hungry people. Can you say that is true of America?'

'No, but at least in America there is a chance of making something of yourself. Here we are all condemned to mediocrity,' Pawel replied.

'I wonder if the poor, illiterate and hungry of America would agree with you?' Irena's voice rose in anger.

'At least they know there is a chance of improving themselves.'

'Then they are full of false hope. You only hear about the successes – what about all the people who fail? They are being cheated but they are just deluding themselves. That is how they keep all the people down, with unrealistic expectations.'

'Of course, Mother, you are a member of the communist party so you have to say that,' Pawel argued. 'You have to be a member to be in your position at the hospital. Do you realise that in America you could be earning a fortune for the work you do? Let's have the truth told for once.'

Zosia listened to this exchange with surprise. No one in her family ever had political discussions let alone became so animated and emotional about it. She was worried she had become the cause of family disharmony.

Chapter 24

Eunice's tiny spare room was really more of a broom cupboard. Wanda had been staying there for almost a month. Roger was away in Chile but would soon be back. The man of her dreams was returning to her. Then a miracle happened – Wanda knew there was a God. The bedsit upstairs became vacant at last. The occupant had disappeared without paying the last month's rent and the landlord had phoned Eunice to ask if her friend still wanted it.

'Of course I want it' said Wanda leaping round the room for joy.

The bedsit upstairs was tiny, dirty and dark but to Wanda it was paradise in a bottle. It had a single bed, two little cooking rings and a sink. There was an old chest of drawers and a chair. She would have to use the bathroom on the floor below. It was worse accommodation than at the vicarage and more expensive, but worth it in every way. She had lived for years at the Greenhalges but she had spent so little time there, it was hardly value for money.

'It will be so much easier to get to work,' she told Eunice. 'We can go in together.' And I will be near Roger, she said to herself.

A week later, Roger arrived back. From her window high up above the street, Wanda saw Eunice fly out of the front door straight into Roger's open arms. He swung her around, grinning and laughing. Wanda tried to replay the scene with herself in it rather than Eunice. No matter how she tried, every time she imagined it, Roger fell over on the pavement with the effort when he tried to swing her round.

She could near the noise and commotion as he brought his bags and camera equipment up the stairs. Should she pop her head round the door and shout hello? She decided she would.

'Hey, Jean, it's just fab that you're living upstairs,' Roger called. 'Come down and celebrate my return with some Chilean booze.'

Wanda was down there like a shot. Eunice looked a little pained but Wanda was past caring. Roger was back, he was happy, she was going to have a drink with him, she lived upstairs. Life was too, too fantastic.

At work next morning, Leonard was reading the *Evening Standard* when Wanda saw a worried expression come over his face.

'Oh, hell. Look at this,' he exclaimed.

'What's the matter,' asked Eunice.

He showed them the headline, *Design firm boss falls to his death* and then read the article below.

Peter Goss, head of the multinational clothing design company Reinhard Goss, fell to his death yesterday from the 15th floor of his company offices in Chicago. Multimillionaire Goss had run the firm since his father's death 20 years ago. The company has described the death as a tragic accident but the police are continuing investigations.

Leonard looked at Eunice and Wanda.

'How on earth could he fall from his office? There's no way that was an accident. He must have jumped – or was pushed,' Leonard said.

'How will it affect Fab Fashions?' asked Eunice.

'It's not good, is it? Maybe Goss has financial problems. I never heard anything, though.'

'Still, to jump out of a 15th floor window, something must have been really wrong.'

Helena had been at her bookkeeping course in the morning and arrived home to take over from the nurse. She gave her mother some lunch, read to her from the Polish newspaper, *Trybuna Ludu*, and waited until she'd fallen asleep. Then she set about doing some housework, preparing a meal for the evening and doing some translations for Kaminski.

Halfway through the afternoon, she decided to sit down for a few minutes with a cup of coffee and read the paper. Brilliant August sunshine was streaming through the sitting room window and an odd feeling swept over her. She tried to determine its source – then it struck her, it was happiness. She loved her new work, enjoyed all the courses she was doing. She was using her brain for the first time since she was 16.

Wanda had phoned the previous evening sounding elated. She was living nearer work now, and was pleased to be away from the strange vicar and his wife. She told Helena she had a new boyfriend who was photographer. Helena had said she would love to meet him but Wanda had laughed and said they should give him more time.

Zosia had even managed to phone from Warsaw. She was enjoying staying in the flat and cousin Pawel had suggested they take the train down to Krakow for a few days. She too sounded so unlike her usual self. Her voice was light, enthusiastic and full of laughter.

Janek seemed to getting on quite well at the grammar school. He had ambitions, he said, to make a great deal of money. He had shown an interest in the stock market and had joined an enterprise club at school. Who on earth did he take after? Helena wondered.

Tadek was his usual self, unchanging as a rock. He was managing to get enough work still, he kept the home supplied with plenty of food from the garden and his watch mending hobby was now actually getting him some paying customers.

Her mother was the only worry but they had managed to get more nursing care and Helena thought her mother seemed a little more accepting of her condition than before.

Helena was woken from her self-contended reverie by the sound of the phone ringing. When she answered it, she knew by the slight delay that it was a call from abroad.

'Pani Helena, it's Robert Kaminski calling. I'm in Chicago – is this a good time to speak?'

'Yes, certainly. Are you really calling from such a long way off? What is it?'

'Have you heard the news? Peter Goss killed himself yesterday. He jumped from his office window on the 15th floor. I just can't believe it. What did he have to do that for?'

Helena closed her eyes and swayed. She remained silent, gripping the receiver till her knuckles were white.

'Hello, hello, are you still there? Can you hear me?'

'Yes, I heard you. What happened?' Helena asked in a hoarse whisper. 'What on earth did you say to him?'

'I never even spoke to him,' Kaminski protested. 'I'd drawn up a list of more than 50 people who are still alive and had worked in his factory including yourself. The Foundation had given the list to Goss's lawyers and some sworn testimonies about conditions at the clothing factory from 1942 until 1945. There were also descriptions of Reinhard Goss's treatment of the slave labourers. I understand the lawyers had simply sent a brief covering letter outlining the claim with a list of the workers. They hadn't even given him all the details.'

'Do they think it was suicide? Do you suppose it was because of that letter?' Helena felt her voice crack in agony.

'It must have been suicide. You don't fall accidentally from an office window like that – unless he was pushed. Maybe one of the people on the list decided to finish him off for revenge. Just a minute – were you in Chicago yesterday?'

'Don't be silly, this isn't a joke,' Helena snapped. 'Will you withdraw the action now that Peter Goss is dead?'

'No, why should we? The Reinhard Goss empire should still pay out.'

'Well, I for one want nothing more to do with it,' and she slammed down the phone.

A few days after Roger had arrived home, Wanda bumped into him on the stairs up to the flat.

'Oh, Jean I wanted to speak to you. Can you come in to the flat for a minute?'

'What now? I'm just off to work,' gasped Wanda.

'Sure, no time like the present,' he grinned.

Wanda followed Roger through the door of the flat. Eunice was nowhere to be seen. She must have left early to get on with some stock taking at the shop. Roger stood in the middle of the room as if looking for something. Wanda stared at him. He had a few days of stubble, his chin was strong, his nose straight, his eyes bluer than blue. She repeated over and over in her head, I love you. Oh, God, what if she said it out loud by mistake. Her heart was pounding and time stood still. She was late for work but she didn't care.

'Well, Jean – let's see, my darling...' he was looking round the room.

Wanda waited, transfixed.

Roger knelt down by the bed and spread himself face down along the length of it. Wanda moved towards him – did he mean her to join him down there? Reaching out, he grabbed something in the corner of the bed by the wall.

'Here we are – got it.' He held up a piece of paper. 'It's a publicity leaflet for my new show. I'm putting on an exhibition at the Indica Gallery. The title is *Through the Looking Glass* and I wondered if I could take some pictures of you for it?'

Wanda stared at the flyer not knowing whether to be pleased or disappointed.

'Pictures of me? Are you sure? I'd love to do that. I've never done any modelling before. That would be really exciting. Yes, I'd love to.'

'Great. I'm going to arrange a studio to do the shoot. I'll let you know when and where.'

Wanda stared at him.

'Is that OK, love?'

'Yes, of course, of course.' Wanda smiled. Life just got better and better.

Chapter 25

Like her grandmother before her, Zosia was finding the old bed on which she had to sleep rather uncomfortable. Her back hurt and her head ached from the hard pillow. Still, she knew she had to put up with a little hardship and it was worth it. Her days were so full and busy. Aunt Irena worked long hours, leaving for the hospital at about five o'clock in the morning and sometimes not returning until the following day when she would go straight to bed. Pawel was with his friends for much of the time so Zosia was often left with Mira for company. They went shopping and stood in queues together, they cooked the meals and cleaned up. Mira took her to the allotment where they collected fruit and vegetables. Zosia almost felt she was back with Babcia again.

One day they went to the Lazenki Palace and sat outside in the grounds to hear the outdoor Chopin concert. Zosia sat listening to the heartbreaking melodies, remembering her grandmother playing the piano to her at home. The huge, sweeping statue of Chopin was in front of her and, although she couldn't see who was playing the instrument because of the crowds, she could almost believe Chopin himself was at the piano. She could picture his young handsome face, elegant long, long fingers and his pained, intense expression. Zosia lost herself in a dream world. When the pianist finally stood up to take a bow, Zosia saw it was actually a little old woman dressed in lime green.

After the concert, Zosia and Mira walked arm in arm down the street, licking ice creams.

'Auntie, you remember my grandfather. What was he like?'

Mira hesitated. 'Well, he was, how shall I say? He was tall and handsome. He had a big handlebar moustache – that was the fashion in those days. But really I didn't know him very well. The first time I met him was at his wedding. Witold and I hadn't been married very long and I felt shy attending one of his family events. It was a big, expensive wedding and I felt quite the little country girl. Your grandfather was very quiet because I think he wasn't very well. But I can't tell you too much about him. Surely, your grandmother told you everything.'

'Yes, but it's always good to get a different perspective. I plan to visit his sister soon. I'm hoping she will be able to tell me plenty of stories about him. Apparently, she is rather eccentric.'

'Yes, she's really eccentric,' Mira agreed. 'She wore a bright red dress at his funeral. It shocked everyone.'

'Why on earth did she do that?'

'Because, as I said, she's eccentric. Well, on the potty side of eccentric actually.'

'She must have been so different from her brother. He sounds so serious and duty bound. Perhaps he was embarrassed by her.'

'Perhaps,' said Mira with a shrug.

'Auntie Mira, could we take the tram to Powazki cemetery today? I'd love to see where my grandfather is buried. Babcia told me so much about it, I feel as if I know the place already. Is Witold buried there as well?'

'Unfortunately not. My dear Witold died somewhere in Germany and we have no idea where his grave is. Come on, then we'll go the cemetery, then we can walk in the park. This weather is so beautiful.'

They travelled together on the clattering tram and started walking towards the cemetery. Outside the gate, Zosia stopped to buy some white carnations from the flower stall. The cemetery was huge and they had to check the map to see which direction they should take. They walked through the gate.

'Auntie Irena works so hard, doesn't she?' said Zosia,

linking her arm through Mira's.

'That's because she is such a dedicated doctor. She and I spent so long alone together when Witold went to fight. Irena was determined to be a useful member of society and especially after the destruction of the war she wanted to build a better and fairer society. She helped with the reconstruction of Warsaw after the war. I mean that literally, carrying bricks and making cement.'

Zosia thought about how useless she would have been doing hard physical work. She began to realise she had had an easy life in comparison – and it was only going to be better. She felt relieved but also a little guilty.

Mira continued. 'Irena then studied so hard at medical school – she's very intelligent. Her one mistake was marrying that good-for-nothing Alexander. He was a drunk and a layabout. He walked out on her when Pawel was only about four years old. Still, he did her a favour really. She was better off without him. The problem was Pawel really needed a father. He has some strange ideas, that boy. He's desperate to get a passport to go the West.'

'What exactly is the problem with it?'

'He's marked down by the police as an anti-government provocateur so they want to do all they can to make his life unpleasant. He hasn't joined the Communist Party so he'll always have problems getting a good job. At the moment he's an eternal student.'

They both laughed, thinking about the hapless Pawel.

'Auntie Irena is a communist, isn't she?' said Zosia, suddenly serious.

'Yes. She really believes in the ideals of communism. She never wants another war – she saw too much of the last one – and she believes in a fair society.'

'How did she get on with my Babcia, then?'

'Irena is the most patient of people. She would never try to force her ideals on anyone. She always tried to help Barbara and make her feel at home. She was aware Barbara grew up in a different era and had different ideas. Now where is the grave – I have to say I haven't seen it since the funeral and that was in 1926. Forty-five years ago exactly. Amazing, look, here it is. I can't believe we've found it so quickly.'

Zosia looked around at the huge headstones and neat paths between them. The sun was beating down and, following a short summer shower before they arrived, moisture evaporated from the grass. She saw where Mira was pointing. It was an enormous black stone monument topped with a huge cross on the top. Enthralled, she stepped closer. A black and white, oval shaped photograph of her grandfather was mounted into the stonework. His sad eyes looked at her. She read the inscription.

Prince Jan Olgierd Poniatowski. 1895-1926
Most beloved son, husband and father
Died in the service of his country

Zosia contemplated the prince's image. She would make him live again, she would find words to speak for him, his voice had been silent for so long but she would resurrect it. She placed the flowers she had bought on the grave, then took out four small white candles, placed them on the grave and lit them. The smell of the wet earth and the blooming flowers made for a peaceful resting place. A soft breeze blew. The candles flickered and died.

'I can never get them to stay lit either,' said Mira.

Chapter 26

Wanda had the address of the photographic studio in her hand as she searched the small streets of Rotherhithe for it. She had never been to this part of London before but was determined not to be late for Roger. She would travel oceans, cross deserts, climb mountains for him so she surely could find her way about Rotherhithe to meet him. At last she found the place in a narrow lane behind an ancient pub.

Roger had told her to come straight up the stairs. She pushed open the door of the studio and there he was, setting up his lights. She stood watching him for a moment, observing him while he didn't know she was there. He positioned the camera on his tripod, frowning and sticking out his tongue a little as he concentrated. He was wearing a black T-shirt and blue jeans, a set of keys dangled from his belt, and a thin gold chain hung round his neck. Wanda watched his hands as they carefully touched the camera, rubbing gently on the lens with a little cloth – hands she wished were touching her.

'Hi, Roger,' she eventually said.

'Jean, just the woman I was looking for.'

That was music to Wanda's ears.

Roger asked if she had found the place OK as it was off the beaten track. Then asked her to put on a particular black and white checked dress. It was one Eunice often wore, plus a white hat and white boots.

Wanda picked up the dress. It was made by Goss.

'You heard about Peter Goss, didn't you?' she said.

'Yeah, Eunice is quite worried how it will affect Fab Fashions. It seems the company is in some financial straits.' He started screwing a lens onto the body of the camera. 'Apparently, there's some big lawsuit against them in the States and they might have to offload a few loss-making businesses. Now, just let me get this lighting arranged ...'

Wanda disappeared into the toilet to get changed. The dress was very tight but she didn't want to tell Roger that. The hat felt silly but the boots were OK. When she came out, Roger had pulled down a huge piece of white paper down one wall and spread it along the floor. Unusual props were positioned round the studio: a mis-shapen wall clock that looked as if it had been melted in a fire, a tea pot with no spout, a record broken in two, a vase of flowers with all the heads cut off.

'How do I look?' she said pulling the dress down over her thighs. 'Is it all right?'

Roger examined her with an approving eye.

'Perfect, just perfect. Exactly the look I was aiming for.'

'What are all these weird things?' asked Wanda picking up the broken record.

'I'm doing a surreal, *Alice Through the Looking Glass* theme. It's meant to be a crazy, topsy-turvy world. Can you just stand on the white paper and hold this teapot for me?'

Tadek came home from painting a large house in Brick Street. His hands were covered in white paint and he was looking forward to a bath. Helena would be going out to her typing class in the evening but he was hoping they could have an hour or so together over dinner. He walked into the sitting to find Helena sitting in the dark with her head in her hands.

'Helenka – what's the matter?' He strode over and put his arms round her. 'What has happened?'

'I've killed someone, Tadek, I'm responsible for someone's death,' she replied in a hollow voice.

'Who? Of course you aren't. Who are you talking about?'

'Robert Kaminski telephoned from Chicago. Peter Goss leapt to his death from his office window – it was 15 storeys up. It was because he received a letter from Kaminski's lawyers about the factory during the war. There was a list of names. My name was on the list. Peter Goss killed himself because of it.'

Tadek sat silent in puzzlement trying to make sense of what his wife was saying.

'But you don't know that was the reason. Maybe there are other reasons – maybe his company is in financial trouble. Anyway, you aren't responsible for what he did. If he felt guilty, perhaps that was his way of gaining absolution.'

'But it wasn't his fault, you see. His father ran the factory. Peter never did anything, Peter tried to help, Peter never hurt anyone, I was hoping, hoping that ...'

'Businessmen like him don't commit suicide over something small. There was probably some huge scandal concerning him – I don't know but it was nothing to do with you. How can it have been?'

Zosia peered at the spidery writing on the yellowing card – Maria Poniatowska. Stoking up her courage, she rang the bell and waited. There were sounds of movement inside, a hacking cough, fumbling with locks. A small woman in a tight black dress with a cigarette dangling out of her mouth was standing there. Oddly she was wearing a black hat complete with a long ostrich feather. She looked up at Zosia.

'Yes?' she barked.

'My name is Zosia Baran. I am Jan Poniatowski's granddaughter, your great niece.'

Zosia waited for a reaction. The old woman stood a while in thought then said, 'Come in. I will talk to you.

Zosia followed her into the flat. She had to stop herself laughing as the ostrich feather dipped round and tickled her nose. Once inside, Zosia noticed the large clock on the mantelpiece and the black and white picture of a young man with curly dark hair. She looked back at Maria when the old woman barked in her rasping voice.

'How old are you? Where do you live?'

Zosia told her she was 18 and staying with her aunt Irena Lato and her aunt's mother Mira Ostrowska. She would be staying for the summer until she started at university in London in September. Zosia told her she wanted to talk about her grandfather, Maria's brother.

'My brother? Ah, I know who put you up to this – your grandmother? Has she come with you? What's she doing now, then?'

'Nothing. She's had a severe stroke and is an invalid. She came back to England for a holiday in '68 and was taken ill. Did no one tell you?'

The old woman was staring at Zosia, she made no indication that they should sit down.

'Ah well, I hardly ever met her,' said Maria finally. 'I saw her a few times when she was married to my brother then I never saw her again until a few years ago when she paid me a few visits. You want to talk about my brother?'

'Yes, I'm really interested in the war between the Bolsheviks and the newly independent Poland in 1920. I don't think many people in the West know about it. I want to do some research about it for my university course. Do you remember those days?'

Maria looked at Zosia for a while.

'What do you want to know? I remember that war. My husband Nathan and I were living here in Warsaw. Nathan was a brilliant man – he was a doctor who specialised in ear, nose and throat but he had so many other interests. He loved literature, psychology, politics.' She gazed around the flat and looked back at Zosia.

'Who did you say you were again?'

Zosia's heart sank. Would she be able to trust anything the old lady said? Still, old people often remembered events of long ago better than the present.

'My name is Zosia, I'm Jan's granddaughter.'

'Ah, yes, the baby girl. Stupid Jan nearly threw you off

the balcony, didn't he? Your mother sorted him out after that, didn't she? I can't blame her, I'd have done the same. Well, you seem to have grown up all right.'

Zosia frowned. The old woman was obviously confused. 'To get back to Jan, your brother. What was he like as a child and a young man? Can you tell me any family stories?'

The old woman turned towards a desk and opened the drawer.

'This is a picture of Jan, with my mother holding him when he was a baby.' She produced another photograph. 'And this shows us on our toboggan in the snow. I'm about nine here and so he would be seven.'

Zosia took the pictures with delight. She had gazed for so long at the few pictures of the Prince that Babcia had. To see these new ones was like a whole new chapter opening up on the Prince's life. A gorgeous baby, perhaps in his Christening robes, being held by a young glamorous mother in a white *broderie anglaise* Victorian dress. The picture had a slightly out-of-focus quality giving it an ethereal glow. The other picture showed Maria and Jan swathed in fur sitting together on a sledge out in the snow. Both were smiling with delight.

'Oh, auntie,' she said. 'These are exquisite. Could I make copies of them?'

'You can have them,' the old lady waved her hand at the pictures. 'I've no use for them. I have others that Nathan took.' She opened another drawer in the desk, rifled through, and handed Zosia two black and white prints. They were almost identical studies of the Prince wearing a plain black suit and sitting in a chair smoking a cigarette. In one picture he was hunched forward over his crossed legs, in the other he was leaning back but in both he was staring at something beyond the camera, a vacant, distant expression on his face. Zosia wondered if this was when he was suffering from the shell shock Babcia had mentioned. Turning them over, she read the words *JP case study 12.*

Zosia frowned. 'Auntie, you said there were some documents about Jan here in the flat. Do they mention his part in the war with the Bolsheviks in 1920? I'm very interested in that conflict. What can you tell me about it?'

'Nathan was disappointed about what Lenin did. He thought he must have been badly advised. The problem is,' the old lady grasped Zosia's arm, 'Nathan went out to get some cigarettes and a newspaper about two hours ago and he still hasn't come back. Would you go out in the street and see if he is coming?'

'Nathan isn't here,' said Zosia patiently. 'I'm your great niece. If you like I could sort through the old manuscripts for you. That would save you the trouble of doing it.'

'I never typed them up. Nathan wanted me to. He told me to keep the book safe until he came back. I'm still keeping it, still waiting. He was writing a book called *The Fragmented Mind*. He was so interested in psychiatry. I had to type up the notes, I haven't done it yet.'

The little old woman looked flustered.

'Look auntie Maria, I'll leave my name and address here on this piece of paper and maybe if you find the documents you could post them to me? I could type them up for you, couldn't I? Anyway, I'd better go.' Zosia was feeling very pessimistic. Perhaps these documents were a figment of her great aunt's confused imagination.

'When you get out in the street, if you see Nathan tell him to come up immediately because I want to talk to him.'

'Goodbye, auntie,' said Zosia.

'Who are you?' asked Princess Maria Poniatowska.

Chapter 27

Wanda was hurrying up Oxford Street toward Fab Fashions. She noticed an ambulance parked near the corner with Poland Street. As she drew closer, she saw a small group of people. Two ambulance men were tying someone onto a stretcher. She stopped and asked one of the bystanders what was happening.

'It's that old tramp – you know the one who always used to sit here. It seems that last night someone threw petrol on him and set him alight.'

'Oh, my God,' said Wanda holding her hand to her mouth. 'Who did that?'

'Callous youths, I suppose.'

'Is he dead?'

'Yeah, burnt to a crisp'

Wanda stood and watched as the ambulance doors banged shut then walked to the shop feeling sick. Eunice and Leonard turned to look at her, their faces white.

'Well, that's it then,' Leonard closed his order book. 'We have to sell off all the stock in four weeks. The Goss Empire has gone tits up. I just had notification this morning.'

'I can't believe it. It's so sudden,' Eunice looked shocked. Do you think there's any connection to Peter Goss committing suicide? Will they pay us for the final month?'

'They better had,' said Leonard. 'I've been told we'll all be paid off but then that's it. We'd better start marking down all these clothes and looking for other work,' he sighed.

'I think I'll finally go to university,' declared Eunice.

'I've had enough of selling clothes, anyway. Time to move on.' She adjusted her skirt while glancing in the mirror. 'Oh yeah, Jean – Roger told me to let you know you're invited to the first night of his exhibition at the Indica Gallery – next Friday evening at 7 o'clock. There'll be wine and party food.'

Wanda's thoughts were in turmoil. She had lost her job but on the other hand she would be the toast of Roger's exhibition and get to spend time with him. That was more important than a stupid job. She smiled.

'Have you seen the pictures?' she asked.

'Yeah, they're great, really great. I think he's captured the *Alice* feel perfectly,' said Eunice.

Wanda looked towards the door and saw a police car leaving. 'Oh, by the way, that old tramp, you know the one who's always in that doorway – he was burnt to death last night. They were just taking away the body as I came into work. Isn't it terrible?'

'How gruesome,' said Eunice picking some fluff from her black dress and wandering off toward the kitchen. Leonard kept staring at his order book and shaking his head.

Zosia stood in the corridor of the train looking out of the window as the train swept past the Polish countryside. Fields and fields of bright yellow sunflowers as far as the eye could see. Head-scarfed women bent double as they worked the land. Pigs, cows, geese, hens – all free-range. And there were hedges, wild flowers, bees, clouds of butterflies. Men hoisted sheaves of wheat onto haystacks with pitchforks, children ran after waddling geese down dirt-rutted roads.

'It looks nice here,' Pawel said, 'but remember most of the industrial south is heavily polluted, the rivers are dead, the air and some food is poisonous and the birds have long given up and flown away.'

They stood in silence. Pawel looked at her and smiled

'Do you want to hear a Polish joke?' he asked. Zosia

nodded. 'In a certain town where there had been trouble, the authorities brought in a 6pm curfew and anyone caught outside after this time would be severely punished. So, two soldiers were walking down the street at 5 o'clock when one suddenly took out his gun and shot a passer-by dead. His companion stared at him, open-mouthed. 'Why on earth did you that?' he exclaimed. 'It's only 5 o'clock!' The other soldier replied, 'Yes, but I know where that man lives and he would never have made it on time.'

Zosia smiled. Pawel raised his hand to stroke the side of her face. She flinched and moved away.

'Don't,' she said.

'I'm sorry – I was just interested in those small brown marks on your face.'

'I hate them. Don't talk about them.'

'I think they're beautiful – just like you.'

Zosia shook her head. She didn't want this kind of conversation. Looking out of the window she saw a man working in the fields. He was holding the handles of a wooden plough as he guided the horse down the furrow. She decided to change the subject.

'I've never seen that before,' she said pointing at the man.

'Haven't you? Well, Comrade Gierek is trying to get the country mechanised – this is the Polish Great Leap Forward. He says we're all going to be rich – ha, ha. That's why I'm at agricultural college – I don't really have a great desire to understand tractors but maybe I'll get a good job at the end of it.' He looked at his watch. 'We should be in Krakow in about an hour.'

'Do you prefer Krakow to Warsaw?' asked Zosia.

'Yes, Krakow is very beautiful but then it was never bombed to pieces. The old market square in Warsaw is nice but it's all fake, you know?'

Zosia nodded. 'I know. I went there with Mira and she told me how they had rebuilt it to an exact copy of the original after the war. She said they used paintings by Canaletto to copy the architecture.'

'Yes, it's a good fake,' said Pawel with a snort. 'Just like the economy of the whole country. I don't understand what it's based on. I can't see how it can keep supporting all these loss-making industries forever. Something will happen – sooner or later.'

'Do your friends live near the station?'

'About a 10-minute taxi ride. Jerzy and Agata Wysocki were colleagues of mother's at the hospital. They have a son, Eryk, who is a little older than me. He wants to practise his English with you so perhaps we should try and speak only English while we're there.'

'Well, that would be just fine for me. We can start now,' said Zosia in English.

Pawel laughed. 'That was much too fast – I didn't understand a word.'

Tadek carried a cup of tea upstairs. He opened the bedroom door and stepped into the darkened room. Helena was lying face down on the bed. Tadek placed the cup on the bedside table and sat on the edge of the bed.

'Tell me what the matter is – please explain to me,' he insisted.

'Don't worry, I'll get over it.' Her voice was muffled by the pillow. She turned and looked at Tadek. 'It's just the past. The older I get the more the past hangs over me. When I was young I was so busy trying to survive the war, or establishing a life here, having a family, working, worrying about my mother. Now I have more time to myself and the past becomes more and more real. I just keep thinking and thinking and thinking.'

'I wish that Kaminski had never come here,' Tadek blasted. 'I never did trust those Poles who went to America. They are not good Europeans – they're only interested in money. He himself said he had a good war, enjoyed every minute of it and now he just wants to make money and get fame from the suffering of others.'

Helena sat up and took the tea.

'I don't think you can blame him. He wanted the stories

to be recorded before they were lost. People who lived through those times are dying off now and their suffering should be remembered. As well as those who caused their suffering.'

'What about Peter Goss? He caused suffering and now he's gone. Why has it affected you so much? He at least was able to choose the time and manner of his death – he denied that to so many others.'

'I didn't want him to die. He didn't deserve to fall from 15 storeys up. Can you imagine how he felt in those seconds while he fell? I'm so afraid he saw my name on the list of the factory workers and died with that memory.' Helena looked into the far corner of the room but Tadek felt she was not really looking at anything.

'But why should that matter? Would he especially remember you?'

Helena looked up at Tadek. Her face was pale, her eyes hollow with lack of sleep.

'No, he wouldn't especially remember me.'

Wanda arrived at the Indica Gallery in Duke Street, opened the door and stood in the foyer. Eunice had helped set up the exhibition so she wasn't at work. Wanda was nervous – this was a seriously upmarket place, full of rich, arty, knowledgeable people, people with university degrees, people who had credit cards, fitted carpets, straight teeth and hyphenated names. Wanda wore a black dress, marked down by 75 per cent, from Fab Fashions as well as a white handbag, high-heeled white boots and a gold chain belt. She'd very carefully applied her make-up, back combed her hair and sprayed it until it was rock solid. She looked around wondering if anyone would be able to tell she was out of her depth.

At the front, a large banner hung that read,

Roger Elliott photographic exhibition – Through The Looking Glass.

Wanda smiled, just the mention of Roger's name was enough to calm her nerves. She presented the ticket Eunice had given her to the woman at the desk and was handed a glass of white wine by a waiter holding a tray. He called her 'Madam' – she was one of the select few. Wanda was directed into the exhibition.

There were a few people already standing round in small groups looking at the photographs, whispering and sipping their wine. Wanda glanced around but couldn't see either Roger or Eunice. She wondered if people would recognise her from the pictures and make a comment. She smiled to herself and walked over to the nearest group clustered round one of the large photographs. She stood behind them and gazed up at the image.

The enormous photo was arranged in two halves separated down the middle with what looked like the edge of an old-fashioned gilt mirror. On the right hand side of the mirror stood Eunice. She was wearing the black and white Goss dress, hat and boots and holding a white teapot. Behind her was a clock on the mantelpiece, a portrait showing a young woman hung on the wall, a dog was asleep in front of the fire place and a cat sat on an arm chair. Eunice was standing casually, her weight reading on one leg, the teapot was held in front of her, resting in both hands and she had a demure smile on her face. On the other side of the mirror stood Wanda. The pictures were life size so it was obvious she was about 6 inches shorter than Eunice and about twice as broad. She was wearing the same outfit, stretched and distorted over her bulky frame. She was holding the black tea pot without the spout and was standing as Roger had directed – both feet placed firmly together, staring unsmiling straight at the camera. Behind her was the broken misshapen clock, a portrait showing some kind of mental defective with enormous ears and slobbering grin. In front of the fireplace a pig lay sleeping on the hearthrug and the armchair, with a rat crawling over the back, was minus one leg and sat distorted on the ground.

Wanda stared in disbelief at the picture and then spun round to look at the next one. It was the same image but in the negative, the next photo was the same but the black areas were replaced with a vibrant purple, the next had bright blue and yellow replacing the black and white area. Wanda looked wildly around the room – the picture, in different colours and variations, was reproduced over and over. She felt her heart race. Roger had tricked her, he and Eunice were using her, mocking her. He'd represented her as a fat, weird product of a distorted other world, while showing Eunice as the elegant norm. How could they have done that to her? It had all been a fake friendship – it had all been a pack of lies. Wanda dropped her glass of wine, shattering it on the hard, polished floor.

'This exhibition is the biggest pile of shit I've ever seen,' she screamed, her voice catching in her throat. 'This is dishonest, it's vile, a betrayal ...'

There was a shocked silence as everyone turned to stare at her.

Two security guards made their way towards her.

'Come on, love. Don't get excited. Let's go outside – you need some fresh air.' They bundled her out of the room followed by the urgent whispers of the guests. Once in the foyer one guard opened the front door while the other pushed Wanda outside onto the street.

'Go on, get out, you nutter. Don't try and get back in again – you're barred.'

Wanda had been thrown out of the gallery and pushed into the street like a criminal. Just as she was propelled through the door she looked back and caught sight of Roger's pale and anxious face behind the two guards. His eyes were wide and he was mouthing her name. The famous smile was gone.

Wanda ran down the street with no idea where she was going. Tears were flowing down her cheeks and smeared black mascara covered her eyes. She had been a fool, a stupid, naïve little bitch. She couldn't believe it. Had Roger and Eunice been laughing behind her back for months? They must have planned this exhibition, it was malice aforethought, it was the murder of her soul.

She half ran, half walked down endless streets, not knowing where she was going. She was completely lost but she didn't care. Nothing mattered anymore. She bumped into passers-by, tripped over the kerb and fell hard on the pavement, bloodying her knees. Getting to her feet, she shrugged away offers of assistance. She knew she was sobbing, mumbling to herself, crying but she didn't care about the concerned looks from people in the street. After walking for an hour, Wanda's sobbing subsided a little and she realised her feet were hurting so much, and that blood was seeping from her knees and the blisters on her heels. She stopped and noticed she was outside a little café. Out of desperation, she went inside, sat down and stared for a while at the red Formica tabletop. Then she picked up the red plastic tomato containing the ketchup and turned it round and round in her hands. She had a ridiculous urge to splash ketchup all down her dress. She jumped when a voice spoke at her shoulder.

'Jean – is it you? What on earth happened to you, where did you go?'

Wanda looked across to see the familiar blue eyes and dark curly hair of Dave the vicar. He was sitting at the table next to hers. She felt shocked to see him and appalled that he was seeing her in this state. She smiled weakly, wiped her eyes and tried to pull herself together.

'Dave – hello. How are you? What are you doing so far from home?' She took a deep breath.

Dave got up and sat down opposite her at the table.

'I'm just killing time really,' he said. 'At present I'm staying on a friend's sofa, in Balham. I had to move, it's a long story. But why did you disappear that night? Why did you leave? I did think I should try and look for you but I had a few problems of my own. I eventually telephoned your parents and they said you'd found a flat near your boyfriend. Why did you never let me know?'

Wanda felt the tears coming back.

'I'm sorry. I had … I had this crazy idea Val was prying around in my room. I kept thinking someone was going in there. Then I even thought you were the culprit. But if I'm honest with myself what I was really doing was searching for an excuse to go after a man – someone I thought I loved. I imagined that if I was thrown out by you, he'd have to take me in. You know, a damsel in distress. It was pointless. I made a fool of myself, I'm really sorry. I should have said something.'

All this information came out in a torrent. She shouldn't be saying this to Dave, she hardly knew him. She looked at him and he put his hand on hers.

'How's Val?' she said eventually, to fill the silence.

Dave said nothing, his fingers drumming the table.

'Let me buy you some tea and a sandwich, you look in a bad way,' he raised his hand to attract the waitress's attention.

'Actually, there's something I should tell you,' he continued, looking back at Wanda. 'I have to be honest, too – it wasn't Val who was using your room. It was me – me and Rachel.'

'What?'

'I was an idiot, too involved with that youth club or should I say with a particular youth in it. Some of them looked up to me, hero-worshipped me. I notice you never fell into that category, though. I did try, you know. Anyway, Rachel was a naïve teenager and she fell under my spell or I fell under hers. It's a terrible thing to confess, but we were using your bed. I couldn't bring myself to use the marital bed, so to speak. Val found out – in fact, she left me the same day you left.'

Dave fiddled with the saltcellar. 'We all have our troubles but we can't tell anyone about them, can we?'

Wanda nodded.

'It was strange that everyone left the same day – you, Rachel, Val, Sarah – even the cat vanished,' Dave continued. 'I was all alone in that house and I just couldn't see how you were connected with it all. I thought it was some vast conspiracy. Then I imagined Val must have told you what I'd done and you left in disgust. Val did tell the Bishop, though, about what I'd been doing with Rachel so I've been thrown out of the vicarage. I have no home, no job, no wife and child. I'm staying with a friend at the moment, trying to work out what to do next.'

'I'm really sorry, Dave. I was so wrapped up in my own problems, I had no idea all this was going on under my nose.'

The waitress appeared with tea and a toasted cheese sandwich. Wanda fell on it suddenly realising how hungry she was.

'Yeah, it's such a terrible cliché. A *News of the World* sexy-vicar-in-teenage-love-romp story. Anyway, Jean, what happened about this man you were chasing?'

'Nothing, he turned out to be a bastard,' she said between mouthfuls. 'But then he had a steady girlfriend, and she considered me a friend so perhaps it's me who is the bastard. When I think about, I was attempting to betray her. The thing is she got in there first. I deserved it, I suppose. Actually, I'm in a pretty similar situation to you – no job, nowhere to live and no partner. But I do have a solution – I'm going home.' She stood up. 'Good luck, Dave.' Wanda held out her hand

'Well, goodbye, Jean,' he said, taking her hand.

'It's Wanda, actually.'

Chapter 28

Krakow, 1971

Zosia stared at Jerzy Wysocki. He was in his early fifties, tall with dark hair greying at the sides, a perfectly formed nose, even teeth and brown sparkling eyes. Pawel, with his long straggly mousy brown hair, pale pimply skin and narrow shoulders, was sitting next to him. Zosia turned her attention to the magnificent food prepared by Agata and for which she must have queued for hours.

'What digestible food, Mother,' said Eryk in English.

Zosia laughed.

'Would I say digestive food?' he enquired.

Zosia laughed again.

'Sorry – no I think appetising would be the right word.'

'Bon appetit,' said Jerzy smiling. 'We learned French at school but now all anyone wants to learn is English. French is such an elegant language. English sounds, forgive me I don't mean to be offensive, but it sounds as if the person speaking has a hot object in their mouth.'

'It sounds like German,' said Agata. 'Like very bad German.'

'I think English best language for the Europe,' said Eryk again in English. 'I listen to all Beatles records and I write all the word songs. I want Zosia explain me some words later.'

'I'd be happy to do that. My sister adores the Beatles – at least she used to.'

She looked out of the window of the small flat at the beautiful old market square in Krakow. Unlike in Warsaw, she felt a great sense of belonging here.

'How are you enjoying your stay in the capital?' asked Jerzy. 'Is it interesting meeting all your relations?'

Zosia told him how she loved hearing her grandmother talk about her childhood and her relations. It was fascinating finally seeing the places she talked about and meeting some of the people. She told him her great aunt, Princess Maria Poniatowska, had a box full of letters and photographs about her grandfather who was killed in the 1920s when the Bolsheviks invaded. Zosia said she wanted to make that conflict the subject of her thesis when she started university in September.'

'You should write about the Katyn massacre instead,' said Jerzy. 'Have you heard of it? Thousands of Polish officers were murdered by Stalin during the war but the Soviets still blame the Nazis. You should write a book about that and tell the West what the Soviets are really all about.'

'I have heard something of that,' Zosia ate her food with relish. 'Do you know much about it?'

'Only that my brother was one of those officers who were tied up with Russian rope, shot through the back of the head with a Russian bullet and thrown into a common grave by Russian hands.' The rest of the group nodded in agreement.

Zosia remembered seeing a documentary about this massacre on BBC2. She wanted to know more and realised, looking round the table, that this was the life she craved – good food, intelligent conversation, historical knowledge, no one ignoring her or putting her down. No one calling her a snob, a show off, a spotty git, miss lah-di-dah, too big for her boots. Zosia fitted in, she was at home, she almost felt she'd never leave.

The next day Zosia, Pawel and Eryk set out for the old town square in Krakow. The weather was extremely hot and the sun beat down on the little canopies over the stalls in the square. Amber jewellery, leather belts, bags, wallets and purses, flowers, ornamental ships were all on sale, while replicas of the Black Madonna were everywhere. Zosia bought a small image of the Madonna painted on wood. It would last longer than her paper picture. She showed it to Pawel.

'The original was painted by St Luke on a piece of wood taken from the house of the Holy Family. This is what the Holy Virgin really looked like,' she said.

'Nonsense,' said Pawel. 'It's been scientifically proven that icon was painted in the eighth century at the earliest. They can count the rings in the wood and find out how old it is.'

'You're wrong, the picture is genuine,' Zosia argued.

'Yeah, like the Turin Shroud. That will turn out to be a fake as well. People just look at things like this and take them at face value but there is always more trickery and deceit behind things than you realise.'

Zosia turned away, annoyed. She was worried that Pawel might be correct. Still, what did it matter what his opinion was? She didn't value it. He was plain, ordinary and lacked soul or imagination.

'It's a lovely souvenir, anyway,' said Pawel smiling and trying to touch her shoulder.

Zosia shrugged him off and went to buy some nuts to feed the pigeons while Pawel and Eryk stood nearby chatting and smoking. Zosia smiled at Eryk and noticed a flicker of annoyance cross Pawel's face. This was a new experience for Zosia – these boys were not mocking her or criticising her. In fact they appeared to be vying for her attention.

Eryk persisted in trying out his English.

'What are called these birds?' he asked.

'Pigeons,' answered Zosia.

They both tried to repeat the word.

'I am feeding the pigeons,' said Zosia. They dutifully repeated her sentence.

'Shall we take a tour round the royal palace?' she asked.

Eryk and Pawel stared at her uncomprehendingly so she resorted to Polish. At the Palace, Zosia walked straight into the ornamental hall exclaiming on its beauty. An old woman sitting behind a desk began shouting at her.

'You can't just walk in here with your outdoor shoes ruining the floor. Who do you think you are? Everyone has to put on these soft overshoes. It's the rule. It says so here quite clearly.'

Zosia turned and took the shoes, blushing. Eryk turned to the old woman.

'Here we have a tourist from England and you shout rude instructions at her. She was overwhelmed by the beauty of our Polish culture and you ruin her day by being so impolite. Can you imagine the impression you are giving of our people?'

The old woman changed at once. She apologised profusely, she offered to find some shoes that fitted Zosia better, she explained in the politest tones that they had to keep the polished floor undamaged.

'The government used to meet here in the old days,' said Eryk.

'Yes, I know,' replied Zosia. 'The Parliament of Sejm met here from 1726.

Eryk realised Zosia knew more about Polish history than he did.

'I'd love to spend a year at the university here when I start my degree. I've read that Krakow has the oldest university in Europe after Oxford and the Sorbonne. I'm sure I'll be back. I feel as if I've come home.' Zosia smiled radiantly at Eryk. Pawel appeared to be in a sulk.

After the palace, the three went to an outdoor café.

'Look,' said Pawel, brightening, ' we have Coca-cola now. Shall I order three?'

'Not for me,' said Zosia. 'I don't like fizzy, brown water. I would like some coffee please and some apple cake.'

Wanda Baran stood on Platform 2 at St Pancras station waiting for the 7.30am train to Derby. She felt a strange kind of elation, probably due to lack of sleep. After seeing Dave, she had rushed back to the flat to pack a bag – leaving most of her belongings that she couldn't carry behind. Then she'd wandered around all evening, finally walking into a cinema and buying a ticket for the first film she saw advertised. She sat in the darkened auditorium where even the unsettling violence of *A Clockwork Orange* couldn't pierce her misery. After spending hours in a late-night cafe, Wanda saw the sun rising at 5 o'clock. London in the early morning mist was just waking up – the milkmen were clinking bottles, the postmen starting their rounds, cleaners headed home after the night shift. This great, teeming city was yawning, stretching and gradually opening its eyes.

It had been nearly five years since Wanda had arrived in London and now she was going home. She looked at the St Pancras station clock, its huge minute hand slowly edging round and summed up her achievements. She knew her way fairly well around the capital by train, tube and bus. She knew how to unwrap clothes from their polythene coverings, how to hang suits on hangers and how to write out price tags. She knew how to fold jumpers, work a till and even how to unpick labels reading 100% Polyester, *Made in Taiwan* and sew in labels reading 100% wool, *Made in England*. She knew how to flatter customers into buying clothes that didn't suit them, and she'd learnt how to be rude to people when they pushed in front of her on the tube. She'd lost her job, her flat and the man she loved. But she did have her parents, her health, her train ticket and her virginity.

As the train came into the station and pulled to a shrieking, scraping rest in front of her, Wanda put down her suitcase, took off her high-heeled shoes and threw them between the train and the platform onto the track. She caught sight of her flabby cheeked face in the dirty train windows.

'Bye, bye Jean. How on earth did you ever imagine anyone would choose you over Eunice. You thick bitch,' she mumbled. 'I wish to announce that Wanda Baran who used to try and used to care and used to compete has, on 15 August 1971, officially ceased to try and ceased to care and ceased to compete.'

And Wanda boarded the train.

Zosia Baran stepped off the train from Krakow back onto the grey station platform in Warsaw. She waited for Pawel who was still in the toilet. Eventually he appeared, holding a handkerchief to his mouth, his hair dishevelled, his eyes blood shot.

'How do you feel?' she inquired.

'I was sick again. I feel a little better now. Hopefully I'll make it back home before I throw up again.'

'Did you have too much to drink at dinner last night?'

'No, I didn't drink any more than usual. I think it was the meat. Sometimes it's rotten here. But then you ate it as well and you're all right.'

'Come on, let's find a taxi.'

'Anyway, did you enjoy Krakow? It's a lovely city, isn't it?'

'It was fantastic. And I really loved your friends. Pan Wysocki is so intelligent and well read. He told me so much about the history, society and culture of Poland.'

'Eryk liked you. He wants you to write to him so he can practise his English. I told him to keep his grubby hands off. I told him you're mine – I saw you first.'

'Oh, you think so do you? Well I'm not anybody's – I'm my own woman, actually.'

'You don't fancy him over me do you?'

'I'm not interested in either of you. Anyway, Pawel we're family, you shouldn't talk like that – it's incest.'

'Rubbish – we're second cousins. Do you know how much of our DNA we share? Probably around 10 per cent. That's neither here nor there. Anyway, haven't I shown you a good time? Haven't I ..?' but Pawel didn't get any further as he clasped his hand to his mouth and rushed to vomit into a waste bin.

Zosia smiled and decided she had nothing to fear from Pawel. He would never harm her.

Chapter 29

At Derby station, Wanda called her father from a public phone. She then sat, shoeless, on a bench on the forecourt as her father's van drew up and out he got. She felt an unbelievable sense of relief and joy at seeing him.

'Wanda – where on earth are your shoes? Did you travel all this way barefoot?' Tadek hugged his daughter. Crying too much to reply, Wanda was so glad to be home, back where she belonged and where she was going to stay. No more pretending, no more humiliation, no more striving for the unattainable. Eventually she gulped a response.

'I was only barefoot on the train. It was ok. I'm so very, very pleased to see you.'

'And so am I to see you. Why didn't you tell us sooner that you were visiting?'

Wanda started laughing and crying together. She was home.

'I'm not visiting – I'm here to stay. The shop went bust and I lost my job so here I am. I'm sure there's a shop in Derby that will employ me. You don't mind if I have my old room do you? Zosia's still in Poland isn't she? And anyway, she'll be off to university in September.'

'That will be perfect. What excellent news. Not about your job I mean but that you're home. Your mother will be delighted.'

They set off towards home. Wanda sat in the front of the van with her father among the toolboxes and old newspapers.

'How is Mummy?' she asked.

'She's all right. She's been a little depressed lately. I've noticed it happens a lot with people who have been through the war. When they get older they have more time to think about it. Nowadays, they encourage people to talk about bad experiences but then we just had to keep quiet and get on with life. She's spending a lot of time with Babcia now, feeding her and reading to her.'

'Mum never told us much about what happened to her but then neither did you, dad. I stopped asking because you wouldn't talk about it and now I worry it's something really bad.'

'Don't worry. I'm glad you're home.' They were silent for a while.

'How is Janek these days?' asked Wanda.

'He seems happy at school, plays football. He's out with his friends most of the time. He's forgotten how to speak Polish, sadly.'

'I heard that. Funny, I seem to be thinking in Polish more and more.'

They drove down the new Babcock Way, speeding under St Joseph's Church.

Wanda saw they had pulled down St Wystan's church and all the little medieval houses that used to stand next to it. There was now a huge hole in the ground with a road running down through it. High above her was a pedestrian foot bridge spanning the road. She couldn't believe it. What had they done to her hometown?

Tadek noticed her amazement.

'I suppose this is progress, isn't it? Pulling down ancient buildings and constructing new roads. I shouldn't complain – renovation is part of my business.'

'Yes, it's sad, though,' said Wanda. 'You never appreciate what you've got till it's gone.'

Wanda took childish delight at seeing 16 Porton Crescent again. Janek was in the sitting room watching football. He was tall, and quite handsome – she hardly recognised him. How sad, Wanda thought. I left home when Janek was so little and now I'm virtually a stranger to my own brother.

She looked at the television screen. 'Hey, it's colour, we've got a colour telly!'

'Yeah, Dad got it for us as a treat. I'm the first kid in school to have one.'

Wanda sat down next to him.

'I hear Derby County are doing pretty well these days.'

'Yes, all thanks to Brian Clough. He's the greatest manager ever.'

'How's school?'

'It's OK.'

'Any plans for what you want to do?'

'Just make as much money for as little work as possible. Yes, pass, ok, goal!!' Janek jumped to his feet.

Wanda could see she wouldn't get much more out of him – but she had been the same at that age, she knew. She looked away from the television. The sitting room seemed much smaller than she remembered it and shabbier. The picture of the Black Madonna still hung over the fireplace, tiny coloured pots, wooden figurines and little ceramic dancing couples covered the mantelpiece. The large sepia photograph of her grandfather, the Prince, was still there as it had always been.

For the first time, Wanda got up and really studied the picture. Her grandfather was dressed in a suit and was sitting sideways on a chair looking at a book. Next to this picture sat one of Babcia taken when she was a young woman. Wanda looked at the smiling, beautiful face. The picture must have been taken when Babcia was about the age Wanda was now. Babcia was young once, a happy smiling girl – Wanda had never taken the time to consider that before. Babcia hadn't been born an old woman.

Helena entered the room and grabbed her eldest child, covering her with hugs and kisses.

Wanda explained how she had lost her job. 'Anyway,' she said, 'I'd had enough of London. Too many people, too much noise, too much competition. I'm glad to be home. How is Babcia?'

'Why don't you go upstairs and see her for yourself.'

Wanda gingerly climbed the stairs and stood outside the bedroom door. She felt the familiar tight knot in her stomach as she knocked, the same small fear. There was no command to enter as there always used to be. She looked round the door. Her grandmother, Barbara Poniatowska, that determined, fierce, all-powerful woman, was curled up at one end of the bed. Her long white hair had been very badly cut into a pudding-basin style, the right side of her body was hunched and crooked and she was shaking. A metal, mechanical device was suspended over the bed. Wanda tried to suppress her shock. She approached and took her grandmother's hand.

'Hello Babcia. I'm home. It's so lovely to see you again.'

Babcia's eyes turned to look at Wanda, she made a small squeaking noise and a little saliva dribbled from her mouth.

'Can I get you anything, Babcia? Are you hungry, thirsty, cold, bored?'

Babcia made another tiny noise and gestured towards the dressing table. Wanda looked but could see nothing on it except Babcia's brush and hand mirror. She picked up the brush and began smoothing her grandmother's rough, inelegant hair. Babcia wriggled and squeaked louder. Wanda looked up as Helena came into the room.

'I don't know what you want, Babcia. Do you know, mummy?'

'It's about time for lunch. Let's go and prepare it. We'll be back in a few minutes, mama,' said Helena leaving her mother wriggling on the bed.

Once outside the room, Wanda asked, 'Who cut her hair so badly, she looks awful – like a mental defective.'

'It was the nurse. She said it would be much easier to manage and keep clean if it was short. She didn't ask, she just did it. To be honest, we never expected Mama to live this long so we didn't complain too much.' Helena looked sad, resigned.

'And what's that metal contraption for?'

'It's to help lift her onto her bedpan.'

'Oh, God, how undignified. Poor Babcia.'

Wanda returned a little later with some soup for her grandmother. As she spooned it into her mouth, most ended up on the bib round her grandmother's neck. All the while the old woman kept murmuring and shaking.

Zosia woke up next morning feeling very weak and tired. She lay still in bed not having the energy to get up. Mira rose and started preparing breakfast.

'Are you all right, Zosia?'

'Yes, auntie. I just feel very tired. I don't know why.'

'Poor child,' said Mira soothingly. 'Did Pawel wear you out with so much sightseeing in Krakow?'

'No, not at all. Did he tell you he was ill on the way back, sick that is.'

Pawel appeared, rubbing his eyes.

'I feel better now so you're feeling ill. What time does Mum get back from her shift, Babcia?' said Pawel.

'About 6 o'clock. She can check Zosia then.'

'Oh, I'm sure I'll feel better by then,' said Zosia and promptly fell asleep.

Irena returned that evening to find Zosia still in bed.

'What the matter, darling?' Irena felt Zosia's forehead. 'You feel quite hot.'

'I just feel really tired. I used to get migraine headaches and felt like this afterwards. But I don't have a headache.'

'I was sick all the way back on the train,' Pawel said. 'I'm all right now, though' He ran his fingers through his hair.

Irena patted Zosia's hand.

'Don't worry. You probably picked up some virus. Just rest for now and I'm sure it will pass in 24 hours. You'll be fine if you don't eat for a couple of days but you must drink plenty of water.'

Zosia smiled weakly and drifted off to sleep. Irena looked at her son.

'Did you have a good time in Krakow? Do you think Zosia enjoyed her stay there?'

'Yes, she seemed really happy. She really liked the

Wysockis – well, she really liked Jerzy. She must go for the older man.'

Irena laughed. 'You're hoping she'll transfer her affections on to you? I suggest you get your hair cut and develop a little culture. Anyway, I'm going to bed. I'm absolutely exhausted.'

Zosia still felt weak the next day. Irena took Zosia's temperature. It was very high. She mixed some rehydrating powder with water for Zosia to drink. When Irena left for work about 7 o'clock she told Mira and Pawel that Zosia should stay in bed for another day.

Pawel went to see his friends but Mira stayed with Zosia, wiping her forehead with a wet cloth and bringing her fresh water. By the afternoon Zosia seemed to be a little better. She took her picture of the Black Madonna from her book and held it to her chest. Mira read the newspaper to her and tried to entertain her.

'Here, you must drink some water. Doctor's orders.'

'I'll try but it's really difficult to swallow. My throat feels dry but somehow stiff and tight.'

'Tell me, Zosia – did you enjoy Krakow? How did Pawel behave?'

'I loved Krakow,' replied Zosia. 'I really think I could live there. The Wysockis were so kind to me. It's strange, my grandmother never talked about Krakow but I felt so at home there.' She paused and looked at Mira with a smile. 'Why did you ask about Pawel?' she said.

'I just wondered. He really likes you. He's a nice boy, you know. He may not be the brightest person in the world, or the best looking but his heart is in the right place. He had a hard time, growing up without a father, in this flat with two women.'

'Yes, I suppose so but I have to tell you I have no romantic interest in him at all. I don't mean to sound arrogant but the man I marry will be a very special man indeed.'

'What will he be like?' Mira laughed.

'He must be tall, of course, and handsome and very well

read and cultured. Maybe I'll meet him at university.'

'Don't go on looks and status alone. Your grandmother probably made that mistake.' Mira stopped and Zosia noticed she was biting her lip as if regretting she had spoken.

'What do you mean?' Zosia was wide-eyed.

'It was difficult for Barbara to fit in with such an aristocratic family.'

'But Babcia really loved my grandfather. He was the light of her life. She spent the rest of her life remembering him.'

'But do you think that's healthy? Perhaps she should have moved on and married someone else. She was very beautiful – I think she had some offers.'

'You never married again after Witold died, did you?'

'No, but he died much later, during the last war, and afterwards I was too busy trying to stay alive and feed my daughter. I got her through medical school, though, and now she's a very successful paediatrician.'

Zosia was quiet, thinking of her mother working in a clothing factory.

'Then of course Irena made a terrible marriage,' Mira continued. 'Your parents are happily married aren't they? In fact, that is more important than a career but Irena wouldn't agree with me. I had to bring Pawel up as Irena was always working.'

'My mother was always working as well, and my babcia looked after us for years, too. She did so much for me, you know. She was such a good woman. I feel closer to her here. I still miss her so much. Why can't I feel my fingers, they are numb and tingling? What's wrong with me?'

To Mira's distress, Zosia turned her face to the pillow and burst into uncontrollable sobs.

Chapter 30

The white plastic table and chairs were placed on the little patio at 16 Porton Crescent and Helena and Wanda sat there together drinking tea and eating homemade cake – homemade by Wanda. Tadek had carried Babcia downstairs and placed her in a large, comfortable chair in the garden.

The young Irish nurse was putting her coat on ready to leave. She called out goodbye and Wanda went to see her out.

'I gave your granny a sheet of paper and a pen this morning,' the girl said in the hallway. 'I thought she might be able to write something – her left hand seems a little stronger. She was all morning writing this – I've no idea what it says but I'll leave it with you.'

Wanda looked down at the piece of paper the girl had given her. Written in a faint shaky hand were the words, *Kochana Wanda.*

Wanda went back out to the garden. 'This cake is lovely – London has really improved your cooking skills.' Helena said leaning over to wipe some dribble from her mother's mouth with the bib hanging around her neck.

'London's got nothing to do with it. I want to make myself useful. As soon as I get a job I'll start paying rent, don't worry.' Wanda bent down and kissed her grandmother's lined forehead.

She saw her mother raise her eyebrows. Wanda had never previously shown her grandmother any affection.

'Don't be silly – I don't charge my children rent,' said Helena. 'Anyway, there are quite a few jobs in the evening paper so I'm sure you'll find something soon. Perhaps you should do the same typing course I did at the Polytechnic.'

'Are you still working on that book with that man – what was his name?'

'Robert Kaminski – no I've finished the work now. I just did some translating and clerical work but it was good that he paid for me to do those courses.'

'So they shut down the shop you were working at,' Helena said. 'I suppose the economy is taking a downturn.'

'Yeah, the company that owned Fab Fashions went bust. It was Reinhard Goss.'

The piece of cake Helena was holding stopped halfway to her mouth and returned to the plate. There was silence.

'I knew Reinhard Goss and his son, Peter,' she said in a strained voice.

'You sound like you knew them personally,' Wanda laughed.

'I did.'

Wanda frowned.

'What do you mean, you knew them? Do you understand who I'm talking about? Peter Goss committed suicide a month ago – I suppose that's why his business went bust or else his business was going bust and that's why he committed suicide.'

'I know why he committed suicide. It was because of me.'

Wanda started laughing and put her cake down on her plate.

'Mum, are you going bonkers. What on earth are you talking about? How did you know him and how, in heaven's name, could you have caused his death?'

'I worked in his factory from 1942 until 1945. It was near Hamburg. Reinhard Goss was the owner and Peter managed the shop floor. I was taken away to work there when I was 16. You knew I worked in Germany and I think you knew it was in a factory. Well, that's what I did – I made German uniforms.'

'Goss made German uniforms during the war. That's incredible. And now they make jeans, dresses, skirts –

everyone wears them.' She looked down, 'I'm wearing a Goss skirt now. The shop was selling them so cheap when I left that I grabbed all I could. So you knew the Goss people from the factory.'

'Yes, I saw Peter Goss almost every day during that time.'

'But how do you mean you're connected with his suicide? What happened? I don't think people know Goss made German uniforms during the war. That's quite funny actually. If all those trendy people knew. Ah, did they find out and is that why they went bust?'

Helena glanced over at her mother who was quivering and mumbling. She wiped away some spittle from the old woman's mouth.

'Yes, and it was me who told them. You know that author, Kaminski, I was telling you about? It all came out when I was talking to him and he decided to sue Goss on behalf of all the slave workers. I think he is still arranging the law suit but I'm not giving evidence – I don't want anything to do with it.'

'Why not? You should get some money, some compensation. You deserve it after all you went through. The Goss people were living off immoral earnings, weren't they?'

Helena paused and looked towards the house. She was lost in thought for a while, then replied, 'Peter Goss saved my life and I have destroyed his.'

'How did he save your life?' asked Wanda beginning to get anxious.

Helena took a deep breath. 'In 1945 when the Germans seemed to be losing the war, Reinhard Goss closed down the factory. He was a vicious old man – we all hated him. The Russians were invading from the East and we were terrified of them. We knew what the Russian army did – especially to women. They wouldn't care that we were Polish and not German. We wanted to find the British or Americans first. But Goss was a Nazi and he decided to go to Berlin and help defend Hitler. He put us in his trucks and we drove East. Everyone else was fleeing West and we were going East. We reached the outskirts of Berlin but the Russians were there already. Peter refused to go any further. His father went crazy – Peter had never, ever defied him before. Peter hit the old man right in front of us and then piled about 20 of us girls into a truck and drove it himself – back west. We met a convoy of British soldiers near Essen. We told them we were Poles and said Peter was a Pole too so he wouldn't be arrested.'

Wanda tried to imagine her mother as a young woman, trapped and terrified. She felt sick with fear.

'Oh mummy, he saved your life but then you saved his. All square.'

'But when Kaminski filed the law suit he gave Peter Goss a list of workers who had been at the factory and my name was on it. Peter must have seen it.'

'Would he even remember you? He probably killed himself because of the shame of having had slave workers or perhaps it was something completely unrelated. Why do you think it has anything to do with you?'

'No reason, really.'

Wanda looked at her grandmother and thought the old woman's eyes seemed moist with tears although maybe that was caused by the slight breeze. She looked over at her mother, contemplating her in a new light. She seemed different, her manner had changed. She had never been able to display strong emotions, was never forthcoming but now she seemed more prone to introspection. Talking about the past was something new. All her life, Wanda could never remember her mother saying more than the vaguest details about her life in Poland. Perhaps it was just a consequence of advancing years.

Zosia was taking a long time to recover. She felt lethargic and tired and was still struggling with the numbness she used to get before her migraine headaches. Irena left for work looking concerned but she had many very sick children to care for at the hospital and she had to go.

Mira spent the day sitting by Zosia's bed. She held her hand, stroked her forehead and read to her. Pawel wandered aimlessly round the flat, he made tea and even went to queue for food.

'Should I telephone her parents?' he asked.

'No,' said Mira. 'There is nothing they can do and it would only worry them. I'm sure she'll start to get better soon. You were ill for about 12 hours when you returned to Warsaw. Do you think it has any connection with your food poisoning? The symptoms seem so different, though.'

'It could be something to do with her migraine headaches. I wish she'd get better – there's so much I want to do.'

'Like what?'

'Oh, there are plenty of people I want to introduce her to, I want her to help me with my English. Just, you know, things.'

'I see. You're not worried about this little girl, so far from her mother, so sick. You're just concerned about what she can do for you,' Mira scolded.

'No, of course not. I want her well for her own good, of course I do. She's asleep now so let's hope she's on the way to recovery. I'll stay here tonight in case you need any help.'

Mira woke with a start in the pitch blackness. A sharp scream had pierced her dreams. She sat up in terror and switched on the light. Zosia was sitting up in bed, shaking. Sweat was pouring down her face and she was making a terrible noise when she breathed. She sank back on the bed, babbling and groaning. One side of her face seemed to be drooping down in a strange manner. Mira got out of bed, went over and took her hand. It was cold and covered in sweat. Zosia was talking in an incoherent moan – Mira didn't understand. Perhaps it was English. Pawel ran in, wakened by the scream.

'What's the matter?'

'She seems much, much worse. What on earth should we do? Ring Irena at the hospital and ask her what we should do.'

Mira fetched a cold face cloth and wiped Zosia's forehead. The girl opened her eyes.

'Babcia, Babcia, help me, please dear Babcia, help me. I can't see, I can't see anything. I can't breathe, help me, help me.' Zosia grabbed the sleeve of Mira's night dress and pulled it towards her.

'It's all right, darling, Babcia's here. You're safe, I won't leave you. Don't worry, everything will be all right. Pawel is phoning Irena. She'll be here soon. She'll make you better. Sweet child, dear girl – it will be all right.'

Pawel reappeared.

'Mum says we must call an ambulance immediately. She won't be able to get back home quickly enough so we must tell the ambulance to take her to the Lenin hospital. She will need antibiotics and must go on a drip.'

'Hurry,' Mira urged. 'Phone them now.'

She turned back to Zosia, who was thrashing her head from side to side and babbling. Mira could make out some words

'Dear God, help me. Jesus help me.'

Mira kept trying to wipe Zosia's forehead but the girl was thrashing about wildly and knocking her away with her fists. She was hallucinating and shouting at imaginary monsters. Mira murmured soothingly and tried to keep her calm.

Pawel came to the bedside.

He told her the ambulance was coming but they had to get Zosia downstairs to save time. He said he would carry her down.

'Oh, God,' he yelled as Zosia retched up black bile all down her night dress. Mira rushed to get a bucket and water.

'Babcia, where are you?' screamed Zosia. 'Mummy, I want my mummy,' Pawel recognised the English. 'I can't see, I can't breathe.' There was a terrible rattling noise coming from her throat, a death rattle, a strangled cry as if some unseen force had its fingers tightly round her throat and was squeezing the life out of her.

Suddenly Zosia became still and quiet.

'England – home and safety' said Zosia. Pawel understood the first three words.

Mira hurried over with a bucket of warm water and a cloth. Pawel ran his fingers through his hair in distress.

Zosia suddenly found she could see again with absolute clarity. A man had walked into the room. She calmed down at once in surprise at seeing him. He was tall with dark hair and dark eyes and she knew him immediately – he was her grandfather. He had a large handlebar moustache and he was wearing military uniform. It suddenly occurred to Zosia that in all the photographs of her grandfather, she had never seen him wearing military uniform before. But here he was, large as life and twice as handsome – a soldier through and through. He walked over to where Zosia was lying. He neither smiled nor spoke but he exuded calm and reassurance as he bent down and picked her up in his arms. She smiled and put her arms round his neck.

Zosia looked at Mira who was bustling around trying to carry a full bucket into the room. She looked so scared. Zosia could clearly see every strand of white hair on her head, every tiny wrinkle under her eyes, the minute blue flowers on her dressing gown. She saw Pawel and smiled at the way he constantly ran his fingers through his hair, she could see the few sparse hairs on his puny chest and the veins standing out on his arms. It was clear they were upset but somehow she felt detached and unconcerned.

Instead she turned her attention to the man who was holding her. There were tobacco stains on his moustache and she could see every tiny stubble of hair on his face. Zosia laid her head against the rough, green material of his uniform. He walked with her out of the room.

Pawel shouted in panic, 'Hurry, I have to get her downstairs. The ambulance might be here.' They turned to

Zosia but her eyes were shut and her face turned to one side. A dribble of black bile trickled from her mouth. And the terrible noise of her breathing had stopped.

Chapter 31

Wanda bent down to pick up the letter from the hall mat. It was addressed to Zosia and was from the London Examining board. It must be her A level results. Wanda brought the letter into the sitting room and put it by the clock on the mantelpiece. Her father was already up, mending his watches. Wanda sat down next to him.

'Good morning, daddy, shall I make you some tea?'

'That would be lovely, darling. What was that letter?'

'It looks like Zosia's A level results. I suppose we'd better not open them until she gets back.'

Irena Lato took a taxi and raced back to the flat. It was 4.30 in the morning. She stuffed money in the driver's hand and flew up to the apartment. The ambulance was outside and the two ambulance drivers were already in the flat.

'I'm a doctor, let me through,' Irena pushed the ambulance men aside.

'It's too late, Pani,' said one of them. 'I'm sorry. She's gone.'

Irena knelt beside Zosia's bed and felt her pulse. The body was still covered in sweat and black bile. She started pressing in her chest.

'We've already tried that, Pani,' said the ambulance man.

Mira was sobbing and rocking back and forth on her chair. Pawel was sitting on the floor with his head in his hands.

'We still have to get the body to the hospital. Can you write out the death certificate?' He looked from Irena to Mira to Pawel.

'Sorry. Was this your daughter, Pani?'

'No,' Irena looked down at the pathetic little body. 'She was my niece. I now have to tell her mother her daughter's dead. How am I going to do that? This child was in my care?' Irena burst out crying.

They wrapped Zosia's body in a white sheet and the ambulance took her to the hospital mortuary. Mira, Irena and Pawel sat in hollow silence in the flat. Irena was rehearsing how she was going to tell the cousin she hadn't seen since they were teenagers that her beautiful, precious child was dead. As a doctor, she had spent her adult life telling bewildered parents their dear children were dead but it had never been anyone she knew personally. This death could have been avoided. She had misread the signs. Zosia was an adult and a strong girl. Irena had thought a few days of vomiting would solve the problem. But she now recognised the symptoms of botulism, probably from canned meat. She had read about a few cases in Southern Poland recently but hadn't put two and two together. Irena booked the call to England and sat waiting until it came through.

Irena looked at her mother. Mira's face was streaked with tears.

'I keep thinking about Barbara,' Mira cried. 'I was so cynical about her snobbery and self-serving manner but the last words of this poor child had been to call to her grandmother. Barbara always boasted about what a lovely girl Zosia was. And she was right – Zosia was an angel, a sweet, gentle beautiful angel.' Mira burst into wails of distress.

Sitting on the floor with his arms round his knees, Pawel was rocking back and forth.

'This is so unbelievable, I can't take in what's happened,' he said. 'Only yesterday I was planning to take her to meet my college friends. I even told them to expect her on Wednesday. Shit – what will my cousins in England say now? Come to Poland and die. Now they'll never want to see me.' He pushed his fingers into his hair and grabbed a handful. 'God, it's so awful. I've never seen anyone die before. In the army they always showed death to be noble and gracious but it isn't. It's dirty, and painful and undignified.'

Irena said nothing. She would have to tell her cousin that the child she had to entrusted to Irena's care was dead – because of a piece of meat. A wholly avoidable death. A ridiculous, pointless death she should have prevented. Irena had been through the war, she'd lost her father in the conflict, she had witnessed the Warsaw uprising, she had helped rebuild the city, she had seen the husband she loved go off with a woman of great beauty but with half a brain, but this was the worst day of her life.

Wanda, Tadek and Janek stood around in a horrified circle. Helena was lying in a foetal position on the floor, howling like an animal. Tadek bent down to her – Helena beat the floor and screamed her daughter's name again and again. Wanda and Janek both had their hands to their mouths – wondering how the family was going to live through this.

Chapter 32

Zosia's body arrived at Goldsmith's Undertakers, Green Lane, Derby. Mr Goldsmith told Wanda that Irena Lato had arranged everything with the authorities in Warsaw. They had paid for the transportation and he would personally see to the body's preparation.

Letters arrived from Irena and Pawel full of sorrow and abject apologies. They detailed Zosia's happy time in Poland, and included photographs of her stay. Wanda intercepted the letters and kept them away from her mother.

The Baran family walked through the door of the undertakers and into the Chapel of Rest. Zosia lay in her coffin, dressed in a white outfit she had bought for her holiday. It had been the first shop-made item she had ever owned, having always worn the clothes her mother had made her. Tadek, Helena, Wanda and Janek stood round the open coffin. The lid was propped up against the wall. A metal crucifix attached to the wood, above which were the letters RIP. Piped celestial music oozed from the walls.

Wanda looked at her little sister. Her long dark hair was arranged around her head and there was a very slight smile on her lips, which were painted red. There was rouge on her cheeks and a little green eyeshadow on her eyelids. Wanda had never seen her sister wear make up before. She would hate that, Wanda thought, she'd be mortified. She winced. Oh God, wrong word. Wanda dragged her eyes away from Zosia's face. Her sister's hands were placed along side her body and there were white roses on her chest. Her breast seemed high up as if she'd taken a breath but never exhaled.

It couldn't be denied – Zosia looked absolutely beautiful. Wanda felt a wave of guilt for being alive. Zosia was the clever one, the beautiful one, the slim one. She was the child Babcia admired, the one destined to go far. Wanda thought about her own failure in looks, brains, achievement as she looked at her sister. All that promise had come to nothing. Which is it better to be – a living failure or a dead saint?

Helena took Zosia's hand and bent her head onto the still breast. Janek stood at the foot of the coffin looking down at his feet. Tadek stroked Zosia's hair. Wanda could bear the scene no longer and she went to sit in the waiting room among the plastic flowers, piped music, adverts for life insurance and examples of tombstone inscriptions executed to the 'highest levels of craftsmanship'.

Mr Goldsmith came into the reception.

'Miss Baran, this was passed on to me by the undertakers in Warsaw. They didn't know who to give it to. It was tightly crushed in your sister's hand when she died.'

Wanda took the scrap of paper and smoothed it out on her knee. It was creased, stained and torn – the Black Madonna.

'Mr Goldsmith, why did you put so much make-up on my sister? She never wore make-up, she would have hated what you've done.'

'I'm sorry, I had to …' he murmured. 'I saw a case of botulism once before, years ago. The body, it looks really bad …I'm sorry.'

Wanda nodded, then went back into the chapel and placed the tattered picture of the Black Madonna on her sister's raised chest.

The funeral took place on a Tuesday. Wanda helped her mother into the church. The traffic on the newly opened Babcock Way roared past, ignorant, unknowing. Wanda stood next to her parents in the front pew, Janek next to her. She looked round the church – it was full to overflowing but she was too numb to register surprise.

She recognised a group of girls from Pinecrest Grammar standing silently to one side of the church. Two of them stood together with their arms around each other crying. There was Mr and Mrs Batorowicz with Lydia who was holding a sleeping baby. Lydia was crying. There also was Mr Nowak from the Polish School and the nuns from the convent. The whole of the sixth form from Pinecrest attended, wearing their uniforms.

Wanda looked at the two statues flanking the altar. Christ was pointing to his sacred heart – red and throbbing. The other statue was of the Mother of God, her child in her arms, a golden crown on her head. From where she stood, Wanda could just make out the Black Madonna portrait in the Lady Chapel. The thin line of her mouth, long face and hollow eyes reminded her of someone. She realised that it was the face of her mother when she heard the news of the death of her daughter. Father Kantor conducted the mass but Wanda didn't register a single word he said. There were anonymous, helping hands all round, her mother's tears, legs almost unable to bear the weight, Janek sweating gently in his black suit, Tadek's expression of silent agony.

After the mass, the funeral courtege travelled to the cemetery on Manchester Road. The coffin was lowered in to the ground. The head stone read,

Zofia Helena Baran, 1953-1971. She was a precious flower lent to us for too short a time.

They picked up handfuls of brown, hard earth and threw them onto the coffin, making a loud, offensive sound on the wood. Zosia must have trembled inside with the noise, Wanda thought.

They returned home to an empty, grieving house, having felt unable to invite anyone back with them. The expressions of commiseration were too much.

Janek went into the garden and started kicking a football against the garage door again and again. Thud,

thud, thud – the relentless beat. Helena sat on the sofa, pale unspeaking. Suddenly she leant over towards the sewing box Babcia had once used to embroider all those delicate flowers and took out a small pair of scissors. She poked the sharpened point deep into her arm. Then she jabbed again and again at her flesh. Wanda leapt forward.

'Mummy don't, don't do that,' as she took the scissors off her mother.

Tadek came into the room holding a cup of tea. He went to get the first aid box from the kitchen and took out a bandage and scissors. Tadek began wrapping the bandage round Helena's yielding arm.

'Why has God done this to me?' said Helena, her voice cracking with distress. 'Why did He want me to be born at a time of such evil in the world, to have never known my father, to live with a cold, distant mother who abandoned me to the Germans. Why did he make me fall in love with a noble, honest man who just happened to be the son of a Nazi?'

Tadek froze briefly then continued with his bandaging. Wanda stood in silence, her arms clasped around herself, her blood running cold.

'I loved Peter Goss and he loved me. He asked me to marry him after we had run from his father but I said no. Do you know why I said no? Because I'm a coward. I couldn't bear the thought of facing the other people in the factory, or my relatives in Poland and tell them I'd married a German, the son of a man who'd run a slave labour factory, a factory that made German army uniforms. I walked away from him – the man I loved, because of his nationality not because of the person he was. I was as prejudiced as they were. I abandoned my Peter after he saved my life and then I pushed him from the 15th floor of a skyscraper. Now my punishment is to have my daughter taken from me. My daughter is dead. Why? Who did this to her? Who is to blame?'

Tadek knotted the two ends of the bandage firmly. He put the scissors and the rest of the bandage back in the little box and lovingly stroked his wife's hair. Wanda couldn't bear to watch. She looked up at the crucifix that hung on the wall above the dining table. A small man suffering in silence for the sins and failings of others. Wanda was struggling to take in what her mother had said, and feeling such love and compassion for her father.

'I'm going to my bedroom. Leave me alone,' said Helena getting up and walking out of the sitting room. Tadek sat down at his little table, still wearing his black funeral suit, and began working on his watches. Wanda stood watching her father. She could hear the thud, thud of the football as Janek continued to kick it against the wall. Each family member dwelt in their own isolated island of grief. The room was full of clocks but time wasn't moving. Wanda's eyes were drawn to the clock on the mantelpiece to see if time still existed. Behind it was the letter addressed to Zofia Baran. She went over to open it and read the white piece of paper inside. It was from the London Examining Board and underneath Zosia's name, address and candidate number it said.

History – A
English – A
Latin – A

Wanda folded the paper and put it back in the envelope.

She went upstairs. The rational part of her knew she was in shock. Her feet didn't feel as if they were walking firmly on the ground, sounds and colours seemed oddly vivid, everything had taken on a dream-like quality. As if in a dream, Wanda thought she saw her mother going into Babcia's room. Helena's expression was strange, fixed, zombie-like. Wanda followed her into the bedroom. Everything seemed to move in slow motion – sound elongated like a record played at a slow speed. Actions became exaggerated and deliberate. The terror and agony in that one little room was palpable. Wanda looked at her grandmother curled in her usual position at the end of the bed by the wall. Helena stood in the middle of the room – taller than she'd ever been before, tall and commanding.

'Mummy, are you all right?' Wanda felt her flesh crawling and her heart thumping in her ears.

Helena turned to look at her. When she spoke, her voice seemed to have increased in volume by countless decibels.

'Am I all right? Do you think I'm all right? My baby girl, my precious little girl, died because she ate some filthy, stinking meat. She died because *that woman* filled her head with nonsense and she went off to a third world country and died in pain without me being there.' Helena pointed at Babcia.

Wanda's breath quickened. 'Mummy, you don't know what you're saying. You can't blame Babcia.'

'I can blame her and I will. She can hear me, she can hear the truth for a change. My beautiful daughter is dead because of her.'

Helena turned and stood over her mother's inert and trembling body.

'You abandoned me,' she screamed.

Wanda pulled her mother's arm.

'Mummy, please this isn't fair, you must stop ...' Babcia wriggled frantically on the bed like a maggot on a fishing hook.

'You were supposed to protect me but you abandoned me. I saw you – don't think I didn't. When they cordoned off the street, you didn't push your way against the soldiers to try and get to me. You turned tail and ran. You ran and ran up the street and away from me. You ran to save yourself – I screamed 'Mummy, Mummy help me,' but you just ran. You dropped the shopping basket and ran. I saw the basket roll down the road and into the gutter. You didn't even look back. You left me to die and now you've killed my precious, precious little girl. How dare you, you evil old witch. You murderer, you false mother, you coward, you traitor.'

Helena's face was now inches from her mother's. Babcia's eyes were huge. Saliva dribbled from her mouth and a large tear was running down her cheek. Her face turned a dark shade of red, her eyes snapped shut, her mouth collapsed to a thin black line.

'Mummy, stop it, this is wrong, stop it at once,' Wanda screamed. 'Stop it, stop it, stop it.'

Tadek came bursting into the room.

'Helena, what's happening? What are you doing?'

Helena suddenly stopped and shrank back until she was sitting on the floor, her head on her knees. She started singing a Polish nursery rhyme in a small, high child's voice.

Tadek bent down over Babcia and took her right wrist in his fingers. She was no longer wriggling and was perfectly, absolutely and finally still.

Chapter 33

Derby, 1975

The little cake shop on Mill Street, opposite the abandoned 'Popular' cinema, was a very convenient place to work. It was only a 10-minute walk from home, the job was easy and could be done without engaging too much brain power. The owner, Mrs Pierce, was a large, friendly woman and although they started early in the morning, they finished at 4 o'clock. Wanda arrived at 7.30 to receive the deliveries of bread, cobs, cakes, scones, sausage rolls, iced fancies, cream horns, éclairs, lamingtons and gingerbread men. She and Mrs Pierce also served tea, coffee and hot soup. They made up fresh sandwiches and warmed the sausage rolls in the little oven.

Their customers were school children, traffic wardens, men working on building sites or little old ladies who came in for a chat and to buy a single cake. Ordinary, friendly local people who didn't need to be flattered or persuaded to buy something they didn't need, couldn't afford and looked dreadful in. Sampling the cakes expanded Wanda's waistline and the pale blue acrylic overall added years to her appearance. At 25, she looked more like 45. She and Mrs Pierce seemed to be merging into one but Wanda had long since ceased to care.

Wanda also had a new Saturday morning job. She had taken over from Pan Nowak at the Polish school. She wasn't especially qualified for the job but they couldn't find anyone else prepared to do it. The numbers in the class had also decreased considerably. Most of the second generation were now too old and the third generation yet too young, even if their parents were considering sending them to Polish school.

Wanda was back home by 4.30 just as Janek returned home from school, having done his final 'O' level that day. He threw his school bag onto the sofa.

'How did the exam go?' she asked.

'It was OK. And now I've finished with school totally and utterly.' He looked pleased.

'But you're going to the sixth form and then to university, aren't you?'

'Nope, I'm not. I'm fed up with school, I want to earn some real money.'

'Mum won't like that. What are you going to do? Work with dad in the decorating business?'

Janek laughed, 'I said earn some real money. Of course I'm not going to work with Dad. I don't want to get my hands dirty and have white paint splattered in my hair. I haven't told mum yet but I'm going to start work as an estate agent. They say a good estate agent can earn brilliant money along with bonuses and commission. That's what I want – no hard physical work and plenty of money. Oh, by the way, this letter was on the door mat when I came in.' He handed an envelope to Wanda and went upstairs to change out of his Broughton School uniform for the very last time.

Wanda looked at the stamp. It was large and showed a group of Polish dancing girls. Wanda recognised the costumes – the letter was from Poland. Wanda took a doughnut from the bag she'd brought from work, stuffed it in her mouth, and opened the letter.

Warsaw, 3 May
Dearest Auntie Helena and Uncle Tadek

I'm writing to send you most affectionate greetings from my mother and myself. I'm sorry to say I have some sad news. My dear grandmother Mira passed away last week. She was suffering from cancer and I think it was a blessed relief for her when the end came. She was a dear lady and a good and faithful wife to your uncle Witold. May she rest in peace.

I also have some happier news. After many years of trying, I have finally been granted a passport so I can visit you all in England. I am so delighted about it. I do hope I will be able to come and stay with you in Derby. First, I have arranged to go strawberry picking in Norfolk for six weeks to earn some money. My friend Eryk did that last summer so he knows the farmer and a place where we can stay. Would it be convenient if I came to see you after I've finished with the strawberries? That would be in the beginning of August.

As ever, your devoted cousin
Pawel Lato

Wanda smiled at the thought of finally meeting the famous Pawel who had been threatening to visit them for so many years. The time had finally arrived. She always remembered the words of Zosia's final letter from Poland – *Pawel's a skinny, long-haired creep.* What would they do with him? Perhaps Janek could keep him company or he could do some work with her father.

Wanda filled the washing machine, and took some clean, freshly ironed clothes upstairs. Pawel could have Babcia's room. Wanda went into the room to see how it would appear to a stranger. The bed had a couple of neatly folded blankets on it. The little dressing table still held Babcia's silver hand mirror and brush. On the mantelpiece was a picture of her grandmother. The smiling young man with his arm around her was her brother, Witold – Pawel's grandfather. Behind stood their parents, the sun shining on their happy faces. Wanda looked at her grandmother basking in the attention of her family. The four of them were on holiday somewhere near a lake and they were barefoot despite wearing formal Edwardian clothes. Thank God they didn't know about the pain and suffering that was awaiting them. Memories of Babcia's pathetic funeral suddenly came back to her. Helena had been too ill to attend so apart from Tadek, Janek and herself, there were just a few curious old women from the Polish community. Babcia had never troubled herself to make friends with those she thought were beneath her.

Wanda turned to the small wardrobe and opened it. Zosia's clothes hung inside – her school uniform, blazer, scarf and hat. Her sports wear, shoes, pumps, a duffel coat, her school bag. Wanda touched the garments – she would have to move them before Pawel arrived so he would have somewhere to put his things. They really ought to go to a charity shop but her mother couldn't bear to part with them. Helena had put all Zosia's things in the wardrobe after the funeral and no one had touched them since.

Wanda picked up the school bag and looked inside. Wanda flicked through the exercise books – the marks were mostly A or A- with scores of Honour Marks. She shoved them back in the bag. Then she unzipped a side pocket and pulled out a few bus tickets, some loose change, a pencil and rubber and a small wooden box.

The box was square, hinged at one side and decorated with carvings on the lid. It was a typical Polish design. Wanda looked inside and saw several pieces of paper folded into tiny squares. Wanda unfolded one piece.

Little Miss Lah-di-da, spots all over your face. You think you're something special but you're just a waste of space.

Wanda unfolded another:

Roses are red, violets are blue, stale sweat smells, just like you.

The next read:

You're a freak, you're a freak, the freak is back.

Wanda unfolded more and more, her body hot with anger. Were these written by the same people who had cried crocodile tears at Zosia's funeral? She wanted to take the hate mail to the headmistress at Pinecrest Grammar and show her what her pupils had done. The trouble was the notes must have been written more than five years earlier and they were all unsigned so she could prove nothing. There was no way she could let her mother ever see them. She took the notes to the outside bin and ripped them all to shreds before throwing them inside.

On the spur of the moment, she boarded a Number 11 bus and travelled up to the Manchester Road cemetery. She bought a large bouquet of white roses from the flower seller outside the gates. Moving along the neat green rows she found the grave of her grandmother and sister resting peacefully together under the green English lawn. She threw away the dead flowers in the vase by the headstone, filled it up with clean water from the tap at the end of the row, and carefully arranged the roses in the vase.

Chapter 34

Pawel sang with happiness as he prepared for his trip to England. Eryk Wysocki was staying the night at the Lato apartment as the two men prepared to take the long bus journey from Warsaw to London – neither had the money to fly. Pawel had received an invitation from his auntie Helena inviting him to stay and if he felt the letter lacked a certain warmth, he chose to ignore it.

Eryk was trying to close his suitcase.

'It's good of your family to let you stay with them in Derby. Don't they hold you responsible at all for Zosia's death?' he said.

'No, of course not,' Pawel snapped. 'It wasn't my fault. In fact, it was more your fault since she ate the bad food at your parents' apartment. I was ill too, remember. No, it certainly wasn't my fault. Anyway, I hope they are sufficiently recovered from her death that they'll welcome my memories of her. I have some pictures of her that I'm going to take for them. That reminds me, there was a parcel that came for her just after she died. I must take it and give it to her mother.'

'Is it just the aunt and uncle, then?'

'No, there's another sister who is about 25, I think, and a boy of about 16. If the sister is as pretty as the other one, I'm well in there. She's not married apparently.'

'So, we'll keep it dark that you tried it on with the dead girl.'

'I did nothing – I'm totally innocent. So what are you doing after the strawberry picking?'

'I'll just move onto the next farm and pick apples, asparagus anything. Last year I earned a nice amount of money. When I get back to Krakow I'm going to open a stall selling craftwork to tourists. What are you going to do when you get back?'

'I don't plan to come back.' And Pawel shut his suitcase with a snap.

One Saturday morning in August, Pawel's train stopped at Derby Station. Carrying his battered old suitcase and a box of strawberries, Pawel wandered down the platform to find his relations. From a distance he saw a short bald man in a white shirt and dark trousers hitched up high over his fat stomach. A woman with frizzy straw-coloured hair, wearing a red and white checked dress from which extended podgy arms and legs stood next to him. The man was holding a sign with the words *PAWEL LATO* written on it.

'I can't believe it,' thought Pawel. 'That is Zosia's sister and that funny little peasant fellow is her father? Who'd have thought it?'

Pawel adusted his grin and threw his arms around a startled Tadek.

'Uncle, I'm so pleased to see you and you must be cousin Wanda?'

He turned to look at Wanda. 'Ah, you look just like your sister,' he lied.

Wanda smiled. 'It's good to see you. How were the strawberries?'

'Small and red. They didn't have much to say for themselves.'

'What about your friend?'

'Oh, he is still picking fruits and vegetables. I left him to it. I wanted to visit my relations most of all. I'm so happy to be in Derby – I've heard so much about it.'

Wanda and her father exchanged glances as they all walked to the car park. Squeezing into Tadek's white van, Pawel kept up a constant stream of conversation – his journey to England on the coach, his adventures at the strawberry farm, his train ride, seeing a stately home from the window, the sights in Derby – anything.

When they arrived back, Helena opened the door of 16 Porton Crescent. Pawel swooped up the steps.

'Auntie Helena,' he bent low to kiss her hand. Helena gave him one of her rare smiles. 'Oh, you remind me of mummy,' he said. 'You and she look more like sisters than cousins. She sends you her fondest love and regards. What a beautiful house! This must be my cousin Janek. A pleasure.'

'We've put you in my Babcia's old bedroom. I hope it will be all right,' said Wanda.

'I'm sure it will be just perfect. Lead on and then you can give me a tour of the house. I just love these English houses. I love everything in this beautiful country.'

Wanda took Pawel up to his bedroom and left him to settle in. He stood there in his own private bedroom – the first time in his life he had ever had a room to himself – and danced a private little jig. He glanced out of the window at the garden lawn below and then looked round the room. Opening one of the small dresser drawers, he found six little picture postcards of the Black Madonna. Pawel shut the drawer with a snap, sat down on the bed and smiled.

At dinner that evening Pawel kept up the conversation. He asked what everyone did, what activities happened in Derby, where he could take some English lessons, could he help Tadek with his work, could he do some gardening? He watched as Wanda distributed the strawberries he had brought between five glass bowls and covered them with cream and sugar.

'This is the way we traditionally eat strawberries in England,' she said.

'And so do we,' replied Pawel, smiling and winking at her. 'You see we aren't so very different, are we?' She smiled back and Pawel could see she was quite pretty under those rolls of fat. She had the most perfect, pale skin – rather like her sister Zosia, in fact.

Pawel was desperate to make a good impression on his English family but even he eventually ran out of things to say and looked round the table. 'God,' he thought, 'this is the most miserable bunch of people I've ever met. Perhaps this isn't a good time to show them pictures of their dead daughter.'

During the following weeks Pawel made himself at home at Porton Crescent. He enjoyed sitting out in the garden, he loved watching television in the sitting room. It was such a novelty to go upstairs to bed and to walk out of the front door and be on ground level in the street. He went to work with Tadek a few times but proved inept at painting, stripping wallpaper, plastering, tiling and hanging wallpaper. He came to Mrs Pierce's cake shop a few times and helped unload supplies, but his English was too poor to serve customers. Janek took him to play football in the park, out bowling and to the pub a few times, but Pawel was rather lazy about learning English which restricted what he could do. Janek's Polish was also extremely poor so he always spoke to Pawel in English with the odd Polish word thrown in. Communication was difficult between them. As a result Janek began to leave Pawel to his own devices.

Most days Pawel found himself lying on the sofa in the sitting room, watching television and trying to work out what they were talking about. He had just dozed off on the sofa when Wanda arrived back home from the cake shop one Friday afternoon at 4 o'clock. She made a cup of tea and went to sit with him.

'I think you're bored Pawel,' she said.

'No, I'm fine. I will arrange some English lessons soon. The problem is English is such a difficult language.'

'Nonsense, it's easy. Words have no genders, all the verbs conjugate in almost exactly the same way, and once you know a word it almost always remains exactly the same, unless you want to make it plural in which case you simply add an s. In comparison Polish is incredibly difficult.'

'Well, I will try I promise.' He lay back on the sofa and sipped his tea. 'I'm starting to enjoy tea with milk in it so I'm making some progress.'

Wanda smiled at him. 'I tell you what – I'll take you to the Polish Club tomorrow evening. There's a dance, so there will be a music group and we can go to the bar restaurant. The music is probably not quite your thing but you might enjoy it.'

'A Polish Club? I heard someone mention it but I find it hard to believe you have such a thing.'

'Oh, we certainly do. My parents don't go anymore. Mummy won't go dancing now and daddy won't go without her.'

Pawel had been staying with the Barans for a month and he knew at some stage he would have to broach the subject of Zosia. 'Your mother has a great problem, doesn't she? Is it because of Zosia?' he asked.

'Yes, I don't think she will ever get over it. She has closed in on herself completely,' replied Wanda with a sigh.

'Would it help if I talked to her? I was with Zosia during her final days and when she died.'

Wanda looked at him. 'Please tell me what happened?'

'The truth is she was incredibly happy. She was fascinated by everything in Poland – the flats, the food, the trams, the countryside. We went to Krakow to stay with some friends. Krakow is beautiful and Zosia fell in love with the place. She told me she felt really at home there.'

'I'm so glad she was happy. I don't think she was ever really happy here. I know she was bullied at school. She was so very clever and pretty. People are always jealous.'

'Were you jealous?' Pawel looked at Wanda's spreading girth and the blue overall she was still wearing. An image of the slim, dark, beautiful Zosia came into his mind.

Wanda lowered her head. 'Maybe I was but I'd give anything to have her back. Her death has destroyed my family. You have no idea.'

'I brought some pictures I took of Zosia in Krakow with me. Shall I show them to your mother? She looks so happy maybe your mother will be able to celebrate her life instead of mourning her death.'

'That's easy for you to say. The pictures may just remind her even more of what she has lost. No, it's best not to.' She looked at him. 'But I'd love to see them,' she smiled.

'Of course, I'll get them. But I think your mother really needs to talk, don't you? My mother said I should try and get her to talk. It will be more healthy psychologically.' He thought briefly of the parcel he had brought with him and was lying unwrapped in his suitcase. No, he would not bring that out – just yet.

'It's still too soon for my mother,' said Wanda. 'Now, I have to tell you must wear a tie to enter our esteemed Polish Club. Do you possess such a thing?'

Chapter 35

'I can't believe that's here,' Pawel whispered, pointing at the image of the Polish Eagle complete with crown, hanging on the club reception wall. 'It's so old-fashioned, imperialistic.'

'Is it? What do mean?' said Wanda. 'It's always been here.' She spotted the club manager.

'Pan Batorowicz, this is my cousin, Pawel Lato, visiting from Warsaw.'

'Ah, good evening. Your cousin, eh? It that on your father's side?'

'No, Pawel's grandfather and my babcia were brother and sister. So he's my second cousin strictly speaking.'

'Ah, I remember your babcia. What a fine lady. How are you enjoying Derby?'

'It's great,' said Pawel. 'Really, um, great.'

'We think so. Anyway, go into the dance hall. The band will be starting soon. Enjoy yourself. Remember the restaurant upstairs will be open in one hour.'

They walked into the darkened dance hall. Pawel bought two glasses of lager and they sat down at a table in the corner. Wanda looked round the room. She had known most of these people all her life. There was Pani Turek, who had always wanted Wanda to marry her son Piotr. The son had gone to Oxford University, so Wanda had heard, and was now a barrister in London. There was no way he'd look twice at someone like Wanda now.

There sat Pani Kuron, her synthetic dress straining against her parted legs. She was in earnest conversation with Pani Zawada and both had obviously noticed Pawel. Pani Kuron had been taken off to Russia during the war on the trans-Siberian railway. Somewhere in the depths of Russia, her husband and daughter had got off the train at a station to find some bread and the train had left without them. The sight of the pair walking down the station platform was the last Pani Kuron ever saw of them. She and her remaining daughter endured four years in a Siberian camp and then were taken to the Middle East before finally reaching Derby. The lady sitting next to her, Pani Zawada, had been caught working for the resistance and was taken to Auschwitz concentration camp near Krakow. Somehow she had survived. After the camp was liberated, she met up with some English soldiers who brought her to England. When she was a child, Wanda had once asked Pani Zawada what the number printed on her arm was for. Pani Zawada had replied that it was a telephone number she didn't want to forget.

All these stories, all these tragedies, thought Wanda. How do we bear it?

Pani Kuron made her way towards Wanda and Pawel.

'Wanda, my dear. We haven't seen you for a long time and how is your dear mother these days?'

'She is well, thank you.' Wanda introduced Pawel Lato.

'I wondered who the young man was. Pleased to meet you. How do you like Derby?'

Pawel looked at Wanda and they both laughed. While the band was setting up, Pawel looked round at the pictures. They were all black and white snaps of Polish pilots during the war. There was an enormous plane propeller mounted on the wall.

'These people seem to live in a time warp,' Pawel whispered to Wanda. 'They have completely ignored the reality of communism in Poland and live in a little Poland they would like to believe in. A Poland that doesn't exist anymore, if it ever did.'

'Well, if it keeps them happy, does it matter? Most of them have been through great traumas you know,' said Wanda. 'War, concentrations camps, Siberia, losing children, wives, husbands. They deserve a little comfort and security now.'

Pawel asked who had created the club and Wanda told him it was the Air Force Association made up of pilots from the Battle of Britain who started it in the 1950s. She said she'd been coming here all her life and it was perhaps strange that the place was still going. She presumed it would close when all the older generation died.

'Those are the people we in Poland call renegades,' Pawel said. Seeing Wanda's look of astonishment, he suddenly stood up, bowed and held out his hand.

'Would madam care to dance with me?'

Wanda smiled and placed her hand in his. He kissed it. As they danced Pawel placed his hand on the small of her back, leaving a warm, damp patch. She looked into his dark green eyes and noticed he was watching pretty young Lydia Batorowicz walk across the dance floor. A confused anger filled her heart.

Tadek was up early on Sunday morning as always and sat down to work on his watches. Helena came in wearing her dressing gown.

'Did you hear Wanda and Pawel come in last night?' she said sitting on a chair near his table.

'Yes, they sounded so happy. Laughing and joking – it was nice to hear.'

'Do you think he's ever going home?'

'I don't know. He hasn't said anything to me. Wanda seems happy that he's here so that's good.'

'Maybe that's his plan. He wants to trap Wanda into marriage so he can stay and live off her and us.'

'Ah, Helena. He brings some much needed life and laughter into this house. He is good for Wanda, taking her out and talking to her. What do you have against the boy?'

Helena paused and tied the belt on her dressing gown.

'Nothing at all but I don't want Wanda to get hurt. I hope he stays in his own bedroom.'

'Wanda is 25, a grown woman. She shouldn't really be living at home at her age. She needs some fun and a little life. Pawel is a good lad. He's a bit lazy but he has a kind heart. Don't you want her to get married and have children? This could be her best chance.'

'I don't want her to settle for second best...'

Tadek looked up from his watches. 'I don't think Pawel is second best. He has a degree, he is kind and friendly and he has quite a nice face. Don't you think so?'

'Zosia didn't like him. Remember her letter. She said he was after her but he'd get nowhere with her. She said he kept going on about coming England. She was obviously suspicious.'

'Look, we were lucky to come here. Why deny it to Pawel? Zosia was planning to come to university in London so obviously she wasn't interested in getting involved with Pawel.'

'Are you saying Wanda should settle for whatever she can get?'

Tadek shook his head. 'Are *you* saying Pawel couldn't possibly want Wanda for herself and he must have ulterior motives? Why wouldn't he want her – she's a warm, witty person with such a generous nature. Leave her to make her own decisions. She is an adult.'

'Adults make mistakes.'

Wanda informed Pawel she was going to teach him English if he wouldn't go to proper lessons. She was teaching Polish to anglicised second and third generation children on Saturdays, so she may as well teach a Pole English. She went to WH Smith to buy a book on English grammar. As she was directed to the reference section by an assistant, a large book display caught her eye. The title was *Fashion and Slavery* and the author was Robert Kaminski. Wanda paused and picked it up. The subtitle read: *How the Goss Fashion Empire was founded on slave labour.* Wanda bought a copy in addition to *An English Primer* for Pawel. She decided she would only speak to him in English in future and they would study some of this book every evening. *Fashion and Slavery* she would read in her room in secret.

When she returned home, Pawel was playing football with Janek in the garden. The weather was warm and Pawel had taken off his shirt. Wanda noticed that he wasn't puny at all, he was thin but strong and wiry. There were pronounced muscles on his arms and he was tanned from working in the sun picking strawberries. When he saw her watching him from the kitchen window, he waved and started fooling around on the swing she and Zosia used to play on when they were little. He climbed on the frame, hung down by his knees, then stood up on top of the swing on one leg.

'You're overacting, Pawel,' yelled Janek.

Wanda laughed. And then ran out in a panic as Pawel fell from the swing with a loud thud onto the grass. He was laughing when she got there, his hair falling down over his eyes, his hands dirty from the soil. He sat on the ground squinting up at her.

That evening Wanda placed a copy of the *Derby Evening Telegraph* in front of Pawel and told him, in English, to read the headlines. He smiled at her, and his eyes sparkled and shone. Wanda hadn't noticed how sweet their colour was before.

New football stadium to be built, read Pawel.

'I'm sure you can easily work out what the first three words mean,' said Wanda. 'Then we can try the next three.'

Pawel made halting progress. He read out the headlines slowly with a very strong accent. His brown tousled hair flopped down over his face as he struggled with the language, his pronunciation making Wanda laugh out loud. She noticed his hair curled at the back of his neck. His finger traced the words on the newspaper and she was surprised to see what beautiful hands he had. Before she could stop herself she said something in English. She couldn't believe she'd said it out loud, she had only meant to think it. But it was there – said and out in the open. There was no drawing it back.

'I love you.'

Pawel's head remained bent over the newspaper trying to work out the words. Then he paused and looked at Wanda with a quizzical expression, seemingly confused. She abruptly got up and ran upstairs to her bedroom, locking the door and throwing herself on the bed – her face glowing, her heart pounding. It was the last days of September and the nights were starting to draw in. The window was open and the breeze was gently swaying her curtains and the branches of the large lime tree at the bottom of the garden. A dove was calling in the tree and she could hear the tinkle of an ice cream van in the street. Two slow houseflies hovered round and round her light fitting. She heard a faint scratching noise and half sat up to see a note appear under her door. Wanda went over and picked it up. It read, *I love you also.*

Wanda looked at it her heart pounding. Could she bear to be hurt all over again?

Wanda took the note and used it as her bookmark while reading Kaminski's book.

Chapter 36

Warsaw, April 1976

My dear Pawel and Wanda

I was so happy when I received your letter. I give you both my heartfelt congratulations and my blessing. I'm sure my dear mother and auntie Barbara would have given their blessing too.

I'm also looking forward very much to coming to England. I have already inquired about the bus journey. It will seem strange living all alone in the flat from now on but I will get used to it. You are all very welcome to stay at any time.

Please pass on my love to Helena and tell her how much I'm looking forward to seeing her after all these years.

My love to you all
Irena

Reading between the lines, Pawel knew his mother was worried about meeting her cousin again, worried she might be blamed. He also wondered how his mother would react to Wanda. Would she too make comparisons to the dark, round-eyed Zosia?

All in all, Pawel enjoyed his time in Derby. He was encouraged because his English was slowly improving. He loved watching football on television and discussing it at length with Janek. He was doing some of the fetching and carrying for Tadek who was getting a little old to do everything himself. At least he didn't have to wear a suit everyday like Janek did now he worked at the estate agents. Janek had recently introduced him to his new girlfriend – Maxine Allsop. Pawel wondered what the attraction was – Maxine was as plain as Wanda but without her wit and charm.

Pawel watched Wanda fuss around preparing for the wedding. She complained to him that she couldn't find any dresses to fit.

'Perhaps your mother can make one – she used to be a machinist, didn't she?' he suggested. Wanda just shook her head.

In the end, she bought one two sizes too small as an incentive to become slimmer.

The wedding was booked at St Joseph's for May 11 and the reception would be at the Polish Club. Mrs Pierce had told Wanda that she would provide the wedding cake. Pani Batorowicz consulted Wanda about the food for the reception and promised to provide the wine free of charge as her present to the couple. Pan Nowak would be providing the wedding photography free of charge as his gift. Wanda organised the flowers, the wedding cars, the invitations and a suit for Pawel. She looked through *The Times* colour magazine for holiday deals in the small ads for their honeymoon and found an inexpensive cottage in the Isle of Wight that would be perfect. Pawel flicked through the magazine as Wanda stood behind him.

'Oh, look,' she said pointing to an article about torture in Argentina. 'I knew the man who took those photos.'

Pawel saw the name Roger Elliott. 'An old boyfriend?' he asked.

'No, a good friend's boyfriend.'

Pawel tried his best to learn the decorating trade from his future father-in-law though he proved to be rather accident prone, falling off ladders, stepping in the paste bucket, knocking paint pots over and hurting himself with tile cutters. Tadek was always patient with him, clearing up the mess and dressing his wounds. Tadek preferred to work in silence but Pawel liked to chat.

'Uncle, we always hear about our side of the family but what about yours? Tell me about them. Do they still live in

Poland?' he asked one day as they were painting a wall in a newly refurbished flat.

Tadek told him about his two older sisters who still lived on the farm he grew up on. It was only a small plot of land but it kept them fed during the war. The place was in a small village, near the Russian border, and it kept changing hands. Over the generations, their ancestors have been Russian, Ukrainian, Belorussian and Polish – and yet they had never moved from where they were born.

'What about your parents?' asked Pawel.

'They are both dead now and my sisters are unmarried. I spent most of the war working on the land.'

'How did you get to England then?'

Tadek stretched up to reach a high point of the wall with his paintbrush. He dipped his brush in the paint pot.

'Right at the end of the war the Russians came through when I was out trying to sell some produce. I had to keep them away from the farm and from my sisters. I knew what the Russian soldiers were doing to women. So I stayed with the soldiers and went through Germany. I was forced to wear a Russian uniform and we marched on Berlin. Later I managed to escape and got on a ship leaving for England.'

'How did you meet auntie? Did you rescue her from the vicious Russian soldiers, or were you part of the glorious Soviet army that liberated her from a concentration camp? Maybe you met on one of those refugee ships coming to England?'

Tadek was silent for a while as he continued carefully painting up near the window frame.

'We met in Catford, south London in the Legal Aliens Office where we were both waiting to apply for residency. Helena looked so thin and pale, I offered her one of my sandwiches. She was a skilled machinist and so we moved to where the clothing mills were – Derby seemed to have the most jobs at the time.'

Pawel looked at Tadek's bald head and fat stomach,

marvelling that he had managed to marry a woman such as his aunt. But then in times of war everything was turned up side down and social conventions went out of the window.

'You're wondering how on earth a man like me persuaded a woman like Helena to marry him, aren't you?' said Tadek looking Pawel straight in the eyes.

'No, no of course not. I can see she loves you. You are a successful, married couple and there aren't many of them around. Look at my parents – my father disappeared so long ago I can't even remember what he looked like.'

'Well, we have our problems like everyone else but we are united where our children are concerned. We want Wanda to be happy and anyone who hurts her …' Tadek glanced at Pawel, who decided the time had come to work in silence.

Pawel and Wanda lay on an old tartan rug spread out on the grass beneath the lime tree in the garden of 16 Porton Crescent. Sticky burs fell on them from the tree, sparrows darted in and out of the rose bushes covering the wall, ants crawled over their bare arms.

'Pawel, would you have preferred Zosia to me? Tell the truth.' Wanda put her head on his chest.

'No, she was odd, too precise, too, well, old-fashioned, if you know what I mean.'

'She was very beautiful. And clever.'

'Stop competing with her – she's gone. It's you I want, witty, bright, funny Wanda.'

'You tried, though, didn't you? You tried to get her?'

'Not very hard. She was difficult to talk to, she was so serious and … intense. She was really purposeful, she had everything planned, and I didn't fit into her plan.'

'She had everything planned except her death.'

'That's why it's best not to make any plans …'

Chapter 37

Wanda knew Irena immediately when she stepped off the coach. She was startlingly similar to Helena although a little taller and slimmer, with darker hair mixed with grey. She beamed with pleasure at her son and embraced him before turning to Wanda.

'And you must be Wanda. I can't believe I'm finally seeing you. How are you? I'm so excited about the wedding. I was worried Pawel would never settle down.'

'It's lovely to meet you at last,' smiled Wanda. 'This is my father.' Tadek immediately took Irena's hand and kissed it. 'Welcome to Derby,' he said.

'How was your journey? Are you exhausted?' said Pawel.

'I'll survive. I'm so excited about everything, I don't mind. We drove through the centre of London – I couldn't believe how fantastic it was,' Irena gushed. 'Tell me, is it always so hot in England? We were brought up with the stories of England being cold, rainy and filled with thick noxious fogs – like in Dickens.'

Wanda smiled. 'No, it's unusually hot – we don't remember a summer like it.'

Wanda listened to Irena's chatter as they got into Tadek's van for the drive home. Her mind, however, was not on the conversation. She had read Robert Kaminski's book from cover to cover and found out all about the factory that made German uniforms with slave labour. Reinhard Goss had been a cruel sadist who'd funded the Nazi party with his wealth. He used and abused the workers. His son Peter appeared to have been different – kind, cultured and humane.

The book included testimonies from workers who confirmed that Peter often tried to protect them from his father's wrath. More than one claimed Peter was romantically involved with one of the machinists but she was never named. Wanda had been relieved – the last thing they needed was for journalists to turn up looking for a story. After the war, Reinhard Goss was never brought before any kind of court and he merely transferred his business to making civilian clothing. He died in 1961 and it was Peter who built up the fashion empire.

The chapter on Peter's suicide was interesting. Kaminski obviously tried to absolve himself from any blame. He claimed he was only interested in gaining compensation from the exceedingly wealthy Goss for his ex workers. His lawyer had sent Goss a letter of inquiry along with a list of a few names of former workers. Kaminski had not even met Goss before the latter killed himself.

Kaminski gave a few hints in explanation of Goss's suicide none of which involved Helena. Goss's third wife was in the middle of divorcing him for a vast sum of money, as his previous two wives had done. It seemed Goss also had a bad cocaine habit. Wanda knew that her mother still thought about Peter Goss and believed he'd killed himself because of her, but the sad truth may have been that he'd forgotten all about her. He was a super rich businessman, he played the field, moving round the world in his private jet, fending off ex-wives and snorting his cocaine. Would he remember a young Polish machinist from 30 years previously? Wanda decided, probably not. And yet, who knew what was going on in his heart?

After Goss's death, the ensuing financial crisis meant the company had to rid itself of some its subsidiaries, including Fab Fashions. The board decided to drop the name Reinhard and just call itself Goss. When in doubt, change your name, as Wanda knew only too well. She had tried the same trick herself. The company decided to be open about their old links with the Nazis but insisted that the new board of governors had nothing to do with the previous regime. They also arranged to provide an undisclosed sum of money to each of the wartime workers or a smaller amount to their families.

Wanda wondered if her mother had received any money and not mentioned it. Kaminski was obviously making a nice profit from the book which had turned out to be a bestseller. There was even a tie-in with a documentary to be screened on BBC2 called *Hitler's Tailors*. Wanda didn't know whether the researchers for the programme had contacted Helena. If they had, she never spoke about it and it was obvious she would want nothing to do with it.

Her thoughts were still with Peter Goss when the van drew up outside the house and Wanda was stirred by shouts of greeting between Helena and Irena. She watched them embrace – the cousins who had once been so close, who hadn't seen each other since they were 16. That was 35 years ago – an eternity away. Irena was so like her mother physically but less nervous, with less emotional baggage.

The night before the wedding, Tadek, Janek and his friends took Pawel out for his final drink as a bachelor. Wanda decided that she, her mother and Irena would have a quiet meal and glass of wine at home. The three women sat around the dining room table.

'Pawel told you my mother died two years ago, didn't he? It is so hard being without her, I miss her so much,' said Irena. 'And I was so sorry to hear about dear Auntie Barbara's death. That must have been a great loss to you.'

Wanda looked at her mother wondering what she was going to say. They had never even mentioned Babcia since her funeral.

'Yes, it was,' said Helena. 'Mama was so good to me, the best mother in the world. She devoted her life to me. She was ill for so long after the stroke. I think she died of shock when she heard about Zosia.'

Wanda looked to see what expression her mother had on her face but it was one of total innocence. The incident in the bedroom seemed to have been wiped from her memory.

'Oh, Helenka,' said Irena putting her hand on her cousin's arm, 'I have to tell you about my deep, deep sorrow concerning Zosia. Words can't express …'

'I know, Irena, I know. But I want to ask you something. Tell me exactly what happened when Zosia died?' Helena sounded eager for the first time in ages.

Wanda looked at her mother in surprise. She had scarcely mentioned Zosia's name in years and never referred to her death.

'But, Mummy, you could have asked Pawel any time. He was actually there,' she said.

'I know, but somehow I didn't want to burden such a young boy with these questions.'

'Pawel brought some pictures he took of Zosia in Krakow but he's never dared show them to you for fear of upsetting you.'

'Well I'd love to see them now.' Helena was actually smiling.

Irena took her cousin's hand.

'I'm so glad we can talk about it. I wrote you a long letter after it happened but I wasn't surprised not to get a reply. I was terrified you hated me and I couldn't bear it.' Tears welled in Irena's eyes.

'I want to lay Zosia to rest before Wanda gets married. I don't want anything to spoil her big day.' She spoke calmly. Wanda felt so relieved she put her arms round her mother and buried her face in her arm before going upstairs to get the photos.

'Zosia was having a truly wonderful time in Poland,' said Irena. 'She paid a visit to your aunt Maria and came back laughing about what an eccentric character she was. Then Pawel took her to Krakow on the train and she stayed with old friends of mine who had a gorgeous flat overlooking the old square. I was so busy working all the time that I had to leave her in the care of my mother and Pawel but she was happy with both of them. I think mother reminded her of Barbara who she was so close to.'

'The death certificate said she died of botulism food poisoning. Did you know it was that?'

'No, not at first. Pawel came back sick from Krakow but I think he had another kind of food poisoning. Zosia became ill in the night after she returned but I thought it was just a virus. People often pick up things when they're in a strange country, new and different viruses that they have no immunity to. I honestly thought she would be in bed for a few days and have a very unpleasant sickness but then recover. Food poisoning is usually only dangerous in small children and the very old. I kept an eye on her and made sure she drank plenty of fluids but I went to work that evening thinking she would be better the next day.'

'So Mira and Pawel were looking after her?'

'Yes. Pawel phoned me at the hospital when he became worried. He told me Zosia's breathing was difficult and I told him to call an ambulance while I organised a bed for her at the hospital. She wouldn't normally have been brought to a children's hospital but I wanted to keep a close eye on her.'

'Did the ambulance come too late?'

'I think it came quickly but unfortunately the poison had reached Zosia's heart and she had a heart attack. It was so sudden there was nothing they could do.'

Wanda came downstairs bringing the photographs. Helena looked at her daughter's image. The first one showed her standing in the old square in Krakow feeding the pigeons as they perched on her hand and flew all around her head. Her face was wreathed in a huge smile. Other pictures showed her sitting on a park bench, listening to the open air Chopin concert, standing on the viewing gallery at the top of the Palace of Culture, her hair blowing over her face and examining an amber necklace while walking round the Old Town in Warsaw. All the pictures showed a beautiful, happy young woman.

Irena went to bed happier than she had been since Zosia's death. Wanda stayed up holding her mother's hand. Helena looked at her.

'You know, Wanda, you don't have to marry this man if you don't think he is the right one. I want you to be certain. Don't settle for less than you deserve.'

'Mum, I've loved three men in my life. The first was utterly unobtainable, the second was fairly unobtainable and this one – well, I'm sure I want to marry him.'

Helena smiled. 'That reminds me' she said. 'I have a wedding present for you from Babcia.' Wanda caught her breath as her mother went to the sideboard and opened a drawer. She took out a pure white linen tablecloth decorated round the edges with intricate blue and yellow flowers.

'She left this for you for your wedding day. It was embroidered by my grandmother,' said Helena placing the cloth in Wanda's trembling hands.

Chapter 38

'Smile please, one more picture of the whole group then we will have the bride's family on their own.' Helena was pleased Pan Nowak knew how to organise chaotic wedding guests, achieving some symmetry out of the melée. Everyone hated the interminable photos, but realised they would love seeing them afterwards. Pawel looked round at her, a rather bewildered expression on his face. An image of Pawel's grandfather, Witold, suddenly popped into her mind, his face wearing the exact same expression. Witold had been sitting at the dining table, staring up at his wife, Mira, and her own mother, Barbara. What had been the cause of his disquiet? It was too long ago, she could no longer remember.

Father Kantor, who'd performed the ceremony, was standing with the wedding party, no doubt hoping for a free feast afterwards. When Helena had first approached him about arrangements for the wedding, he'd barked, 'It's not a good idea for cousins to marry. It amplifies any bad genetic traits, you know.'

Helena had managed to keep her composure and respond gently, 'But they're only second cousins and they don't have any bad traits.'

Pan Nowak was ordering Helena and Tadek to stand to Wanda's left while Irena stood to Pawel's right. Helena became aware of inane giggling from behind her. It was Janek's new girlfriend, Maxine Allsop. Helena glanced at her. She was quite large and plain, given to relating very long and very boring stories about trivial incidents. Helena thought she was ordinary, dull and dim. She looked at her son – tall, blond and handsome and hoped against hope that Maxine wouldn't get him.

Helena greeted Mrs Pierce and said a cheery hello to Wanda's school friends with their respective husbands and children. Eryk had managed to come over for the wedding as well as some of Pawel's friends from college. Pan Nowak snapped the shutter and so on a hot May day in 1976, the hottest on record, the wedding group was captured forever.

The wedding procession moved on to *Dom Polski*. Helena had not set foot in the place since Zosia's death. She hadn't felt like dancing and she hadn't been able to face people in the Polish community. She didn't want the sympathy, she didn't want to talk about it. She blanked out the sound of Irena's excited exclamations, took a deep breath and went inside.

After the meal, Tadek stood up to speak. Public speaking was not his natural territory, yet he made the speech of his life.

'Dear family and friends. We are here today to celebrate the wedding of our precious daughter, Wanda, to this fine young man, Pawel. I have to tell you that her mother and I are more delighted than we can say. Wanda has been a model daughter – she is kind, dutiful, witty and charming. Life has not always been kind to our family, but we have renewed hope with this wedding and pray for the blessing of grandchildren.' Tadek raised his glass and nodded towards his daughter.

'To my precious girl – may she have every happiness.' Wanda struggled hard to keep the tears from falling on her white gown.

When Mr and Mrs Lato returned home from honeymoon, they continued to live at Porton Crescent until they could save enough money to buy a small flat. Wanda carried on working at the cake shop and Pawel, who spoke English with tolerable ease now, worked with Tadek.

By June the following year, Derby was agog with the news that the Queen would be coming as part of her Silver

Jubilee celebrations. She would be presenting the old town with a charter enabling it to call itself a city. Helena went with Wanda down to the market place to hear her speech. A short, fat man with a double chin and a large wart on his forehead, was seated on a platform with the Mayor and other local dignitaries.

'There's Maxine's dad,' whispered Wanda. 'You can see where she gets her good looks.'

The Queen came forward to a raised dais to give her speech. She spoke about the 'ancient city of Derby, one time home to the Romans, the Saxons, the Vikings and many other immigrants who, throughout the ages, have given the city its vitality, industry and innovation.'

'That's us,' whispered Helena to her daughter. 'We're the immigrants who've given Derby its vitality.'

Wanda looked at her and they both started laughing. Helena gently patted Wanda's swelling stomach. She saw Wanda was blooming, her face shining with unalloyed happiness.

On the night Wanda gave birth to her daughter, Anna Zosia Lato, Pawel came back from the hospital elated. He had been with Wanda during the birth and had finally left Derby Royal Infirmary at 9pm while his wife and daughter slept. He arrived back at Porton Crescent and Helena hugged him with genuine warmth. She suddenly felt great affection for the boy, the father of her granddaughter. Helena poured them both a small vodka to toast the baby's health and they settled down on the sofa to talk.

'I'm so excited, I can't believe the miracle I've just seen. That sounds so sentimental, doesn't it,' said Pawel sipping his drink.

'No, I understand perfectly. And it is a miracle.'

Pawel stared at his glass.

'Auntie Helena, there is something I must give you. It has been at the back of my mind since I first arrived in England but I never found the right time. It is a parcel that arrived for Zosia the day after, after she … passed away.

I'm afraid in all the panic I just pushed it in a drawer. I have it in my room.'

'A parcel? Who sent it?' asked Helena.

'I'm not sure. It wasn't very well wrapped and was half open. It appears to be old letters and manuscripts and bits of paper – I'll go and get it.'

Pawel returned holding the parcel still in its original brown paper packing. He handed it to his mother-in-law. Helena tore the packaging open completely.

'There's a note,' she said.

I thought this might be of interest to you. I have no children to pass my things on to, so you may as well have it. M

Helena took the manuscript. She looked puzzled. 'Who sent this?'

She looked at the packaging. On the back was written Maria Poniatowska and the address.

'Ah, it's from my aunt Maria. I had a letter from the concierge at the flats she lived in to say that she died last year. Yes, I know Zosia visited her. Thank you Pawel, there may be some interesting bit of family history in this. Who is JP? Oh, it must be my father, Jan Poniatowski.'

Helena put on her glasses and began reading the sheaf of handwritten notes, held together with green tags.

Notes on the mental condition of JP, May 1923. Recorded by Dr Nathan Weinberg.

I have been making studies of the condition called Dementia Praecox (that is dementia in the young) and also recently called schizophrenia (or fragmented mind). It constantly amazes me how great the power of the human mind can be, how the brain can create an entirely new reality, how it can even produce physical symptoms extending from that other reality. JP is a 28-year-old male who has suffered from delusions, hallucinations and erratic behaviour for 10 years. As a result he has always been unfit for military service and for any useful occupation. His parents are first cousins and I wonder if this has any bearing on what is perhaps a hereditary condition. His sister tells me JP was quite normal until the age of 17. He was outgoing, confident and friendly. He changed suddenly at around this age when attending military school and had to be brought home. His problems seemed to stem from the time he fought a duel with another student and killed him. Could this have been the trigger? His moods seem to go in cycles, he can be quite lucid and normal for a time, then almost completely insane the next. For a year he thought the whole of Warsaw was under 10 metres of water and he often made spluttering noises as if he were drowning. He is occasionally aggressive, particularly towards his mother, but never in the extreme so far. Mostly he withdraws into himself and hides in his room. He dislikes strong light, loud noises, crowds of people, and confrontational situations.

I am talking to him while he is sitting in the corner of his bed, leaning against the wall with a blanket covering his head.

NW: What are you hiding from?
JP: The whisperers.
NW: Who are they?
JP: They whisper to me all the time telling to do things.
NW: What are they telling you now?
JP: The bed is covered in spiders and ants. They are crawling all over the covers. Snakes are climbing up the curtains. The whisperers tell me to hide and not to move then the spiders won't hurt me.
NW: Are the whisperers always talking to you?
JP: Not always. Sometimes they go away. But I know they will be back.
NW: What else do the whisperers tell you? What do the whisperers think of Barbara?
JP: They tell me Barbara is a good woman. They tell me I

*should marry her. They tell me she will be the one who will
save me.*
NW: *Is that what you are going to do?*
(JP has pulled the blanket from his head.)
JP: *Barbara treats me like a person not like someone who is
ill. She treats me like a normal human being. No one else
does that. My parents think I'm mad, my sister patronises
me. I have some problems but I'm not stupid. I feel safe
with Barbara.*
NW: *Your parents think she's a social climber.*
JP: *The voices tell me Barbara is a good person and she
won't harm me.*
NW: *Do you love her – does she love you?*
JP: *What is love? She is my nurse. She will look after me.*
NW: *What would happen if the voices changed their minds
about Barbara?*
JP: *I think the voices tell me the truth.*
NW: *And what if they stopped liking Barbara?*
*(JP says nothing but pulls nervously on the buttons of his
jacket. He never meets my eye.)*
NW: *The voices would never tell you to harm her in any
way, would they?*
JP: *(giggles) They might.*
NW: *But you wouldn't do it. You wouldn't harm your
fiancee?*
JP: *I wouldn't, but they might.*
NW: *They can't do anything without you though, can
they? Did the voices tell you to attack your mother? You
threatened her with a knife, do you remember?*
JP: *I never hurt her. I never hurt anyone. My parents made
it up. They want to put me away in a lunatic asylum. My
father hit me hard on the head with an iron bar just because
I was talking to my friends. They are ashamed of me. I
never hurt anyone – they hurt me. They are all against me,
ganging up on me. Them and the secret police.*
NW: *You have never attacked anyone, then?*
JP: *No, never. Even though I know things about people – I
know who you are for instance.*

NW: Who am I?
JP: You work for them, you work for the secret police. I know you can read my thoughts. They taught you that in the Cheka – in the secret police.
NW: Who told you that?
PJ: The whisperers. They are never wrong.
NW: What do the whisperers look like?
JP: I'm not sure I ever saw them. Once when I looked in the mirror I thought one was behind me. They may look just like people or perhaps they are small and black – like little devils. Maybe you are a whisperer.
NW: Perhaps they are not real but just like a dream.
JP: That's what I think sometimes but then they talk to me so loudly I can't ignore them.
NW: Do you think that you are mad?
JP: Sometimes I wonder if the whisperers are mad. Perhaps they tell me to do crazy things because they are crazy.
(JP has now pulled the blanket back over his head): JP: Stop looking at me, you can read my thoughts if you see my eyes.
(I decide to suspend the questioning for now.)

Helena took off her glasses and sat a while in silence. The thoughts were tumbling, racing in chaos through her brain. Her father – that distant, solemn, perfect, unavailable man – was mad. He was never a hero, never in the army, never anything but a lunatic. Helena couldn't take in the enormity of it. Her mother had lied all these years. But father couldn't help it, of course he couldn't help it.

Helena couldn't think straight. She frantically rifled through the rest of the papers. There were more notes about her father, and others seemingly about different people, pages of other case studies. Then she found a pile of letters – written in a familiar hand. Helena read them greedily, hungry for information.

Warsaw, 24 January 1924

Dear Dr Weinberg

I am in receipt of your letter of 22 January. You claim that you have my best interests at heart and that you only want to spare me future suffering. I am amazed at your impertinence at presuming to know what is best for me and for my fiancé. Jan and I love each other and that is why we are going to be married. I believe that your reasons for suggesting otherwise are simple snobbery on the part of Jan's sister who thinks that because my father made his money through trade, I am not worthy to be part of her family. Has she, by taking up with you, never heard of the phrase 'the pot calling the kettle black?

Yours sincerely

Barbara Ostrowska

Warsaw, 6 January 1925

Dear Dr Weinberg

I was grateful for your visit last evening. Jan seems to calm down after you talk to him. He stops being aggressive towards me. As I told you, I am expecting a child in the summer. When you said I should therefore consider my position – what exactly did you have in mind? I have no one else to turn to for advice. My parents know nothing, I cannot tell them after their objection to my marrying and Jan's parents have cut me adrift. I feel I have been used.

With fondest regards

Barbara

Warsaw, 15 June 1925

Dear Nathan

Please, please help me. I am so grateful for your past help, please come to my aid again. I am so afraid – I have no one to turn to. Please can I come to your surgery – I will try to telephone you but it is difficult.

Barbara

Warsaw, 24 June 1925

Dear Nathan

I'm very grateful to you for tending my injuries and so relieved when you told me my child was safe. I am keeping the 'goods' safely in the flat. I am going to my parents for the confinement next week. They suspect nothing so far. Jan will stay at the flat while I'm away. Can anything be arranged for that time? Do whatever you can.
love, Barbara

Warsaw, 25 October 1925

Dear Nathan

It is done. I am at my parents. I have locked the flat but there is a key with the concierge. Oh, God, Nathan, he very nearly dropped my baby from the balcony – please God forgive me. He said the child was evil, that she was put in the apartment by the Cheka to harm us. What could I have done? I had to save my child, I had to save myself. Can you arrange the death certificate? How will Maria react? What have you told her? He is her brother, after all. I don't know what to think, what to do. I'm caring for my baby. Witold said I mustn't go back to him when he heard how Helena nearly died. We must not make contact again – can you keep Maria under control at the funeral?
In haste, Barbara

There was a copy of the death certificate signed by N Weinberg. Cause of death was listed as –

self-administered acute morphine intoxication leading to asphyxia, coma and death.

At the bottom of the pile was a small piece of blue note paper, an ancient paper clip had left a red rusted mark at one corner. The writing was in a shaky, large print – an unfamiliar hand.

<u>My scattered mind</u>
They cut my thoughts, they unravelled my brain
Logic and consequence, damaged
I cannot think, my ears implode
But with your deft needle, you sewed me back together
Barbara, seamstress of my mind

In the small, neat hand of Dr Weinberg was written
below –

I found no suicide note but this poem was left on the table
next to the deceased.

Helena felt the tears flow, she couldn't read any more.
She looked over at the photo of her father standing on the
mantelpiece and muttered slowly the words she never
previously had any reason to use – 'Oh, daddy, oh daddy,
my poor, poor daddy.'

Chapter 39

Mr Reginald Allsop was a small businessman (he stood 5ft 4in high), a freemason and the Conservative council leader. He had a neat moustache, a pouch of double chins and a jovial manner. He'd worked in his family's business, Allsop and Son Printers, a well-known Derby firm, all his adult life and despite the booms and busts that had buffeted the city over the years, the business had kept going.

Maxine invited Janek to have dinner at her parents' house after they had been going out for six months. Janek knew he had to make a good impression.

'Daddy will just love you,' said Maxine hanging onto his arm. Janek thought differently. Mr Allsop would have deduced from his name that he was a foreigner and probably, as he would no doubt put it, a papist. Janek knew he was going to have to do some nifty footwork. He looked up at the elegant, detached house with its garden sweeping down to the river. This place smelled of money.

'Mr Allsop – I'm so pleased to meet you finally. I'm Johnny Baran.' And Janek put out his hand and fixed his most disarming smile on his face.

Mr Allsop paused for a second, then smiled and returned the handshake. 'Pleased to meet you Johnny. Call me Reg and this is my wife Lily,' he said, indicated a small woman with tightly permed hair.

Janek debated his next more, then decided to chance it. He kissed her hand.

'Oh, Maxine said you were a charmer, and she was right,' giggled Lily. 'I'll leave you men to talk over sherry while Maxine helps me in the kitchen.'

Janek felt relieved – this was going better than he'd hoped. He directed the topic of conversation – Reg and his business. As they talked, Janek could feel Mr Allsop's intense pride in the printing firm. Their discussion also ranged between Mr Allsop's activities in his local Masonic lodge, his passionate belief in new roads, smart shopping centres and suburban life. He worked hard at the council to push this agenda.

As they sat down to dinner, the conversation turned to Maxine.

'A great pity she has no brother, but there we are,' said Reg.

It was only mentioned in passing, but it was obviously a blemish in Reg's otherwise perfect life, like a streak of yellow urine in the white virgin snow. Mr Allsop had never had his longed-for son. Lily had given birth to Maxine in 1957 after eight years of marriage but for some reason no other child had ever appeared.

'Anyway, Maxine's a chip off the old block, aren't you girl?' said Reg, laughing.

Janek could vouch for that – she and he were soulmates. Maxine had left school at 15 desperate to work in the family firm but her father had advised her to find a job elsewhere first to broaden her experience. So she had taken a job as an estate agent and was taking a business studies course in the evenings, at which she'd met Janek.

'I've only heard good things about you from your boss Ken Cavendish,' said Reg. 'He's a good friend of mine, you know. He says you've got a fine business brain. You know how to make money – that's a skill to be proud of. That way I know Maxine here will always be cared for.' Janek glowed with pleasure.

Six months later when Maxine told her father she and Janek wanted to get married, Mr Allsop approved. He would pay for the wedding, they need do nothing, he would be glad to take the project over in its entirety. He would arrange the church, the reception, the honeymoon, he would set them up afterwards. In short, they could not hope for a more generous benefactor.

'You know St Wystan's, don't you?' said Mr Allsop. 'The building of that church was my project – so much better than the gloomy old St Wystan's. That's where you'll get wed.'

Janek tried to remember the old church. The magnificent Anglo-Saxon edifice with its columns lovingly sculpted by armies of stone masons who passed their craft down from generation to generation. He vaguely recalled its tower and two iron bells, the crypt, the stained glass windows and huge, rivet studded oak door. The church had been demolished to make way for the Babcock Way underpass in 1970.

But Janek certainly knew the new church in Turney Road. He had driven past it many times and had once peeped inside with a client who was thinking of buying a house nearby. The new St Wystan's had a slim, blue steeple, whitewashed walls, blond-wood pews, a modern stained-glass window depicting St Wystan, handkerchief at the ready, standing over a leper, a pulpit which had won an award from the Design Council and a very large car park.

Reg Allsop, through his contacts at the Council, had played a huge part in the design and construction of the church and so it was not surprising that, in early August 1978, Janek and Maxine's wedding was held there. Mr and Mrs Allsop had arranged everything, the clothes, the cars, the reception at Bingham Lodge Hall. Janek hand delivered the embellished white and gold invitation printed by Allsop Printers to his family. It read:

Mr and Mrs Reginald Allsop
Request the pleasure of the company of
The Baran Family – Tadeusz, Helena, Wanda and Pawel
At the wedding of their only daughter Maxine
To Mr John T Baran.
St Wystan's Church, Saturday 25 August 1978 at 2pm and
afterwards at Bingham Lodge Hall, Chelston

'It's a lovely invitation, isn't it Mum?' said Janek. 'Do you like it?'

Janek was trying his best to placate his mother. He knew she thought he wasn't old enough at 19 to get married and that she was annoyed that he'd refused to go to university. To top it all, he was getting married to a very young girl in a Church of England church.

'Well,' said Helena. 'Yes, it's lovely. I'm sure your father and I will turn up at the appointed date and time.' Janek could feel her stiffness, her reluctance to participate in the proceedings.

'What are you going to wear, Mum?' asked Wanda.

'I think I'll buy a new suit. It will be the one thing I'll have control with over this wedding.'

'You'll look lovely whatever you wear, Mum,' said Janek.

'You could make something. You always used to,' said Wanda.

'I really don't want to sew anymore. What are you going to wear?' asked Helena.

'Looking at me, it will have to be something between a tent and a marquee. But I will buy a nice little pink dress for Anna.'

Helena took Anna and walked up and down the room with her while Wanda buttoned up the front of her dress.

'Last week would have been Zosia's 25th birthday,' said Helena patting Anna rhythmically on her tiny back.

Janek was worried on the day of the wedding. He knew his family would feel a little out of place among all these rich Anglo Saxons, with the men in penguin suits and the women in flowery hats. He knew the bride's family would take up almost all of the church and he worried about how his parents would get on with Reg and Lily at the top table. But his greatest worry was the after-dinner speeches.

The three white Rolls Royces left St Wystans and made their way to Bingham Lodge. Once inside Helena was placed on the head table next to Lily Allsop and Tadek was put next to Reg. Janek and Maxine sat between them with Ken Cavendish, the best man, at one end of the table and Linda Allsop, Maxine's cousin and bridesmaid, at the other end. Janek overheard Lily talking to his mother.

'I can't believe my little girl is married. It's so difficult when you have only one child. You are so lucky to have two,' she said.

Janek winced.

'Actually, I have three children but ...' began Helena.

'Oh, Maxine, don't start displaying your garter, love,' Lily interrupted, laughing and got up to talk to her daughter ignoring Helena's response.

Janek turned his attention to the other side, where his father and new father-in-law were talking.

'How's business, Ted?' inquired Reg.

'Oh, not so bad. And you?'

'Thriving, Ted, thriving. In fact I've got some news about that particular subject which I think will be of interest to you.' He patted his nose with his index finger, winked and stood up. Janek swallowed hard. His mouth was dry and he felt his heart rate speed up. There was nothing he could do about it now – the deed was done, signed and sealed.

'Ladies and gentlemen,' said Mr Allsop clinking his champagne glass with a knife, 'Can I have your attention please. I want to thank you all for coming and celebrating with us the wedding of our lovely daughter, Maxine, to this fine young man here. Now I have a few things to say about Maxine. I know this may embarrass her but if you can't say these things at your daughter's wedding when can you say them? As you all know, Maxine is my only child and so is rather special to me, to put it mildly. I hope you're all having a good time and enjoying this excellent meal. I also want to thank you on Maxine and John's behalf for all the wonderful presents. I just hope there are some baby clothes among them, if you get my drift.'

Helena and Tadek stared at each other in alarm.

'Only joking, folks, only joking. I'm sure that pure white

wedding dress meant what it said, eh Maxine' and he winked at his daughter.

Janek kept his gaze firmly on his mother's face.

'But let's get down to some more serious business,' continued Mr Allsop. 'I just want to say how delighted Lily and I are that John is joining our family. He is a fine young man and I'm told by all at Cavendish's that he has a superb business brain. Ah, business – now let's get serious. Allsop Printing is a flourishing business and I want to make sure it will be in safe hands when I eventually retire – so I can spend more time playing golf, preferably in the Costa Del Sol.'

Laughter.

'So, I want to announce that John and Maxine will be gradually taking over the running of Allsop Printing over the next five years. It's a decision I've been happy to make. You two have a very bright future ahead of you and we all wish you the best. Allsop Printing Works will, one day, be all yours.'

Applause and shouts of, 'Well done,'

Janek looked at his mother. She smiled and whispered to him, 'That's wonderful.' Janek nodded and closed his eyes as he listened to the next bit.

'And that's not all,' continued Mr Allsop, once the applause had died down. 'As I said, I have no son and it will be a tragedy if the ancient name of Allsop died out. My ancestors have lived in Derby for generations and my great grandfather, Joseph White Allsop, started the Allsop Printing company way back in 1830. The name Allsop Printing is synonymous with fair prices, fine quality and fiscal rectitude. So, I have to say that I was extremely honoured when my new son-in-law here agreed to take the name Allsop so it wouldn't be lost to the family business or to posterity. I can't say how delighted I am that John agreed to do this and his generosity will be richly rewarded. Allsop and Son will continue to be Allsop and Son. So, everyone please stand and toast the bride and groom, John and Maxine Allsop!'

Helena, Tadek and Wanda sat, open mouthed with their glasses half way to their mouths.

'Mum, dad drink a toast,' said Janek urged. 'Come on.' He tugged at his mother's arm.

Helena and Tadek remained seated. Wanda stared at her brother in wide-eyed astonishment. Everyone else was standing, cheering. Tadek stared down at his drink, Helena brought her handkerchief up to her eyes.

Wanda called out, 'But Janek, you're *our* father's only son, too. What about his name?' but against all the applause, her voice seemed like a small sad howl in a gale.

Chapter 40

Derby 1978

A wet Tuesday afternoon in October found Wanda playing with 18-month-old Anna in the sitting room of 16 Porton Crescent. She was singing her a Polish nursery rhyme she remembered her grandmother singing to Janek when he was a baby. Wanda copied the exact same lilt in her voice, the same pre-war Polish accent. Anna was just starting to form her first words and they were all Polish. That was the only language Wanda spoke to her for now – she knew her daughter would learn English soon enough at school.

Wanda generally spoke Polish to her mother now, too, after years of insisting on speaking English. Her mother was watching her from her armchair, listening to her singing. Helena had recently been made head of administration at the Polytechnic and had begun studying for a part time degree in psychology with special emphasis on schizophrenia. The doorbell rang and Helena let a very excited Maxine into the room.

'I've just come from the Royal Infirmary and guess what? I'm going to have a baby. Isn't it wonderful news? I can't believe it. I did one of those home tests last week and then went to the hospital for a blood test. They have just confirmed that I'm pregnant.' Helena got up and kissed her.

'We are so happy, dear Maxine. When can we expect the happy event?'

'They've given me a date of 11 June. That would make the baby, let's see, yes Gemini. Oh, what if it was twins? Wouldn't that be just fantastic?'

'Congratulations,' said Wanda.

'And, look I bought a book of names that they were

selling in the Friends shop at the hospital. I've been looking through it and I've decided if it's a boy I'm going to call him Clark. I think that's a really nice name, don't you? Maybe Clarke with an E would be classier. And the best thing about that name is that you can't shorten it.'

'Well, that's not really a recommendation, is it?' said Wanda. 'I mean, you can't shorten 'shit' but you wouldn't call him that, would you?'

'Wanda, really,' said Helena, shocked. 'We know what you mean, Maxine.'

Maxine looked put out. 'Anyway, I can't stop. I'd better get back, bye now.' And she was gone in a flash of paisley print and strong perfume, driving her Ford Escort off down Porton Crescent.

Wanda waved her off at the door, 'Bye, Max,' she called.

'Really, Wanda – that was a bit cruel. Your sharp tongue …' said Helena.

'Yes, but Clarke Allsop – what a nightmare. I have to do something to protect my poor nephew.'

'It's her decision what to call the poor little scrap. Don't be too hard on her. She seems so happy.'

They heard voices in the hall. 'Hey Anna, daddy and granddad are back,' said Wanda scooping up her daughter.

The two men were talking excitedly as they came into the sitting room.

'Quick, put on the news,' said Pawel rushing over to the television set. 'Have you heard – they've elected a Polish Pope. I can't believe it, this is fantastic news. What on earth will the Soviets do? What excellent news.'

He laughed loudly.

'Really? But what difference will it make?' said Helena.

'I thought only Italians could be Pope,' said Wanda.

'This is tremendous news for Poland,' said Tadek. 'Let's get out some vodka and drink a toast to our new Pope.'

As the BBC confirmed the news, Wanda, Pawel, Tadek and Helena stood to attention and raised their glasses of vodka in celebration. The Black Madonna looked down at them, dark, brooding, inscrutable.

Anna Zosia Lato looked around at the adults towering above her. They were all looking at the television and no one was paying her any attention. But even at only 18 months of age, she knew how to get someone to notice her.

She tugged hard at Helena's skirt and said in a clear, high voice, 'Babcia'.